STO

FRIE ✓ W9-BAT-596

OF ACPL

3 1833 0065

THE SECRET OF
THE UNDERSEA BELL

Winner of Boys' Life-Dodd, Mead Prize Competition

THE SECRET OF THE

UNDERSEA BELL

by

JOHN SCOTT DOUGLAS

jD7458s

Dodd, Mead & Company · New York · 1951

Copyright, 1951, by John Scott Douglas. All rights reserved. No part of this book may be reproduced in any form without permission in writing from the publisher. Printed in the United States of America by Vail-Ballou Press, Inc., Binghamton, N. Y. Designed by Stefan Salter.

TO IONE—

who not only encouraged her husband in venturing into the depths in diving dress and copper helmet, but also wished, with all her heart, that she herself might visit that strange and beautiful world beneath the sea

U. S. 875792

CONTENTS

The characters and situations in this book are wholly fictional and imaginative; they do not portray and are not intended to portray any actual persons or parties.

1.

STORM WARNINGS

RONNIE NORDHOFF pulled the dripping oars into the skiff as it glided alongside the small motorboat. Clambering over a thwart, he picked up the mooring line, and sprang aboard the *Sea Spray*. He was securing the line to her towing bitt when he heard the rattling of planks and a thin, piping voice.

He glanced around and saw his younger brother running along the old Seal Cove pier. Bounding beside him, his coat glinting like copper in the brilliant California sunlight, was their Irish setter, Mr. O'Malley.

Skip cupped his hands, and shouted, "Wait, Ronnie!" His voice was barely audible above the lapping surf and the grinding of pebbles on the beach. "Mr. Romano wants to see you. He says it's mighty important."

"Okay, Skip," Ronnie answered, his voice lacking its usual spirit. "I'm not going anywhere. I just came out to check on Dad's boat."

Ronnie could guess why Joseph Romano wished to see him. Romano was branch manager of the Seal Cove Bank and a family friend. Only a few months past, Ronnie had learned from his mother that the banker was also executor of his parents' estates. "Executor," his mother had added with a smile, "just means that Mr. Romano will carry out the terms of your father's will and mine, Ronnie. But nothing will happen to us, so don't worry about it."

But something *had* happened. A reckless driver, passing at high speed on a curve, had collided with his father's car, leaving Skip, Mardie and himself without mother or father. After seeing his parents laid to rest, Ronnie had driven Skip and Mardie home, and then, throwing a sleeping bag into the old jalopy, the Bouncing Betty, he had gone off alone.

Stunned with grief, he had no clear memory of where he went in the days that followed. In his mind was a picture of rolling out his bag one night beside a moonlit stream, and he was sure he must have seen Mardie and Skip from time to time. But he could not bear to face Joseph Romano. He shrank from the thought of seeing old friends, even such close friends as Bill Ballard and Pud Dart.

Early that morning he had awakened to find himself lying on a beach. Soaring cliffs and a stream plunging in a series of white cascades through a gap in the rock walls suggested that he was on the San Simeon coast, though he wasn't sure of that until he climbed a steep trail and found the jalopy beside the highway. His heart seemed dead within him, but his mind was once more clear.

His world had crumbled, and he saw that it was time he salvaged what pieces he could to make a new life for Mardie, Skip and himself. And so at daybreak, without breakfast, he had driven south on the San Simeon highway to Seal Cove. He had stopped at the old pier to visit his father's abalone boat. The *Sea Spray* was one of his assets, one of the pieces he must use in rebuilding his life, and he wanted to be sure that no one had molested it.

But now that he was aboard, he could not bear to disturb anything that had belonged to his father. The *Sea Spray*, like the other abalone boats that sailed along the mid-California coast, was a tiny craft for open sea, and would have fitted cornerwise in a moderate living room. Only small boats, however, could work among rocks. And it was in close quarters between rocks that the deep-sea diver of an abalone boat often went down to search for the large, ear-shaped shellfish. The boat had no rails, making it easier to pull a diver aboard any part of the boat if he were pursued by a predatory creature. It had a small engine cabin amidship, and fore and aft were hatches for storing shellfish.

Thor Nordhoff, Ronnie's father, had been the diver on the *Sea Spray*. And now, when Ronnie reluctantly lifted aside the cover of the after-hatch, he could see his father's red and black diving dresses, two copper helmets, rubber air-hoses and other diver's gear pushed back under the deck. With heavy heart, Ronnie replaced the cover, and walked over to lift the tarp from the air-compressor that had supplied his father with air when diving. He saw no sign that anyone had tampered with the machine.

The cabin door stood ajar, but when Ronnie looked inside, the engine did not seem to have been disturbed. Had he visited the boat recently and failed to lock up? He couldn't be sure. He snapped the padlock, and stood looking out through the opening of the cove, rubbing the mist from his eyes.

Ronnie was tall for eighteen, with a slender build that concealed a wiry strength, a muscular coordination that made him a natural athlete. Freckles, a shade lighter than his wavy red hair, as well as an expression of cheerful good humor, usually tempered the rugged contours of his face.

But now there was pain and bewilderment in his countenance as he watched the rolling blue Pacific flashing with silvery lights. On such a day he could imagine his father crying boisterously to his line-tender and boat-operator, "It's a good day for digging, boys!"

"Digging" to Thor Nordhoff meant going down in diving dress to pry abalones from undersea rocks, ledges and crevasses. No abalone diver would work in heavier seas than he did, or as long. No diver would work at greater depth, either, for at times he descended 125 feet to find shellfish. It seemed unbelievable to Ronnie that his father's boat lay here at anchor while the other Seal Cove craft were out fishing. It seemed unbelievable that Thor Nordhoff would never sail again, for his great vitality had made him appear like an elemental force, as much a part of nature as the winds, the seas and the storms.

In silence, Ronnie freed the mooring line of the skiff, and stepped into it, picking up the oars. He rowed to the pier, tied up the boat, and climbed the switchback stairs.

Upon his reaching the top Mr. O'Malley jumped up on him, his body wriggling with ecstasy, his feathery tail waving. Ronnie hugged the dog, his face against the setter's glossy head. A lump rose in his throat as he thought of how fond his pretty mother had been of Mr. O'Malley.

"Mr. Romano wants you to sign some important papers, Ronnie."

"I know, Skip. I'll take care of things now. What day is it?"
Skip thought a moment. "The seventeenth."

"Ten days since the services," Ronnie said, aghast. "Have I been gone that long?"

"Nope," said the twelve-year-old. Skip's eyes dropped and he kicked absently at the rough planking. "You've been home every day or so, but you don't seem to hear anything Mardie or I say to you. You act like you were walking in your sleep."

Ronnie felt ashamed. Overwhelmed by his own grief, he had forgotten his younger brother and sister. He felt a tug of remorse as he looked at Skip, a wan and disheveled youngster now. His face and hands were in need of soap and water, his shirt was dirty and lacked two buttons.

"Ronnie," Skip added anxiously, "what's to become of us?"

"We'll manage, Skip."

"Yes, but . . . *when?*"

The question embarrassed Ronnie. His arm went around Skip's shoulder and tightened. "Right now!" Ronnie said, and as he started along the dock, he added, "I didn't mean to, but I guess I've been running away."

The younger boy followed at the skipping, hopping gait that was his usual substitute for walking. "You're really going to take care of things, Ronnie?" he asked in a worried tone.

"I promise," said Ronnie.

Skip looked relieved as he hopped into the old jalopy parked at the end of the pier. But Ronnie paused, looking wryly at the Bouncing Betty. It had cost twenty-five dollars when he and Bill Ballard and Pud Dart had bought it three years before for camping and fishing trips, and only Bill's ability as a mechanic had kept it running. The old car had no top, and over Bill's protests, Ronnie and Pud had painted ladders along the sides and hung a bell from a bracket over the hood to make it resemble a fire-truck. Bill always had more common sense than Pud or himself, Ronnie thought now. In his new position as head of his family, he would look ridiculous driving such a car. He decided to repaint it as soon as possible.

He climbed in behind the wheel, and the setter jumped in back. The Betty clattered and chugged up a short rise. There Ronnie paused, viewing his home surroundings for the first time with the seeing eyes of a stranger. The cove, partially protected to the northwest by a curving spit of land thinly treed with wind-gnarled cypress, lay shimmering in the dazzling sunlight. To the east of it stretched a valley, sheltered between long ridges green with radiata pines. Here and there, beneath their spreading branches, Ronnie caught glimpses of small, quaint cottages buried in masses of bloom.

"Do we have to leave Seal Cove?" Skip asked anxiously.

"I'm afraid so," Ronnie said with regret, realizing how much he loved the town. "I expect to enter Cal this fall."

The Betty rattled down the slope, turned over the bridge, and onto the main street, which followed the meandering course of San Pasqual Creek. They passed scattered houses, the grammar school, a feed store and the Seal Cove Cafe. Through the open door of Ballard's Garage, Ronnie saw Bill Ballard working on a car, but his friend did not glance their way. Ronnie waved to other friends as he drove past the drugstore, the hardware shop and Plimm's Grocery.

After they passed the bank, Skip asked, "Aren't you going to see Mr. Romano?"

"When I'm cleaned up, Skip."

Stores and business buildings gave way to old houses, set back in spacious yards and shaded by giant oaks and sycamore. Walking stiffly along the path serving pedestrians was a tall, thin figure of a woman wearing a large hat abloom with artificial flowers. Ronnie started to raise his hand in greeting, but the expression of icy disapproval in Miss Amelia Prindle's sharp old face made him change his mind.

"The old busybody's been snooping around," said Skip indignantly.

"What for?" Ronnie asked in surprise.

"She says Mardie and I are running wild like Injuns. We didn't invite her, but she came busting right in and looked at everything, and it's kind of a mess right now. She says she's going to have a good talk with you. And she asked Mardie how she'd like to go to an insti—to an institution."

"An orphan asylum? She's not sending you kids to any such place! I'm taking care of you!"

Though Skip looked relieved, he asked, "How can you stop her?"

Skip's question made Ronnie wonder. Miss Prindle had taught school in her younger years, but upon the death of her father, one of the prosperous farmers of the valley, she'd devoted much of her time to meddling in her neighbors' affairs. She'd tried to prevent Ronnie's father from building his abalone plant in Seal Cove. And though she'd failed in that, as in many other unpopular causes, she had given his parents a bad time of it. Could Miss Prindle enlist enough support to send Mardie and Skip to an orphan asylum? The thought frightened Ronnie. It was time he faced responsibilities!

He turned into their driveway. The comfortable old redwood house was built U-shaped around a patio, with a drive along the east side leading to a bare, spacious yard behind. Set well back in the yard, on the brink of San Pasqual Creek, was the old stable their father had converted into an abalone-processing plant. Its overhead door, comprising most of the north wall, was down as always when the plant was not in operation.

Two old trucks, one cannibalized of parts to keep the other running, stood in the west side of the yard. And beside one of them stood a forlorn eight-year-old with their pet rabbit, Peter, in her arms. His sister's appearance made Ronnie uneasy, for he knew how it would impress Miss Prindle. Mardie's hair, usually brushed until it gleamed with buttercup brightness, straggled about her wistful face. Her dress was as rumpled and soiled as Skip's shirt.

Before he could speak to her, however, a truck rumbled around the corner of the house and stopped beside the jalopy. Ronnie was surprised when Orrie Shumaker stepped out. Shumaker was an able abalone diver, and one of the few fishermen besides Ronnie's father who had also operated a first-class abalone plant. However, he was no friend of the Nordhoffs. More than once he had spread rumors that Thor Nordhoff was about to go into other work, in an unsuccessful effort to replace Ronnie's father as leader of the abalone fishermen.

Because of his powerful build and short stature, Shumaker was sometimes referred to as "Mr. Five-By-Five." A long-billed flyer's cap emphasized the roundness of his brown face, and his dark eyes moved restlessly in the slits beneath his cavernous brows and plump cheeks as his glance swept the closed plant, the old trucks, and the two neglected children.

"I drove over to say how sorry I was about your folks, Ronnie," he said, a false note in his voice betraying his pretense of sympathy.

"Thank you, Mr. Shumaker," Ronnie said.

"Anything I can do for you kids?"

"No, thank you. We're getting along."

After a reproving glance at Skip and Mardie, Shumaker said dryly, "Not too well, I'd say. What are your plans?"

"College this fall, if I can afford it. I hope to find rooms near the campus so that Mardie and Skip can be with me."

"Think you'll have enough for that?" Shumaker asked brusquely. "Money always burned your father's hands, and I doubt if he left much."

Mardie hugged her pet rabbit, looking tearful. Skip's eyes were brimming as he drew patterns in the dust with one toe. Ronnie resented the diver's comments, and wished Shumaker would leave.

"Thinking of selling the place?" Shumaker asked casually.

"I hope to," said Ronnie.

"Pretty heavily mortgaged, isn't it?"

For a moment Ronnie stared in astonishment at the stocky little diver. "Why, not that I know of!"

"I know differently," Shumaker stated bluntly. "Your father slapped a $4,000 mortgage on this place when he built his plant. If you're serious about selling, I'll assume that mortgage and pay you $2,000 clear. A mighty generous offer."

"*Generous!*" Ronnie exclaimed. "But Dad said that this place, with all improvements, was worth more than $10,000!"

Shumaker gave a short, dry laugh. "Your father was an

optimist."

Ronnie stared at the diver in confusion. Was Shumaker trying to befriend him? Was $2,000 a liberal offer? If that was all the property would realize, would there be enough to pay his father's debts? It seemed doubtful. And if there was nothing left after paying the debts, how could he finance college? How could he raise Mardie and Skip?

Anger welled up in Ronnie as he suspected what Shumaker was trying to do. The diver hoped to take advantage of his youth and inexperience to buy an abalone plant cheaply! But why did Shumaker want a second plant? It was rumored that he was already in financial difficulties with the bank at Morro Bay, was slow paying his fishermen. There was something strange about that, too, for though Shumaker's pack was inferior to that of the Nordhoff plant, it had been selling well, and he should be in comfortable circumstances.

"If $2,000 clear is all this place will bring," Ronnie said, an angry tremor in his voice, "I'll dive for abalones and operate this plant myself!"

It was the first time such a thought had occurred to him. He was almost as startled as Shumaker when the words spilled out. Clearly the man had never expected a refusal. His dark eyes narrowed beneath the heavy brows. Color crept under the deep brown of his cheeks. He thrust out his lips, and then uttered a short, mocking laugh.

"You don't even know whether you'd black-out under the pressure of a dive!"

"I can soon find out," Ronnie said with warmth.

"As for diving and operating an abalone plant," Shumaker went on, "I manage because my sister takes charge when I'm out fishing, and your father got by because your mother helped out. But both jobs are hard, and you're not up to either."

"What do you mean by that?"

"You've been out on your father's boat only a few times, from what I've heard, and you've never been down in diving dress. You haven't even worked in this plant. Summers you've chased around in this old wreck of a car, taking jobs for brief periods but mostly having a good time with the Ballard and Dart boys. Could you stick at any one thing? I doubt it. You're a playboy, an athlete, and there's no place for your kind in anything as rugged as abalone fishing. Better be smart and take my offer, or I'll get your place later after the bank takes it over. And I won't pay as much then!"

There was partial truth in what Shumaker said. But there were also reasons for Ronnie's apparently happy-go-lucky existence in the past which neither he nor the townspeople of Seal Cove fully understood. Ronnie's cheeks grew hot with suppressed anger as he listened to the diver's outburst, but with an effort the boy kept control of his temper.

"Is that all, Mr. Shumaker?" he asked.

"That's all!"

The stocky little man climbed into the truck, slammed the door, kicked the starter, and drove out of the yard.

Mardie nuzzled Peter with her pointed chin, a curious, faraway look in her blue eyes. Skip stopped petting Mr. O'Malley and raised a strained face.

"Golly, are things as bad as he says, Ronnie?"

"I doubt it, Skip. I think he's trying to scare us into selling the property cheap. I've got to get cleaned up now."

Skip trailed behind as Ronnie entered the kitchen by the back door. The phone buzzed, and Ronnie strode into the living room to answer it.

"Aw, let it ring," Skip said behind him. "Mardie and I don't pay any attention to it any more."

"You don't?" Ronnie asked in surprise.

"Naw! Dozens of people called up every day to say how sorry they were about Mom and Dad. We couldn't stand it!"

That wouldn't do, Ronnie decided, if he were to continue running the abalone plant. It was time he started picking up the pieces!

Lifting the receiver, he heard the warm, friendly voice of Walter Bonnell, manager of the Seal Cove Inn. Bonnell asked where Ronnie had been, and then expressed his sympathy.

Finally he said, "If you feel like talking business, Ronnie, could you tell me how much abalone you have on hand?"

"Not much, Mr. Bonnell. Several hundred pounds, I believe."

"Put our name on all of it. Your father's Seal Cove abalone has been a specialty of the Inn, and no other plant could supply as good a pack. We must figure out a new specialty now."

"Maybe I could supply you, Mr. Bonnell," Ronnie suggested. "I may take up diving and run the plant."

Walter Bonnell laughed as though he thought Ronnie were joking.

"You know too much about abalone fishing to go into anything so rugged, Ronnie. You'd better try to make a name for yourself in college football, and maybe some alumnus will give you an easier job."

———

Ronnie hung up with a feeling of shock. Walter Bonnell, like Shumaker, thought he couldn't stick a hard job! Ronnie wouldn't expect Shumaker to have much confidence in him, but the manager of the Inn was a friend. Bonnell had been a famous college athlete not many years back, and in off season at the Inn, he still sometimes relieved their coach to teach the boys of Seal Cove High the finer points of football, basketball and track. Often he played tennis or basketball with Ronnie and other boys of the town to keep in physical trim.

Quickly Ronnie took a shower and changed into clean clothing. And then, in a thoughtful mood, he left the house. He stared with distaste at the jalopy and its garish decoration. It had played its part in making the townspeople think he was a carefree boy with no serious purpose! So now it was into the truck that he climbed, and drove westward.

Parking across the street from the bank, he stepped out, and heard a voice call, "Wait a sec, Ronnie."

He turned and saw Marsh Marple, a former classmate at Seal Cove High, hurrying toward him. It struck Ronnie that no one would mistake Marsh for a playboy. A suggestion of stubbornness about Marsh's jaw and something decisive about his eyes and mouth made him appear much older and more mature than his years. In reality, he'd been born two months before Ronnie.

Now, in a grave, almost fatherly way, he laid a hand on Ronnie's shoulder, and said quietly, "I'm mighty sorry about what happened, Ronnie. I know we've been crosswise many times, but if there's anything I can do to help, I'd sure like to do it."

Ronnie was so touched that his eyes stung. Never would

13

he have expected such an offer from Marsh, after their years of rivalry. Yet, now that he thought of it, every time he'd beaten Marsh for a school office or the captaincy of a team, Marsh had supported him to the limit. And he'd backed Marsh the same way when it was he, Ronnie Nordhoff, who lost.

Those days of high-school rivalry lie behind us, reflected Ronnie. *We can at last be friends! Except,* he added as an afterthought, *where Ginger Dart is concerned.*

"Thanks, Marsh," Ronnie said gratefully. "But we're making out. Have you found a job yet?"

Marsh regarded him soberly for a moment. "Didn't you hear? I've bought an abalone boat, and I'm going to start fishing tomorrow. I've been an abalone diver for the past three summers, as you know, and I made a mighty good living at it."

"I wish you luck," Ronnie said. "I may be diving myself."

Marsh's gray eyes widened. "I thought you were going to college. Its more your style, Ronnie. And maybe I could help out by buying your father's plant, if you could make the terms easy enough."

"I'll have to see how things stand, Marsh. If Dad's affairs are in as bad shape as Shumaker says, I may have to fish. And then I'll need the plant."

A fleeting smile lighted Marsh's rough-hewn face. "Diving takes tenacity, Ronnie. Try it, and you'll find out."

Here it was again, thought Ronnie—the suggestion that he couldn't stick at a difficult job. And despite Marsh's kindly intentions, Ronnie could not keep a trace of annoyance from his tone, "Maybe I will try it."

"You won't go down more than once," Marsh predicted.

"Of all the fellows who started diving when I did, three summers ago, only two stayed with it."

"What makes you think I can't handle a tough job?" Ronnie demanded with warmth. "Do you remember that you were quarterback of the squad in your sophomore year, and that I'd improved so much by the end of that year that I was quarterback in our junior and senior years?"

Marsh stiffened at being reminded of his defeat. "That was play!" he snapped. "Fishing is work."

Here we go! thought Ronnie. *Wherever Marsh and I start, we always end the same way—in disagreement.*

"I have a half mind to go out tomorrow with Dad's crew and let them put me down to prove you're wrong, Marsh!"

"With Hammerhead Halvorson and Ken Carlson?"

"Of course."

"Ronnie, they never dreamed you'd try abalone fishing," Marsh said earnestly. "And neither did I. Halvorson is now my line-tender. Carlson is my boat-operator."

Ronnie's mouth parted in disbelief. "They wouldn't sign up with you without asking me!"

"They must eat—and of course they didn't think you'd fish!"

"Why 'of course'?" Ronnie cried. "I'll tell you frankly, Marsh, that I'm getting burned up at hearing, 'Of course, Ronnie Nordhoff won't fish. Of course, he can't handle a hard job. Of course, he's just a playboy.' Don't I have any chance to prove myself?"

Simmering with anger, he started to turn away. But Marsh caught his arm. "I still can't believe you intend to fish, Ronnie, but I won't take your father's crew from you, if you're serious."

15

"You keep them! If they don't have enough confidence in me to say a word before changing to another boat—"

"There's another thing," Marsh broke in. "If you don't care to sell your father's plant, I'll have no choice but to build my own and go into competition with you."

"Building an abalone plant," Ronnie suggested, "takes money."

"First-class plants like your father's, yes. But I can set up a woodshed operation behind the cottage I'm renting. Though it won't be too efficient, it will allow me to process my own catches—and those of any other fishermen who will sell to me."

Marsh's words momentarily left Ronnie speechless. If Marsh established a successful woodshed operation, it might be impossible to find a buyer for the Nordhoff plant! There weren't enough fishermen in Seal Cove to supply both! Perhaps he should have taken Shumaker's offer.

"You have the first touchdown, Marsh," Ronnie declared heatedly. "But if I should decide to fish, watch for holes in your line. I may be coming through them!"

"What do you mean?"

"Remember why my play improved so much at the end of my sophomore year that I was made quarterback the next? My opponents started kicking me in the scrimmages, and I resented it. I'm getting annoyed at the kicking I've been taking today! If I can't go to college, you'll have a competitor here who means business!"

Marsh's gray eyes grew stern. "If that's the way you want it! You usually came out ahead in high-school. Now maybe it's my turn!"

———

Ronnie said, "We'll see," and turned toward the bank.

His face felt hot when he entered, and within him was a warm upwelling of emotion. It was a feeling he'd often experienced in the past when a football opponent had kicked him in the pile-up and he could scarcely wait for the chance to hurl himself against an opposing line. ·

2.

"THE RONNIE NORDHOFF TREATMENT"

J OSEPH ROMANO, manager of the Seal Cove Bank, was talking to a customer at the counter. When he saw the tall, redheaded boy approaching, he said, "I'll see you in a minute, Ronnie."

Romano was a man of medium height and strongly built, with iron-gray hair and mustache. The son of a Swiss-Italian farmer of the valley, he looked more like a tiller of the soil in Sunday clothes than a banker. Several times he had passed up opportunities to manage larger branch banks of the chain he worked for because of his devotion to the people among whom he was born.

Presently he beckoned Ronnie to come through the swinging gate to his desk, and said, "Draw up a chair." He peered at the boy briefly, his brown eyes warmly sympathetic.

"This isn't only your loss, Ronnie," he said gently. "The town has lost two of its best people." He paused, his strong brown hands stirring slightly on the desk pad. "They were my finest friends. Your mother—that sweet, quiet woman, looking like a girl with the green scarf she always wore over her fair hair—managing your father's plant, putting out the best abalone pack on the coast. And your father—that untamed man with blue seaman's cap set back on his wild mop of red hair, coming into the bank in a faded shirt, his powerful arms bare, and roaring, 'I need money to meet my payroll, Joe'!"

Romano's eyes glowed. "I would say, 'Nordhoff, this is undignified. Be patient!' And your father would just grin. He knew I loved it. He knew I enjoyed seeing strangers look at him, startled, and the new clerks asking themselves, 'Who is this wild man?' "

"That was Dad, all right," Ronnie said, and the banker's words somehow eased his sense of loss. His mother and father would never be gone so long as they lived in the memories of men like Joseph Romano!

"Ah, but that was but one side of your father, and there were so many," went on Romano. "Thor Nordhoff was a man with little schooling, but he studied, he observed, and all the time he kept learning. To you and Mardie and Skip, he was a good father; to your mother, the most colorful man she ever knew. To Army engineers building breakwaters, Thor Nordhoff was the man who understood most about the shifting of sand and the currents on our coast. To the marine scientists who study the oceans, he was the final authority on seaurchins and abalones. To the state, he was the diver best qualified to make California marine surveys. To legislative committees, Nordhoff was the authority to consult when abalone conservation measures were being drawn. To the fishermen, your father was a leader who would always assist with a generous hand when a wife or child was sick, who would help a man down on his luck or in need of money to overhaul or repair his boat. And to me," said the banker, "he was both a great friend and a great trial."

Romano frowned as he drew some papers from a desk box. "This is what I feared might happen. Your father earned thirty, sometimes thirty-five thousand a year, from diving and his plant. Time and again, I begged him to lay something aside for a rainy day. But it was always for some other fisherman's rainy day your father's money would go. For scientific instruments and books on marine biology. For weeks in Sacramento, which he paid for from his own pocket, while he fought for conservation measures. And now what is left? Debts, debts, debts!"

He tossed the sheaf of papers across the desk, but Ronnie was too stunned to do more than glance at them. He stirred uneasily.

"Isn't there anything left, Mr. Romano? The boat, the house, anything?"

The banker shook his iron-gray head. "All mortgaged, Ronnie," he said heavily. "Your father carried no insurance—too expensive for a diver. There's insurance on his car to collect, of course, and a few unpaid accounts. But against the thousands he owed—" Romano spread his hands in a helpless gesture.

The room began wavering before Ronnie's eyes like the ground from a banking plane. He felt dizzy and sick at heart. With an effort, he got a grip on himself.

"Then there's . . . no college?" he murmured faintly.

"Worse than that, Ronnie," the banker said unhappily. "Even the house must go to meet these loans of your father's.

Of course," he added quickly, "you and Mardie and Skip will come to live with me until you can get on your feet."

"You already have six children!" Ronnie protested.

"All right," said Romano. "Now I have nine."

Slowly Ronnie's head cleared. He thought of something his father had once said: *"A diver can always wrest a living from the sea."*

Ronnie wasn't a diver, but he might learn. Marsh had become quite good at the work. And hadn't he proved himself Marsh's equal at football, at basketball, at track?

"I'll never forget your offer," Ronnie said, gripping the arms of his chair. "But I think we can make out where we are, and pay Dad's debts too, if you'll only give me the chance."

"And how will you do this?"

"By diving and running the plant."

"Be practical!" said Romano, in the weary tone of a man desiring to put an end to an unpleasant matter. "I know more about you than you think, Ronnie. Unlike many people in this town, I realize that you didn't try various jobs each summer from choice. You did that because your father wanted you to learn about different kinds of work to discover what you were fitted for. I also am aware that your father gave you several hundred dollars at the beginning of the summer, and you returned it to him untouched when you came home."

"Dad must have told you that!" Ronnie exclaimed.

"Yes—that, and other things. He admitted to me that he wouldn't allow you to go out often on his boat because he was afraid you might want to follow his footsteps and become an abalone fisherman. He thought you ought to go to college and have the chance he missed. For that reason, too, he never allowed you to work in his plant." Romano stared steadily at Ronnie for several moments before adding, *"But you did!"*

Ronnie was startled, believing that had been a well-kept secret.

"Yes," Romano continued, "your mother likewise confided in me. At times when your father was away and she was short-handed, you insisted upon helping her. She said you could do any job in the plant, but that you were best of all at detecting a tough abalone steak. She claimed that you could do it by sight, or by feel, blind-folded."

"She tested me once on that," Ronnie admitted, flushing.

"So? Well, it convinces me you might in time be able to run the plant profitably, Ronnie—if there were only enough fishermen here to supply you. But when you must both dive and process abalones—no; I do not believe you can do it."

"That's what everyone said when my father moved here to build his plant," Ronnie declared with a trace of warmth.

"Ah! but your father was already a diver!"

Ronnie said grimly, "The bank's going to take quite a loss on the money loaned to my father, is that right?"

"That is correct."

"Would you lose much more if you gave me just one month to prove what I can do? Allow me to use my father's boat and plant for thirty days?" And seeing the banker starting to shake his head, Ronnie, without being conscious of it, lapsed into his father's speech, his voice rising as he slapped the desk with the flat of his palm. "Land's end, Mr. Romano, are you a man or a banker? Thirty days is all I ask! If I'm cut out for an abalone diver, the bank will recover its loan, every penny of it! And if I'm not, what have you lost? *Only one month!*"

Romano stiffened in his chair, and stared at Ronnie as if he were seeing an apparition. Then he settled back, and a glimmer of amusement appeared briefly on his face and vanished.

"This is undignified! Be patient!" And these words, with which he had so often reproved Thor Nordhoff, seemed to give Joseph Romano intense satisfaction. "Thirty days you shall have! And may I not live to regret it!"

Ronnie's step was brisk, his spirits soaring as he left the bank. For one month he had a home, a plant, a boat! With the right kind of luck, he might start to clear up his father's loans and regain possession of these properties for Mardie, Skip and himself.

But after starting home in the old truck, he saw a serious obstacle to his plans, and his spirits plummeted. Marsh had taken his father's crew! Where could he find another? Experienced line-tenders and boat-operators usually turned to diving after a time because an abalone diver received half the boat's catch. It was true that some men had made their first dives with crews no more experienced than themselves —Ronnie's father and Bill Pierce among them. But they had taken long chances until their tender and operator had learned their jobs!

Ronnie was still concerned with this problem when he parked behind the house and walked into the kitchen. He felt discouraged at the pile of dirty bowls, cups and plates in the sink. A box of corn flakes and several empty milk bottles stood on the table, and the remains of some sticky concoction covered the stove. Remembering that he'd not eaten since the previous night, Ronnie walked over to open the refrigerator. It held nothing but mustard, mayonnaise, a leathery piece of cheese, and a package of dog meat. There was not even any milk; they bought it at the store when slack periods in the abalone plant allowed their mother time to prepare meals at home. Ronnie hoped that Mardie and Skip had used the money he'd given them to eat properly.

Stepping into the living room, he found more disorder. Wilted flowers drooped from the vases. Skip's beanie and jacket dangled from a chair. Old newspapers littered the carpet, and on a turned-back corner reposed a knuckle-bone of Mr. O'Malley's. Ronnie picked up the dry bone and punted it into the fireplace, raising a plume of dust that settled slowly on the hearth.

I must clean up this mess! he thought. *No wonder Miss Prindle thinks the kids would be better off in an orphanage!*

He was starting for the kitchen broom-cupboard when a car hummed down the driveway and stopped in back. He had just time to put the milk bottles in the sink before the bell rang.

Ronnie opened the back door. His pleasure at seeing Pud Dart was swiftly dampened when he spied Pud's younger sister. Pud was nearly as large as his father, the sheriff of Seal Cove, and normally his expression was as happy as a child's, but he looked somewhat anxious now.

Ginger resembled her small and beautiful mother. Her golden hair fell in soft, natural waves to her shoulders; large green eyes and a small, pert nose gave her a deceptively angelic expression. She had been cheer-leader at Seal Cove for the past three years, but her cheers for Ronnie ended when she left the sidelines. For some reason he could not fathom, she would rarely go with him to a school party, box-supper, or a square dance.

Pud raised his brows and gave a jerk of his head to suggest that bringing Ginger had not been his idea. He tried to speak, and then, unable to find words, he gripped his friend's shoulder so hard that Ronnie thought for a moment his ribs would crack.

Even Ginger appeared more friendly than usual, for her green eyes glowed with sympathy as she said, "What are friends for if not to help in trouble, Ronnie? We've set three extra places at the table for you Nordhoffs every night. But there's no answer when we phone, and no one is here when we've come by—"

Ginger stopped abruptly, thoughtfully looking at the dishes in the sink, the sticky stove. Without a word, she moved on into the living room, standing in the doorway to survey the disorder.

"Pud," Ronnie whispered, "if I could find a well big enough to drop you in—!"

"She insisted on coming," said Pud helplessly.

At that moment there was a clatter outside, and Mr. O'Malley bounded into the kitchen, followed by Skip and Mardie. The disheveled little girl still carried her pet rabbit. Ginger turned at the commotion, and then quickly hurried over to put one arm around Mardie and the other about Skip. She kissed the little girl's tousled head. Both children began crying.

"Now, don't you worry, darlings," she murmured, and Ronnie thought he'd never heard a voice so tender. "I didn't realize things were so bad. I called and called, but . . . What did you have for breakfast?"

Mardie rubbed a small fist against her eyes. "Hot dog and coke," she said tearfully.

"Same here," said Skip.

"And for dinner last night?" Ginger asked.

"Two dogs and a coke," Mardie said.

"Me, too," said Skip.

"Weren't any of your neighbors kind enough to invite you to dinner?" Ginger asked, aghast.

"Sure," said Skip. "Mrs. Jones asked us over a couple of times, but her old police dog acted so mean we were scared to go past him. The Camerons next door have been trying to get us to come over but they're new here and we don't know them very well. And Miss Prindle, too . . . only we wouldn't go because she wants to put us in a place where kids who don't have any homes have to stay."

"Over my lifeless body, she will!" And despite her quiet tone, Ginger's voice held an explosive quality that made Ronnie uneasy. "Haven't you had anything but hot dogs and cokes since your parents—?"

Mardie sniffed. Skip blinked the tears from his eyes.

"Sure," he said. " 'Burgers and cokes a couple of times."

"No vegetables, no salads, no milk?" Ginger pursued. When Skip shook his head, she asked, "I don't understand this. Were you ordering all your own meals? Where was Ronnie?"

"Off somewhere," said Skip.

Ginger's arms went protectively around the children, but there was no mistaking her fury. Her face had gone white, her green eyes blazed.

———

"*Hot dogs and cokes!*" she cried. "I can understand what a shock this has been to you, Ronnie, but these youngsters must have a balanced di t! Do you think they can build sound bodies on what they've been eating? Have you ever heard of milk, meat, vegetables, lettuce, cheese, cereals?"

"Now, Ginger!" Pud begged her. "Remember your promise!"

"I promised to count ten before losing my temper! Well, I'm starting now! One—two—three—"

Ronnie explained desperately, "Honest, Ginger, I thought Mardie and Skip would use the money I gave them to buy regular meals at the café."

"—four—five—six—" went on the redheaded girl.

"Ginger!" pleaded Pud.

"—seven—" chanted Ginger and releasing the children, her flashing eyes swept the room.

"She's going to throw something!" yelled Pud, dragging Ronnie toward the front door.

They bolted through the living room, and flew through the door at the count of ten. Sprinting around the house, they scrambled into the Bouncing Betty. Ronnie kicked the starter. The jalopy, shaking and rattling, shot down the driveway and onto the street.

"*Whew!*" Ronnie sighed. "As if things weren't bad enough without bringing *her* around!"

"I begged her to behave, Ronnie. But she's been worried frantic about you Nordhoffs . . . saying I had to find you and see if everything was all right."

"I'd believe you, Pud, if I didn't know she thinks I poison the ground I walk on!"

Pud gave Ronnie an odd glance. "You think so? Ginger would slay me for telling you this, but she has your picture in a football helmet on her dresser."

"Does she stick pins in it daily?" asked Ronnie bitterly. "How many pictures does she have of Marsh?"

"None," said Pud. "And that's funny, because she square-dances with him nearly every Saturday. You'd never think a sobersides like Marsh would let himself go the way he does when dancing."

Ronnie turned his head, wondering if Pud were joking about the photograph. But Pud's round, bland face was innocent of humor.

"Why does she keep that football picture, and go *pffft* every time she sees me, Pud? And why'd she give up all her dates last spring to coach me in math so I could stay on the track team, and then rush to congratulate Marsh when I beat him out of first place in the mile?"

"Ginger's full of contradictions," observed Pud. "Would you expect a kid sister lively enough to be cheer-leader also to be smart enough to graduate at seventeen? And since I last saw you, she's started her own business, keeping books for small shops and stores here and in Morro Bay. Now she rubs it in that I'm still without a job."

"Jobs are scarce in Seal Cove!"

"Are you telling me! If you can't work at the Inn or in a store, what's left but abalone fishing? I'm not mechanical enough to be a boat-operator, and I sure don't want to tend a diver's line. If anything happened to him, I'd never forgive myself."

Ronnie grinned, knowing that, despite his great size and

---

strength, Pud was as soft-hearted as a girl. Often in a football game Pud had sent two opponents crashing to the turf, and had then good naturedly lifted the winded men to their feet. Sheriff Dart had discovered the same quality in his son when he'd tried to train Pud for the work of a deputy sheriff. Pud became a remarkably accurate shot with all types of guns. But Sheriff Dart had reluctantly abandoned his plans after realizing that Pud could not bear to hurt anything that walked or swam or ran.

Ronnie stopped the Bouncing Betty at Plimm's Grocery. "If our credit is still good, I'd better stock up with groceries before we see Ginger again."

Fifteen minutes later Ronnie emerged from the store with two large cartons of groceries, which he put in back. He slipped behind the wheel and looked at Pud.

"How long does it take your sister to cool down?"

Pud smiled ruefully. "Let's go see Bill."

"Coward!" Ronnie cried with a grin, starting the car.

They drove along the main street to the Ballard Garage and hopped out. Bill was staring at a greasy part he'd removed from a sedan. His brown eyes and genial bulldog face lighting, he hurried over. There was always something amusingly purposeful about his gait, in part due to the fact that his legs were somewhat short for his stocky body.

"Long time, no see, Ronnie," he exclaimed eagerly. "But it does my eyes good. As for you, Fat Boy,—"

"I resent that," yelled Pud. "Put up your dukes, sir!"

Bill Ballard ducked Pud's deliberately wild swing, and they all grinned. It was like old times.

The three of them had been backs on the Seal Cove football

squad for three years. Marsh Marple had been the fourth back, but he'd never been a close friend. There had been some doubt in their coach's mind as to whether Bill should have a place on the team. He was a little light for football, and his short legs slowed him up. But when given a chance, Bill had proved his worth. He was too slow for a spectacular run, but with a tenacity that always surprised his teammates, he could stop bigger men, and usually he was able to wriggle through his opponents for the yard or two needed for a first down. He was at his best on defense, or when a game was going against them, for he seemed to grow more confident, more cheerful in adversity.

Ronnie would never forget how Bill had rallied the spirit of their team in the final minute of a hard-fought game with San Luis Obispo High.

It had looked as though they were going down to a six-to-nothing defeat when Bill had recovered a fumble on their opponents' thirty-six. With but sixty seconds of play, the weary Seal Covers had taken time out to go into a huddle. Ronnie privately doubted if their squad had enough fight left to make another yard. Bill had come up, dragging one foot slightly, his left arm pressed against his chest. On his homely face, heavily smeared with dirt, there had been a funny, twisted grin.

"They're all in," he had surprised his teammates by saying. "Their line is going to crumple like a paper sack."

The words had had an electrifying effect on Ronnie; he had laughed and asked, "Did you get a bump on the head on that last play, Bill?"

Bill had wrinkled his short nose, before continuing confidently, "Let's feint a pass. They'll be expecting it. Then we'll break their line wide open so that Ronnie can go through."

It had gone exactly as Bill planned. He took out his man, and Pud laid two others on the sward. Through the hole they made, Marsh had run interference and had removed the last man blocking the way. Ronnie was able to cross the line standing. But Bill had to be carried unconscious from the field before Marsh could kick the winning point.

Afterward, when the team had visited the hospital, they'd found a doctor taping up Bill, who had a cracked rib.

"When did you smash that rib?" Ronnie had asked suspiciously.

"Recovering the fumble," Bill had admitted with a grin. "Think I wanted to be pulled from the line-up when the game was in the bag?"

That year, to the astonishment of the student body but not to his teammates, Bill had been voted the most valuable player on the squad. . . .

Now, Bill held up a greasy part. "Say, look at this!"

Pud clucked sympathetically, and winked at Ronnie. Trying to appear interested, although he knew no more about mechanics than Pud, Ronnie asked with a straight face, "Oh, a mud-guard pump, isn't it?"

"*Awk!*" Bill cried with a pained expression. "If it was up to you two, the Bouncing Betty would fall apart in a week!"

"We didn't use a piston ring for teething the way you did," Pud said with a grin.

Matt Ballard drove the tow-car into the garage at that moment and jumped out. He was of medium height and stocky like his son, and he moved in the same purposeful way. He gripped Ronnie's arm in a gesture of sympathy, and said, "We're mighty sorry, boy."

Bill thought it best to change the subject. He said, "It didn't take you long to fix the Taylor car, Dad."

Matt Ballard's black mustache quivered indignantly. "Ten-mile drive, and what do I find? A loose distributor head that old farmer Taylor could have fixed in a minute." No more than his son Bill could the elder Ballard understand unmechanical people. "How are you getting on with the Fleming car?"

Bill held up the greasy part.

"What in thunderation are you doing, boy?" his father yelled. "I put a new timing gear in the Fleming car just last month!"

"Oh, you did, did you?" drawled Bill, grinning. "Look at this."

Matt Ballard examined the part and grunted. "Defective, wasn't it? Don't charge Fleming for the work."

"Take back that crack about my not knowing what I'm doing?"

Matt Ballard grabbed the peak of Bill's cap and pulled it down over his nose, and then went off chuckling to the office.

Bill raised the cap with difficulty, and grinned as he glanced after his father. "He's a great guy," he said. "But he doesn't need me here any more than radar on his tow-car. I wish I could find a job where I was really useful."

Bill's mechanical aptitude was something that Ronnie had always taken for granted. Suddenly he saw how it might be put to work.

"You helped for two months on Dad's boat one summer

when his operator was laid up with a broken leg!"

Bill nodded. "Your dad said I kept the engine in top condition, too. But I don't know of any abalone boat that is short an operator."

"I am!" Ronnie exclaimed.

"Do I hear right?" inquired Bill.

"I'm trying abalone fishing."

"Who are you kidding?" asked Bill. "You're going to college."

"I can't. Miss Prindle is trying to put Mardie and Skip in an orphanage, and if I don't prove I can make a home for them, she might do it."

In their long years of friendship, Bill had never failed him. And now, without a moment of hesitation, Bill said, "You've got a boat-operator! If you need a line-tender, Pud's your man."

"Not me!" cried Pud, frightened by the suggestion. "I couldn't do it! If I made a mistake, and anything happened to Ronnie—"

"You'd better not make a mistake!" said Bill ominously.

"New tenders are bound to make mistakes while they're learning," Pud insisted. "Look at what happened to Bill Pierce! His line fouled, his air-hose was cut, and because his crew was green they weren't able to get him up before he strangled in his dress."

"Yes, that happens," Bill said calmly. "On the other hand, both Pierce and Ronnie's father and others have made their first dives with inexperienced crews. Their tenders and operators learned their jobs before they faced their first emergencies."

Pud's plump face was damp. "And what if something had gone wrong the first time Pierce or Ronnie's father went down?"

"Don't you understand that's the chance I have to take?" Ronnie pleaded. "Dad's affairs are in an awful mess, and I can't earn enough at anything else to straighten them out and support Mardie and Skip. I'd trust you more than anyone I know except Hammerhead, and he's working for Marsh."

"I've had two months' experience," Bill added. "I'll teach you how to do the job, Pud. Every tender is inexperienced when he starts out."

"I can't do it," Pud wailed. "I'll try to find Ronnie an experienced tender."

"Where?" demanded Ronnie. "Jim Algrove's been looking up and down the coast for a line-tender. All the good ones are fishing."

"I'll find one somehow," Pud promised hoarsely.

"Pud," Bill said grimly, "would you like the Ronnie Nordhoff treatment, or will you help our pal, now that he needs us?"

The redhead stared at Bill in astonishment. "What's that?"

Bill tried to whistle but his homely face puckered with a repressed grin. Pud's bland face had an expression of innocence that would not deceive anyone.

"What's the Ronnie Nordhoff treatment?"

"Should we tell him?" Bill asked.

"Why not?" said Pud. "Our football days are over."

"Well, Ronnie," Bill declared with a grin, "you weren't a very aggressive football player in your frosh and most of your sophomore year. But in your last two games of your second year, you were terrific."

"You know why." And Ronnie's eyes clouded angrily in recollection. "In my last two soph games, our opponents started kicking me in the scrimmages and in my junior and senior years they kept it up, no matter who we played."

"They never did," said Pud. "It was your teammates who kicked you."

"My pals!" Ronnie cried indignantly. "What was the idea?"

"You were too easy-going," Pud explained. "When anyone pushed you around, however, it made you mad and then nothing could stop you. It was Ginger who first noticed that, and she suggested that if we kicked you now and then to keep you stirred up—"

"It would be *her* idea!" Ronnie exploded.

"Now don't blow up," Pud said hastily. "You became a great quarterback, and helped turn our losing team into a winning one."

"I can't give Ginger the Ronnie Nordhoff treatment," the redhead snapped. "But when a fellow needs a job, and won't tend my line—"

Pud and Bill had never seen Ronnie so angry, not even when he'd risen from a pile-up and was determined to teach a lesson to opponents that he imagined had kicked him. Heavier though he was, Pud knew he was no match for his friend when Ronnie was blazing mad. He turned to flee, but almost immediately realized that he was exposing the broadest part of his anatomy to attack. Wisdom dictated that he surrender!

"All right," he sighed. "I'll be your tender!"

The angry flush faded from Ronnie's freckled face and he

chuckled. Never one to harbor resentments for long, he clapped Pud on the back.

"I didn't mean to lose my temper, Pud. But so many people have been giving me the Ronnie Nordhoff treatment today that I was beginning to feel like plunging through someone's line."

"We'll make a crew," Bill prophesied.

But Pud's plump face was troubled. Clearly he didn't relish the prospect of putting one of his two best friends down in diving dress on his first dive.

"Let's meet at my place at six in the morning," Ronnie said, as he left the garage with Pud. "If I'm lucky, I'll be a diver by this time tomorrow."

And what if he weren't lucky? What if he blacked out under the pressure of a dive? What if he had the misfortune to meet one of the predatory creatures of the deep on his initial descent? Well, those were the hazards an abalone diver must face, and he'd better not think too much about them!

3.

WHAT THE RED MEN STARTED

RONNIE was almost dressed the following morning when he heard the rattle of gravel against his window-pane. Quickly he pulled on a faded blue wool cap of his father's and buttoned up his new pea-jacket. To avoid waking the sleeping children, he slipped from the patio door and closed it quietly. Bill and Pud stood beside the truck.

As he crossed the yard, Ronnie noticed that the pines rimming the valley were tipped with light by the rising sun. But the valley still lay in shadow, and there was a chill bite to the air.

With a nod to his friends, he climbed behind the wheel, and observed wryly, "The trouble with six o'clock is that it comes at such an unearthly hour."

"Doesn't it, though!" Bill agreed, chuckling.

Driving from the yard, Ronnie turned onto the deserted main street, and the old vehicle clanked noisily through the slumbering village. Ronnie parked at the end of the pier. The three boys jumped out, and for a few moments peered in silence across the water.

Suddenly the sun climbed above the hills like a burst of fire, making the cove sparkle with silvery lights. Out beyond the protecting spit, however, the gray seas were feathering in a brisk wind. Two little abalone boats rounding the hook of land climbed and fell in the swells. Another boat to the south would bob into view and then vanish, except for its swaying mast.

"I—I can't put you down on your first dive when—when the seas are like this, Ronnie!" faltered Pud. "Shall we call off fishing today?"

"I suspect our well-fed friend is a little nervous, Ronnie," Bill said with a grin. "But I believe he's right."

Ronnie gave an impatient shrug. "You're not easily discouraged, Bill, and perhaps I should wait for a better day. But Marsh's boat is out, and he's one of the people who has been giving me the Ronnie Nordhoff treatment. If he thinks he can dive today, I'm going to try it."

"Why not practice in the cove first?" suggested Pud.

"That's just ducking the issue; there are no abalones in the cove!" Ronnie started thoughtfully out to sea. "This is working up to a storm. It may be a week or so before we'll have another chance to fish. Mr. Romano gave me only thirty days to show what I can do!"

"You're the diver," Bill said, walking at a purposeful gait toward the truck.

They gathered up numerous sweaters, sleeping bags, an extra can of gasoline, and lunch sacks. And then, loaded like pack-mules, they walked to the end of the pier. Cautiously, because their hands were occupied, they descended the switchback stairs to the loading platform, and dumped their gear into the public skiff.

Ronnie dropped to a thwart, and when his two friends were

settled, he picked up the oars and rowed out to the *Sea Spray*. After climbing aboard and stowing away his luggage, he unlocked the cabin so that Bill could start the engine.

Presently Bill began growling. Ronnie looked in to see what was wrong.

"Can't start it! Have you been using the boat?"

Ronnie hesitated. "Honest, I can't remember, Bill. Everything's been so confused since Mom and Dad—"

"You must have," Bill interrupted. "Every time you or Pud touch anything mechanical, it stops working. I hope the motor doesn't lay down while you're diving!"

Bill worked until the engine started. Gasoline vapor rose in a blue cloud astern; the propeller stirred up milky suds. Crouched in the small cabin, Bill listened with a critical expression on his grease-stained face. He regulated the carburetor until there was a rhythmic throbbing.

"Sounds all right," he said doubtfully, emerging from the cabin. "But I don't know what you've been tampering with. Mind leaving the engine to me after this?"

"Okay, chief," said Ronnie with a laugh.

After Pud had heaved up the anchor, Bill took his place at the railed operator's station on the cabin. He ran the boat up to the loading platform, so that Ronnie could secure the skiff, and then headed across the cove.

At the entrance a whistling sou'wester made the *Sea Spray* pitch. She rose and dropped away, spray exploding in flashing showers over the bow and flying back in stinging gusts.

Swaying on his stocky legs, spinning the wheel first one way, then the other, Bill seemed to relish the punishment. But Ronnie and Pud saw no purpose in sharing it with him.

They retreated to the after-deck, rolled out their sleeping bags, and crawled in to keep warm. Pud reached for a lunch sack that appeared to have been packed for a crew of laborers. He offered Ronnie a thick sandwich, but Ronnie shook his head.

"I haven't even had breakfast, Pud. You run the risk of getting bends if you eat before diving."

Bill had turned southward, and now Ronnie saw the green walls of Seal Cove Valley disappearing astern. Off to port the breakers boomed, splintering into fans of spray against the low bluffs. The slopes beyond rolled away in golden waves, patterned here and there with a dark-green tracery of live oaks.

Lying in his warm sleeping bag, gazing at the bright-yellow hills, the spreading oaks, the deep-blue sky, Ronnie was aware that in some strange way his senses had sharpened. With every nerve of his body, he felt the twisting and rolling of the boat, the violent impacts of the seas. With unusual clarity he heard the breakers cracking before they cannonaded thunderously against the cliffs. He was conscious of his cold hands, the labored quality of his breathing. This quickening of his senses was something he had often experienced before important football games. Perhaps his mind was summoning the defenses of his body to meet a threatened danger. But the dangers he would face today were greater than any encountered in the past.

The truth was that he was distinctly uneasy about making his first dive!

So many people had tried to discourage him from following his father's work, and now he wondered whether they were right. Even Ginger, after bringing order to the Nord-hoff house the previous day, had begged him to reconsider. How angry she had been when he refused! Ronnie winced on recalling her biting comment: "Oh, I should know better than try to talk sense to you!"

Only one person had offered encouragement, and she was their new neighbor, Mrs. Nellie Cameron. Bringing over a bread pudding for their breakfast, she had stopped to talk of the days when Bill Pierce and the other young fishermen of Morro Bay had broken the Japanese abalone monopoly. She had also spoken of the evening his father came to her, brimming with excitement, to describe his first dive. Before leaving, Mrs. Cameron had said, with a confidence that still warmed Ronnie's heart, "You'll make as good a diver as your father. It's in your blood!"

He was still thinking of her heartening words when Pud drew another sandwich and two bananas from his lunch sack. "Who started this industry, Ronnie?" Pud asked. "The Japanese?"

Ronnie shook his head. "Once Dad tried to trace its beginnings from fragments of history, scientific evidence and Indian legends. He concluded that abalones had been the favorite food of the coastal red men long before Columbus discovered America."

He paused, struck by the thought that any part of the coast now gliding by might in bygone days have been a primitive encampment. But he pushed the idea aside, and went on:

"The coastal Indians had no domestic animals, and in this arid country they couldn't raise much. They must have had trouble getting enough food to keep alive, Pud. Probably they killed a few deer, but more likely they had to depend on rabbits or ground squirrels. They ate the pods of the mesquite, and ground up acorns for meal. Their principal diet must have been the mollusks they took at low tide—mussels and abalones pried from exposed rocks, clams dug from the sand, and the smaller octopuses captured in tidal pools—"

"Wait a minute!" Pud protested, throwing overboard a banana skin. "Do you expect me to believe an octopus is related to a clam?"

"I thought Dad was pulling my leg when he told me they were both mollusks," Ronnie admitted. "But it's true, Pud. An abalone is really a big sea-snail, with a single, large, ear-shaped valve or shell, right? Bivalves like clams or oysters have two shells. And the octopuses and squids have an internal shell."

"I wouldn't know what's inside an octopus," said Pud. "But I don't see any family resemblance to other shellfish."

"There is, though," Ronnie insisted. "An abalone has a muscular 'foot' which is really a suction surface covering its entire under side. It resembles the suction disks of an octopus or squid, or the suction foot of a clam or an oyster."

"I get it," said Pud, taking a large bite of his sandwich. "How do you suppose the Indians got abalones?"

"Pried them from the rocks uncovered by the receding tide, I suppose. Dad thought the squaws must have cut the abalones from their shells, cleaned them, and hacked the chunks of meat into thin slices with pieces of shell. After pounding the slices, they could have put them on hot rocks around a fire to cook. But to the red men, abalones were more than just a nourishing food. You've seen the shells of different species of abalones in Dad's collection, Pud—the threaded, the pink, the green, the black and the red abalones—with mother-of-pearl ranging in color from milky-silvers, pale green, and warm pinks shot with swirls of emerald. Well, the coastal Indians worked pieces of abalone shell into dress ornaments, and any not needed that way were used as a shell currency in trading with inland tribes."

Ronnie paused, probing at his memory for other stories his father had told him.

"Abalones remained an Indian food until Chinese were brought to California to help build the railroads," he recalled. "Once that work was done, some Chinese formed a small abalone industry. They'd slice and dry the shellfish, and ship their product to China. Before laws could be passed to regulate the size they could take, the Chinese had stripped the rocks in shallow water of abalones large and small. There were so few left that the industry died a natural death."

"There must have been plenty left in deeper water," Pud suggested.

"Yes; that's where the Japanese came into the picture. They started to fish for abalones with power-boats and deep-sea divers. First they fished in Monterey Bay. Then they worked southward along the San Simeon Coast. Before long they had processing plants at Morro Bay and Santa Barbara, and were working even farther southward, out of San Pedro, Newport Beach and San Diego. They were good fishermen, but they kept out everyone who wasn't a Jap. They owned the boats, the plants; they even controlled the marketing of abalones. That's what Bill Pierce had to buck when he decided to break the Japanese monopoly in the mid-twenties, Pud."

Ronnie thought of his father's stories about the first leader of the abalone fishermen. The colorful Bill Pierce had strongly resented the Japanese control of the industry because he was half coastal Indian, and could never forget the part abalones had played in the diet of his red ancestors. In defiance of the Japs, he bought a patched diving dress and a rowboat. Then, accompanied by two friends as ignorant of diving as himself, he went out to see what he could do.

An utterly fearless man, he became an expert diver. Soon he purchased a motor-boat, equipping it with an air-compressor to relieve his companions of the hard work of supplying his air with a hand-pump. Pierce prepared his first catches in his own kitchen, selling his pack from door to door. When he earned enough, he built the first American-owned abalone plant. And in time he acquired boats which he rented to friends on shares.

During this period Ronnie's father appeared in Morro Bay —a young man of twenty who, though ragged, footsore, and hungry, had an unquenchable spirit that had quickly won Pierce's sympathy. Thor Nordhoff was a child of the depression. The oldest son in a large family, he had run away from the Montana ranch where he was born to avoid being a burden. Wandering from place to place, he had taken whatever odd jobs were offered.

Pierce set him to work pounding abalone steaks. Within a short time Thor Nordhoff was so skillful at it that when his thoughts turned toward becoming an abalone diver, his employer wouldn't hear of it. Growing impatient, the young man persuaded two fellow workers in the plant to help him achieve his ambition. They borrowed one of Pierce's boats and sailed from the bay to try their luck. When they stopped close to some rocks that seemed a likely place to find shellfish, they had a hard time trying to discover how to put the diving dress on Thor Nordhoff. On his initial descent he proved a natural, however, having no trouble either with his gear or in gathering abalones.

The three new fishermen returned to Morro Bay to discover that Pierce was awaiting them somewhat anxiously. Ronnie's father cried eagerly, "Bill, can I rent your boat?"

Pierce countered with, "How did you make out?"

"Thirty-odd dozen this time, Bill. But with practice—"

"You're wasted in my plant," Pierce interrupted. "You've rented a boat!"

Pierce never regretted his decision. Within a few weeks Ronnie's father took more abalones than any other diver, and he remained among the top fishermen to the day he died. . . .

Now comfortably full of food, Pud appeared to be sleeping. But suddenly he roused himself, reached into his sack for an apple, and began shining it on his sleeping bag.

"Pierce, your father, and the other American fishermen must have had quite a time getting control of the abalone industry from the Japs, Ronnie."

"It was a small-scale war, I guess, but Dad would never talk much about it. Maybe he was afraid I'd get ideas. Occasionally he would let something slip out, though, and last night Mrs. Cameron told me more about what happened."

Thoughtfully Pud bit into the apple. "None of the fishermen will say much. Do you suppose there was any shooting?"

"I doubt it. But there were fist fights. Mostly the fracas was confined to rough pranks—as if diving weren't dangerous

45

enough!"

Ronnie chuckled in recalling something he'd learned the night before.

"Mrs. Cameron said that once Dad saw a Japanese diver on the other side of a rock prying off abalones. To give him a pleasant surprise, Dad reached over and grabbed his shoulder. The Jap thought an octopus was attacking him. After slashing in all directions with his knife, he signalled his tender to draw him up fast. Reaching the surface, he saw another boat alongside his own, and suspected what had taken place below."

"Did the Jap ever get revenge?" Pud asked.

"He sure did! A short time later, when both boats were close together, the Japanese wrapped Dad's life line around a rock. The little Oriental then had his tender take him up so he could watch the fun. Hammerhead nearly pulled his arms from their sockets trying to tear his diver loose. Chet Thomas, who was then Dad's operator, came to help, thinking the line had snagged. They couldn't understand why the Japs near-by were convulsed with laughter. After a time Dad filled a basket with shellfish, but when he tried to signal Hammerhead, the rope resisted his pull. My father soon worked back to the rock where his line was tied, and freed it. Well, one thing in that abalone war always led to another. Dad and some other American divers felt they had to retaliate for the scare Hammerhead and Thomas had gotten. They secured a sling of rocks to the propeller of a Japanese boat. And the next day every Jap in Morro Bay surrounded her, trying to figure out why she moved so slowly with her engine wide open. Those must have been lively times, Pud!"

———

Ronnie paused, staring uneasily up at the sky, now largely overcast.

"The rough tricks that they played on one another didn't really decide the conflict," he continued. "The American fishermen spent more for their boats, motors and equipment. And they took greater chances, too, losing one out of ten boats every year—as they still do. By greater daring than the Japs, by having better engines and finer gear, the Americans took more abalones than their rivals. Other things being equal, Pud, the side that could produce the larger pack was bound to seize the other fellow's markets. The last Japanese gave up the struggle several years before the sneak attack on Pearl Harbor."

Hearing Bill Ballard shout, they slipped from their bags and stood up. Off to port was an L-shaped building of unpainted boards wedged into a cleft in the cliffs. Ronnie's father had once pointed it out as the dwelling of "China Charlie," who gathered seaweed and shipped it to his homeland. But in a moment Ronnie realized it was not the weather-beaten old house that Bill was calling to their attention. Offshore, and to the south of it, under the looming shadow of the great rock known as Blacktop, another abalone boat bobbed on the swells.

"Whose boat, Bill?" Ronnie shouted.

Bill glanced back. On his bulldog face, now damp with spray, was a wry grin. "You can't escape him, Ronnie. It's Marsh Marple!"

Ronnie groaned. "Sail south of Blacktop, Bill," he cried, after a moment. "I don't want Marsh to know if I flub my first dive."

"Might be handy to have him near-by," Bill pointed out. "Just in case you should black-out."

Grimly, Ronnie answered, "I'll take that chance!"

He climbed onto the cabin beside Bill. It irked him to see his father's old crew helping Marsh into his diving dress. Naturally, Halvorson and Carlson had every right to fish with Marsh. What was annoying to Ronnie was that they thought he lacked the qualities that had made his father a great diver. "Hammerhead" Halvorson had been Thor Nordhoff's line-tender for twenty years; he had acquired his nickname by popping up and denting his helmet on the boat on his one and only dive. Ken Carlson had been operator of the *Sea Spray* for a shorter time. Carlson had had to hold his weight in check during the time he was piloting Flying Fortresses over Europe, but in the years since leaving the service, he had placed no restraint on a long-repressed appetite. His great girth, as a result, had become the butt of considerable humor wherever abalone fishermen gathered.

A minute later Bill shifted into neutral and allowed their boat to drift alongside the *Bubbles*. Hammerhead—a rangy man with a scraggly yellow mustache and a squashed sea-man's cap—glanced up, his china-blue eyes widening in alarm at seeing Ronnie.

"You can't begin diving in such heavy seas!" he protested. "Besides, that fat Dart boy has no experience as a tender!"

"He believes I'll make a diver, which is more than you do, Hammerhead!"

The old man wrung his gnarled hands helplessly. "After tending your father's line so long, Ronnie, would I desert you if I thought for a moment you were serious about diving?"

"You're not the only one who believes I can't be serious about anything but having a good time," said Ronnie grimly, although impressed by Hammerhead's sincerity. "Let's sail south of Blacktop, Bill."

"Not *there!*" cried Hammerhead.

"Why not?" demanded Ronnie.

"Your father was diving south of Blacktop one time, and he gave an emergency signal. I pulled him up fast, and he looked scared half out of his wits. When he said we'd better move to a new location, I asked him what had happened. 'Hammerhead,' he answered, 'you'd think I was crazy if I told you.' That's all he'd tell me."

Ronnie wondered if his father had played a prank on the old man, but it didn't seem likely. He stared at Marsh, who sat with his feet in the open after-hatch, waiting for his crew to finish putting on his diving dress.

"You'd be smart to listen to Hammerhead," Marsh advised. "I'm not even sure I can stay down long when it's this rough."

While Ronnie debated whether to heed Marsh's advice, another abalone boat sailed around the seaward side of the great rock. Orrie Shumaker stood on the diving ladder suspended from the port side. The folds of his rubberized dress rose and fell, and as the other boat drew nearer, Ronnie could hear gasping breaths coming from the diver's bloodless lips.

"My number . . . was almost called," he announced hoarsely, when his boat came to a stop. "Ran into an octopus . . . nearly as large as my boat."

"Twenty-six feet across?" Ronnie demanded in a startled voice.

"Closer to twenty-four . . . would be my guess." Still breathing heavily, Shumaker turned his small, dark eyes on Ronnie. "You'd be wise to take that offer I made you yesterday for your father's plant and boat. Go into something less dangerous, my boy!"

"If I took your offer, I couldn't support Mardie or Skip, or pay my father's debts."

"I doubt if you'll get a better offer," Shumaker snapped.

"Maybe not," Ronnie said. "But it doesn't matter now. I'm going to become an abalone diver."

"You'll never make the grade," Shumaker stated bluntly.

He motioned to his tender. The man slipped a copper helmet over Shumaker's head. The stocky little diver lowered himself a few rungs and then, with surprising agility, jumped sidewise to land with a splash. As his tender paid out the life line, Shumaker's helmet grew more dim until it vanished beneath a pale-green swirl of rising air bubbles.

Air-hose peeled from the coil on deck. It could scarcely be distinguished from the weaving strands of bull kelp as it slithered downward. Seconds later, there was a jerk on the life line. Holding the line with one hand, the tender reached for the kelp knife. Thrusting the long pole down close to the black air-hose, he began cutting away kelp that might become entangled with the line or hose. At each upward stroke, the scimitar-shaped blade on the end of the pole severed a stalk, and it drifted away, supported by its big air bladder.

"How do you avoid cutting the air-hose?" Pud asked. "In the water, it looks almost like a kelp stalk."

Shumaker's tender glanced up, his face expressionless. "Green tenders sometimes do cut a hose."

Pud looked as if he were going to be sick.

But Ronnie, still smarting from Shumaker's words, was not to be discouraged. "Take the boat northward a few hundred yards, Bill. I'm going down!"

He stalked aft, lifted aside the hatch cover, and pulled out his father's diving gear. The red dress was patched in several places, so Ronnie pushed it back under the deck and chose the black one. After removing his shoes, he pulled it up to his waist and sat down on the edge of the hatch. Seeing Pud staring helplessly at the outfit, Ronnie kicked at a pair of cast-iron shoes with heavy tire-casing tops.

"Buckle these on, Pud. Bill will show you how to bolt the collar-strips and breast plate."

Bill shifted the gear-lever into neutral, came aft and dropped to deck. He grinned when he saw Ronnie trying to force his hands through the tight cuffs. Grasping the suit, Bill hauled it down again. He picked up a jar of petroleum jelly from the hatch, and handed it to Ronnie.

"Grease your hands and wrists with this, and they'll slide through. To think I'd be explaining that to Thor Nordhoff's son!"

"You know how it was, Bill," Ronnie said. "Dad was afraid that if he let me come out with him on the boat very often, I'd want to dive instead of going to college. Now I have to learn the hard way."

"I'll say you have," Bill agreed sympathetically.

As soon as Ronnie had worked his hands through the cuffs, Bill showed Pud how to fit the copper collar strips between the divided neck flaps. Screws on each strip had to be driven through holes in the outer flap. And over the screws went the breastplate. The top of this plate had a half-circular collar, and when the other half had been put on behind, Bill bolted both plates with a wrench. Then he tied the life line around Ronnie's waist, leaving an extra length at the back to fasten around the heavy leather belt after it was strapped over the line.

"Just an extra precaution," Bill explained. "The life line could be attached to the belt, but if it should snag and break, we'd still have a line around Ronnie's body."

"It's good one of us knows what we're doing," said Pud, with a pallid smile. "How can we haul him up if the line parts?"

"Use his air-hose." Bill wrapped the life line around one hand. "Giddap, horsie!" he said to Ronnie. "I'll keep a tight grip on your reins in case you fall overboard."

Awkward on his shoes, which had high cleats under the balls of the feet and smaller ones under the toes, Ronnie stepped to the deck. The ladder was still aboard, blocking his way, and he kicked it overboard. It struck the water with a splash, slanting down from the cross-brace extending off to port. One slow step at a time, Ronnie made his way along the narrow deck until he was past the cabin. Kneeling then, he grasped the ladder support and eased his body over the side until he could feel the rungs under his feet.

Bill handed the line to Pud and went aft to start the gasoline air-compressor. Presently it popped with a skipping beat. Bill came forward with the copper helmet, and tossed the coil of air-hose attached to it on deck. He picked up a dilapidated tobacco sack, dipped it into the sea, and scrubbed the insides of the three glass plates in the helmet. Then he lowered the helmet overboard with the hose, filling it with water, which he dumped out a moment later.

"The tobacco leaves a thin film of oil on the plates," Bill explained. "Now they won't fog up. How are you feeling, kid?"

"F-f-fine," Ronnie said, ashamed of the hoarse, nervous quality of his voice. He tried to grin but he was afraid he made a grimace instead. His heart was pounding with rapid, heavy beats. The pulse in his throat was throbbing. His mouth was dry. And when he pulled on his cotton gloves and strapped an abalone-bar to his right wrist, he was conscious of the shaking of his cold hands.

Bill turned the monel valve of the helmet, and there was a brief, sharp hiss of air before he screwed the valve closed again. He suspended a heavy lead weight from the knobs of the breastplate, and slipped a cord over Ronnie's head to hang another weight on his shoulders.

"Is this getting your wind up?" Bill asked.

"A l-little," Ronnie admitted. This was understatement, for he felt as if some unruly mice were scampering about in his stomach.

Bill gave him a long, steady glance, then looked up at Pud, and chuckled. "You two look like a couple of anemic ghosts. Let's talk this out and get some things straight. How many times did your dad go down, Ronnie?"

"Maybe twenty thousand dives in twenty years, counting those made in marine surveys and work on breakwaters, as well as in fishing."

Bill clucked. "Dangerous business!"

Ronnie got Bill's point and was able to laugh. "I guess *one* dive won't hurt me!"

"I hope not," said Bill. "Now, I can't tell you much about what to do under water, except to duck down so that the blood will go to your head if you should get woozy. Everything else you'll have to learn from experience, as other abalone divers do. But I can set your mind at rest about several points.

"Pud isn't likely to make any mistakes today. Accidents usually happen when a tender becomes so familiar with his job that he grows careless. But suppose Pud does cut your air-hose with the kelp knife. Don't get rattled; just close your exhaust valve. You'll have enough air to remain alive five minutes or a little longer, and we'll have you up by then."

"If my life line hasn't fouled," amended Ronnie.

"Your line snags in a crack only when it's pulled at an angle or becomes slack. I'll try to have the boat right over your bubbles whichever way you go. And I'll see to it that Pud keeps your line taut at all times."

"How will I know if Ronnie should black-out?" Pud asked nervously.

"His bubbles won't move around, and he'll ignore your signals. And those signals, by the way, are very simple. Ronnie gives a tug on his line when he reaches bottom; two, if he wants a basket; three, if he decides to come up."

"Don't I send any messages?" asked Pud.

"Of course you do. You repeat every one he gives you, first of all, to show that you have it straight. But you also 'talk on the line' when it's necessary. You might give a single jerk, for example, if Ronnie forgets to report that he's reached bottom. If he answers, you know he's all right. There are also other reasons to signal him. You yank three times if you think he's staying down too long, or if, for any cause whatsoever, you believe he'd better come up."

Turning to Ronnie, Bill added, "Grip your line as you descend, because it's at the back of your belt and hard to reach at that time. If you start to lose consciousness, give three quick jerks. Pud will bring you right up." His homely face sobered abruptly. "Oh, I almost forgot the most important thing!"

"W-what's that?" Ronnie quavered.

"I want you to bring me a pretty little green-haired mermaid!"

The unexpected nonsense was exactly what Ronnie needed. He laughed, and with that reaction his stomach relaxed. Picking up the rope basket, he struck Bill on the head.

"That's better!" Bill said. "You were looking too jumpy!"

He opened the air-valve of the helmet and slipped it over Ronnie's head, giving it a quarter-turn to lock it to the collar. The sudden roar of air was like a dynamo.

Bill's matter-of-fact approach to diving had dispelled much of Ronnie's earlier misgivings. Feeling confident now that he'd have no serious trouble, he lowered himself clumsily down the ladder. Water clamped the rubber dress around his legs, then his waist.

Ronnie released the ladder, intending to slide backward into the sea. And then something quite unforeseen by Bill occurred. His legs swiftly rose, so that he lay spread-eagled on the water, staring upward through his grilled vision plate at the rolling black clouds that now covered the sky.

First bobble! he thought with despair. *But what did I do wrong?*

He tried to force his feet down to regain an upright position. Air had ballooned the legs of his dress, however, so that he might as well have tried to sink an inflated life-raft. He put out a hand to grasp the ladder but was unable to locate it.

A swell lifted him, rolling him slightly sidewise as it flowed under his body. He had a brief and startling glimpse of the *Sea Spray*, across not less than a dozen feet of foam-laced water! For the first time real panic stirred in Ronnie. He was drifting away from the boat, and helpless to do anything about it!

4.

FIRST DIVE

Bobbing on the sea like an inflated rubber animal used by bathers, Ronnie was both frightened and puzzled. Pud was in part to blame for allowing so much slack that his diver could drift away from the boat. But Pud had no reason to expect anything like this to happen! What mistake had allowed him to assume a prone position after leaving the ladder?

Annoyance flowed through Ronnie at realizing that his father's old crew were witnesses to his clumsiness. Hammerhead and Carlson probably expected something like this! Angrily, Ronnie raised both legs and brought them swiftly down. Though the impact made them sting, it accomplished nothing more.

He felt himself being towed toward the boat. Seeing the ladder rising and falling with the *Sea Spray's* rolling, he grasped it and once more tried to force his legs down. No use! Strain as he might, he was still a horizontal diver!

Through his oval vision plate, he saw his operator descending the ladder. When Bill turned the monel valve, the roar in his helmet dwindled to a faint hissing, then finally ceased. Rapidly air bled from his dress. With nothing to keep him afloat, Ronnie's cast-iron shoes sank, bringing him back to a vertical position. Grateful though he was to Bill for thinking of this obvious solution, he was at the same time uncomfortably aware that without any air he might sink like a chunk of iron should Pud lose his grip on the life line for even a few moments.

Leaning over, Bill placed his mouth close to the face plate, and shouted, "Listen, pal, allow yourself to sink in leaving the ladder. If you *sit down,* air flows to the legs of your suit —and up they'll come!"

Glad to know the nature of his error, Ronnie waved to show he understood. Bill turned the valve, and once more his ears were bombarded by a thunderous roaring. Water no longer clamped the rubber outfit so tightly to his body that each breath was an effort. He was relieved to find himself becoming more buoyant.

Part of his assurance, however, had ebbed away. Diving wasn't as simple as Bill made out! And while their first mistake hadn't been serious, they might, in their inexperience, make other blunders that could have grave consequences. Badly shaken now, Ronnie's hand trembled as he made final adjustments with his air-valve. Then, with faltering heart, he waved.

Pud paid out his line, and a swell shattered like silver tinsel against his vision plate. The bottom of the boat rose and vanished. Through the pale-green water Ronnie saw nothing at first but shimmering specks of sediment, but presently he was gliding through kelp. The blades changed from brown to purple, then back to brown as they swayed like draperies in a gentle breeze.

———

Ronnie's earlier nervousness was replaced by a zest for this strange new world. But his feeling of elation was quickly driven away by a throbbing in his ears. Violent streaks of pain shot through his head. Momentarily he lost consciousness, and the life line slipped from his limp fingers. When yellow balls of fire burst through the darkness before his eyes, when the roar of his air faded to a far-off rumbling, he knew what was happening.

He was blacking-out!

Blindly he groped for his line so that he could signal Pud to pull him up! But as Bill had warned him, it was tied to the back of his belt, and not easy to locate while his senses were wavering. Reaching upward and backward during the brief intervals between the intense, probing pains, Ronnie tried to find the rope but it continued to elude him. Then his hand closed on something solid. His tug met not the slightest resistance! Dimly he was aware that he must have grasped a kelp stalk.

Through the swimming sea of blackness rose a picture of the Bouncing Betty, climbing a mountain road. Pud was driving, and Bill, on his other side, saw him lean over, holding his head. The memory was so vivid that he thought he heard Bill shouting, "Your ears are blocked, Ronnie. Blow and swallow!" Now he tried the remedy that had given him relief then. Clamping his lips tightly, he blew until his cheeks swelled out, and swallowed repeatedly. Moments later his ears popped. And with the equalizing of pressure inside and outside his head, the darkness receded, the pain was gone.

Gliding upward past his vision plates were sandstone walls. He was descending into a submarine crevasse.

As lightly as a feather, he struck the rough, rocky bottom. When his weight was no longer suspended from the life line, however, he felt the torrential current sweeping through the undersea canyon. He stumbled and floundered on the uneven, slippery stones while trying to maintain his balance.

Finding a precarious purchase for his shoes at last, Ronnie braced against the thrust of the invisible river, and looked about. There was a dreamlike quality to this marine world in which he found himself. The soft, luminous light changed constantly with the shadow-play of the swells, perhaps thirty feet above.

Strange, vividly colored plants and small animals intensified his feeling that this was a fantasy which might vanish. Great purple sea-urchins, with long swaying spines, were like porcupines in weird masquerade. Scarlet starfish formed intricate designs on the beige walls. In a protected crack, sea-anemones waved brilliant, questing tentacles in search of food. Hermit crabs in another recess dragged whorled shells with jerky movements while crawling through an elfin forest of lacy red seaweed. A school of tiny fish, shimmering in the subdued brightness, swam before his plate. Ronnie remembered that the inner knob of his monel valve would spill excess air. Now he bumped it with his head to discover what the fish would do. As a shower of silvery bubbles spurted upward, the school scattered in fright.

Belatedly he recalled that he had not signalled. If he delayed much longer, Pud would think he had lost consciousness and pull him up! Ronnie gave a sharp tug on his line, and was reassured by his tender's prompt answer. Awkwardly as a child learning to walk, he began to flounder along the crevasse. After a dozen steps, he stumbled and reached out to steady himself against the sandstone wall. Expecting support, he was astonished when his hand touched nothing, and he nearly fell.

This was a dream world in more ways than one! Why couldn't he touch a wall apparently within arm's reach?

After a moment's thought, he understood. Water acted like a gigantic lens. It brought distant objects closer than they were in reality. And looking at a sea-urchin of grotesque proportions, he decided that water must also magnify everything to make it seem deceptively large. He must remember that!

Starting on again in his search for abalones, Ronnie no longer found the high cleat under his instep a hindrance. Though it tipped him forward, making it difficult to maintain balance while standing straight, it was of tremendous help when he drove his feet against the bottom, fighting the opposing current. After rocks gave way to sand, he mistakenly concluded that he could pay less attention to his footing. Startled flatfish scuttled away at his approach, trailing sea-dust in their wakes.

Advancing with careless haste, he had the misfortune to step on a sting ray. A diamond-shaped fish, perhaps four feet in diameter, it was so perfectly camouflaged in the sand that Ronnie failed to see it until its tail whipped back. The poisoned spine lodged in the tire-casing top of his shoe. Retreat then became impossible.

The sting ray rose like a giant bat, beating the water into swirls and eddies with its wings. Ronnie was turned upside down, so that the air flowed to the legs of his dress. Only for a moment did he remain in that position before the creature's dive for the sand again brought him upright. Then, whirling in terror, the ray spun Ronnie about like a human pinwheel. Only the grills over his vision plates prevented them from being broken as his helmet repeatedly thudded the crevasse walls. Fortunately, he was upright when the sting ray at length tore its spine free and fled, stirring up clouds of silt along the bottom.

Stunned and trembling, Ronnie watched the fish disappear around a turn of the undersea canyon.

This sure isn't my lucky day! he reflected.

He thought of the uncomfortable minutes when he lay spread-eagled on the sea . . . the intense pain that had almost brought about a mental black-out . . . this recent experience, which might have ended disastrously if his plates had broken and his air had been lost. If this was what diving was like, he wanted no part of it!

He grasped his life line, intending to give three emphatic tugs that would leave no doubt in Pud's mind that he wished to come up—and quickly, too! But with his hand on the rope, he hesitated.

Wasn't it possible that every diver felt this way after his first mishaps? Things were bound to go wrong while you were learning. But he knew how to slip from a ladder now, he'd solved the problem of changing pressure, and in the future he could watch for the revealing bulge of a sting ray's eyes in working along a sandy bottom.

If he survived his early mistakes, there were rich rewards. At times his father's share of a single day's haul amounted to $400 or more. And while an increasing number of fishermen,

and a growing scarcity of abalones would make such bo-
nanzas rare indeed in the future, he could still count on a
substantial income as a diver. Nor could he think of any
other work in which he could earn enough to support Mardie
and Skip, and pay his father's debts.

Another reason for Ronnie's hesitation was his townspeople's belief that he could not buckle down to a hard and de-
manding task. By quitting now, he'd confirm his critics' opin-
ion that he couldn't take it! Maybe his high-school teammates
had been right in giving him the Ronnie Nordhoff treatment!
Perhaps he was too happy-go-lucky! But at least he could give
himself a fair chance to show what he could do!

Still uneasy, but angrily determined now, Ronnie stumbled
on.

Where the crevasse forked, he chose the north branch. Soon
it brought him to a marine grotto formed by an overhang of
rock. Only a little light penetrated this cavern, so that it was
as shadowy as a cathedral. Protected from currents, it offered
an ideal lodging place for the plants and animals of the sea.

Crowded for space on roof and walls and slanting floor,
they formed a living palette of colors. Golds and scarlets stood
out in brilliant rebellion against subdued mauves and browns
and greens. Spotted among this profusion of marine plants
and animals were seaweeds as glowing as a rainbow. Bare,
oval spaces spoke of another abalone diver's visit, and the re-
moval of shellfish from the walls.

Cautiously Ronnie peered about to discover whether any
predatory creature inhabited this dead-end of the crevasse.
Seeing nothing that might harm him, he pushed aside sea-
plants with his abalone-bar. Presently he located an oval shell,

streaked with red, and slightly ajar. Slipping the point of the bar beneath the shell, he pried quickly to break the hold of the abalone's suction foot. He raised it before his plate, astounded at its size, for it appeared as large as a basketball. But, to his intense disappointment, the shell passed easily between the jutting prongs on his bar. They were set eight inches apart, and any red abalone of smaller diameter was below legal size. The magnifying power of water had once more deceived him!

Replacing the shellfish, he searched for others, clambering up the sloping floor, parting and looking among the stalked hydroids and large, flower-like anemones. Though he pried away a number of abalones, only one, perhaps nine inches across, was big enough to keep. Still, he felt a tingle of excitement as he dropped it through the circle of hose forming the mouth of his rope basket.

Leaving the grotto, he now retraced his steps to try the south fork of the crevasse. It angled seaward, at times becoming so narrow that air was squeezed from his dress as he forced his way ahead. Bare spots bore evidence that another diver had fished here. Beyond reach there was an occasional abalone he had missed, but at first Ronnie could find no way to take them. His initial attempts to climb the sheer rocky faces always ended in failure, despite the buoyancy of his dress. Quite by chance he discovered the secret of climbing when one prong of his prying bar caught on a projection. He could use it like an alpinist's pick to pull himself up the walls! Then, while clinging with fingertips, he was able to collect a few more shellfish.

His meager success, however, was discouraging. When his way was blocked by a large mound of rocks, he wondered whether it was worthwhile to go on. Was he searching in the wrong places? Why hadn't he asked his father where to look? Without much hope, Ronnie squatted to peer under the bottom rock of the barrier.

His heart-beat quickened at seeing several oval reddish shellfish attached to the lower side. Eagerness made him clumsy. Failing to pry loose the nearest one, it clamped so tightly to the rock that he could find no place to slip the bar beneath its shell for a second try. But four other abalones came away easily enough. And all exceeded ten inches in diameter! Encouraged, he searched on the under surfaces of other rocks in the pile. Abalones clung to nearly all. And when he'd crossed the tumbled heap, his basket was full.

He gave two jerks on his line. After a short delay, it descended, bringing him an empty basket which he untied and replaced with the bulging one. Two tugs on the rope sent this gliding upward.

As he advanced, the crevasse grew narrower and deeper, so that only a pale-blue glimmer of light seeped down from above. Ronnie found it disturbing to be so closely confined, and he suspected that it was no place for a beginner. Doubtful about his ability to free himself if he were trapped between the walls, he was still so buoyed up by his recent success that he hated to leave. He was taking abalones in quantity on his first dive, something that only his father, Bill Pierce and a few other fishermen had accomplished.

Regardless of the poor light, he could make out the oval shells of abalones among the sea grasses. And nearly all that he found were large enough to keep—strong evidence that no other diver had visited this part of the crevasse. After dropping another dozen shellfish into his bag, he was snatched from the floor, then slowly settled back. He stood motionless, his heart pounding heavily, wondering what had happened. Pud must be keeping the life line too taut, he decided, so that the boat had lifted him when she rose on a swell.

A moment later, he felt three jerks on his line. Pud wanted him to come up! Perhaps Bill was having trouble following the rising air bubbles. It was so calm in the crevasse, however, that Ronnie couldn't believe conditions above were severe. In no mood to quit, he repeated the signal, and followed with a single jerk to say he intended to continue fishing. Three more abalones went into his basket. Then, when he was dragged from the bottom once more, Pud repeated his urgent signal.

With a feeling of reluctance, Ronnie worked ahead to a wider part of the crevasse and gave three jerks on his line.

The response was prompt. Ronnie was plucked from the bottom and glided upward between the sandstone walls. Within a few moments, he emerged from the crevasse into sunlit water glittering with golden particles. Fish, blazing blue and silver in the soft, brilliant light, wove among the stalks of bull kelp through which he was passing.

Barely in time, Ronnie recalled that his father always exercised while coming up. What reason had he given? In a moment the half-forgotten explanation flashed into his mind.

The compressed air he'd been breathing was composed of oxygen and nitrogen. While the excess oxygen absorbed through his lungs could do little more than exhilarate, the nitrogen was dangerous. It might froth at his joints in a quick ascent, exactly as soda bubbles do when a pop bottle is opened. Undissolved nitrogen bubbles were the cause of the paralysis known as diver's bends! And the best way to get rid of them was by vigorous exercise as you were pulled up. To make up for his forgetfulness, Ronnie began to kick frog-fashion and flex his arms like an irate Punch in a puppet show. He was still doing these gymnastics when the bottom of the boat slipped by him.

Instants later a swell crashed over his head and he was bobbing beside the boat. Grasping the ladder, he tried to lift his partially filled basket aboard, but found it too heavy. Pud leaned over to snatch it with a heavy wire lifting-hook.

The ladder was plunging so wildly with the boat's rolling that Ronnie was afraid it might break his face plate. Finally he took a chance and caught hold of a rung, laboriously drag-ging himself up with hands alone until he could use his feet to climb. Fatigue struck him like a blow upon leaving the water. Encumbered with over two hundred pounds of gear, it was all he could do to pull himself up high enough so that he could lean wearily over the deck. Pud unscrewed his hel-met.

It was a relief no longer to hear the constant roaring; to feel the cool, salty breeze after the hot compressed air. Never had Ronnie felt so drained of strength, even after the fourth quarter of a hard football game.

"Why didn't you come up when I gave three jerks?" Pud angrily demanded.

Lying with his cheek pressed against the deck, and gasp-ing for breath, Ronnie made no attempt to answer. Within minutes his breathing became more normal. When his strength returned, he straightened up on the ladder and looked at Pud. His friend's broad, plump face was still white with strain.

"You might give me more than ten minutes to fish, Pud, before you start signalling me to come up."

From the forward end of the engine cabin, where he still stood at the wheel, Bill exclaimed, "*Ten minutes!* You were down an hour, Ronnie! Divers lose all sense of time when they're below."

Ronnie glanced at Bill in disbelief, but could discern no glint of humor to suggest his operator was joking. He turned to his tender again.

"A slack line is dangerous, Pud, but don't hold mine taut enough to drag me from the bottom with every rise of the boat. Keep that up, and sooner or later you'll pull me against a sharp rock and rip my dress!"

"How could I help that when it's this rough?" Pud demanded indignantly. "Sometimes the boat was swept back twenty feet or more from your bubbles!"

"That's right," Bill admitted. "We haven't enough horses of power to hold position in these seas. You've proved yourself a natural by taking about four dozen abalones on your initial dive, Ronnie; even your father did little better his first time down. Let Pud help you aboard, so we can start back."

Ronnie glanced westward, and saw that a sooty cloudbank was building up across the horizon. The stiffening wind, which had hauled around to that quarter, lashed the seas into crested swells. He turned to look at the other boats. Only the *Bubbles* rose and sat in the rollers. And Hammerhead was having a hard time keeping his footing as he pulled a heavy basket of abalones aboard, and dragged them aft to dump into the hatch.

"Where's Shumaker?" Ronnie asked in surprise.

"Sailed south to Morro Bay," said Pud. "He has sense!"

"Let's see what Marsh will do," Ronnie suggested.

"Now, none of that!" Bill cried anxiously. "I know you two! Neither of you will ever admit that the other is the better man."

Watching the boil of bubbles beside the other boat, Ronnie made no answer. Moments later Marsh's helmet bobbed up. Slowly he climbed the ladder and leaned on deck to have his helmet removed. He lay breathing heavily for minutes before he stood up and gazed toward the *Sea Spray*.

"Had enough?" Ronnie called.

"How do you feel after your first dive?" Marsh countered.

"Fresh as a spring breeze now. But you look exhausted."

"I'll feel fine in a minute," Marsh answered wearily. "But you'd be smart to knock off, Ronnie. You look terrible."

"Speak for yourself," Ronnie snapped, growing annoyed. "Do you think you're the only diver with any stamina?"

"I've been at this longer than you have."

"That's right; I can't get experience on a ladder. You're just too stubborn to quit. . . . Put on my helmet, Pud!"

"Don't be like that, Ronnie!" Pud begged in a whisper. "Can't you see that Marsh wants to call it a day? If you stop fishing, he will."

"Any time he will! He just thinks I can't take it!"

"Be reasonable," begged Bill.

"Who's being *un*reasonable?" yelled Ronnie. "Marsh is building a competing abalone plant in Seal Cove, and he's determined to take the biggest catches and put me out of business!"

Ronnie tried to slip the helmet over his head. And when Pud saw there was no dissuading him, he took it and pleaded, "Don't stay down too long!"

Ronnie didn't release the ladder this time until he was floating upright in the water. He felt no qualms when a silver sheet of water slipped past his vision plate and the bottom of the boat appeared and vanished. He blew and swallowed as he glided downward, and the changing pressure caused him no distress.

He had the comforting knowledge, gained on his first descent, that he was a natural diver. Ronnie wondered what made "a natural." Strength alone failed to explain it. Once, after an abalone boat had lost its diver, a boy of fourteen, slight in build, volunteered to replace him. On his novice dive he dropped into a hole where abalones were plentiful. Although he floundered around somewhat until he became accustomed to his heavy gear, the teen-ager was soon sending up basket after basket of shellfish. Men starting the same way had done as well or better on their first descents. They were "naturals."

Yet there were others, seemingly as well qualified to become divers, who bled from nose and mouth upon going down, blacked-out under pressure, suffered from compressed air, or became terrified to find themselves locked in a rubber diving dress with only a thin cushion of air between themselves and the surrounding water. Practice enabled some of these men to overcome their handicaps. Ronnie's father had believed, however, that "made divers" never equalled the "naturals." And because they did work for which they were unfitted, they were more likely to have accidents.

Ronnie dismissed the problem. It was enough to know he was one of the lucky few who had little difficulty adjusting to the unnatural conditions of undersea work. Bolstered by that knowledge, he had greater confidence.

When he touched bottom, he discovered that the boat had drifted while he was resting. He was now in a wilderness of tumbled boulders, many higher than his head. They were encrusted with barnacles and entwined with the "hold-fasts" by which the kelp gripped rocks. These hold-fasts, like snarls of exposed roots, promised such difficulties to a beginner that Ronnie decided he'd do better to search for the crevasse in which he'd fished on his first dive. He clambered over the boulders, stumbling, tripping and slipping on the tangle of root-like creepers. Laboriously he progressed for a hundred yards, and then, working around a boulder too high to climb, he came abruptly upon a fissure in the ocean floor, opened perhaps by some past earthquake.

Was it the crevasse in which he'd met with fair success on his earlier descent? Or was it another? He had deliberately avoided giving Pud a signal that he'd reached bottom because he wanted his tender to keep a taut life line in case he stumbled into a hole. But now Pud, apparently worried at receiving no signal, gave a tug on the line. Knowing his tender was alert, Ronnie decided to take a chance.

Without responding to the signal, he stepped from the edge of the crevasse and started gliding down between its walls. The move apparently took Pud by surprise. Ronnie realized that he was going down too rapidly.

Fearing a "squeeze" from the suddenly increased pressure,

he blew and swallowed. His ears popped with the opening of his aural passages. But after a few more feet of descent, they closed again. This blockage, which allowed the pressure to become greater outside than inside his head, grew extremely painful. Ronnie swallowed repeatedly, and blew until his eyes seemed to bulge from their sockets before his ears cracked loudly to relieve the pain. Knowing he must act quickly to avoid a squeeze, he opened his monel valve wider to build up a stronger bulkhead of air in his dress. The intensified roar was deafening.

Abruptly he was jerked to a halt. The line he gripped was pulled upward once. Still he failed to respond, hoping Pud would understand that his diver had not yet reached bottom. There was a short pause, as if Pud might be consulting with Bill. Then, far more slowly, the walls once again glided upward past Ronnie. His shoes soon touched bottom. Promptly he gave a single tug on his line.

After the sudden descent from the brighter water above, he could see nothing for many moments. Then, slowly, his eyes adjusted to the dim light and he made out oval spaces in the thick sea growth covering the walls. He must have removed the abalones from those spots! As he worked seaward, he felt sure that this was the same crevasse he had visited before. He spied a sea-urchin on a jutting ridge similar to one he remembered having seen before. And above a ledge, which looked like one he'd had difficulty in climbing, were several blank spots on the walls.

Presently he reached the point where he thought he must have ceased fishing, for he began to find abalones. In some places he flipped off one or two shellfish before moving on;

in others, he'd collect a dozen or more within a space of a few feet.

As the crevasse became more and more narrow, Ronnie grew increasingly aware of the risk he ran of becoming wedged between the walls. Pud still held the life line too taut, with the result that every time the boat was lifted or carried backward by a big swell, Ronnie was dragged upward by his line. It was bad enough to be snatched from an abalone he was about to pry free and hauled over sharp edges of rocks, barnacles and sea-urchins that might rip his dress. But it was worse to feel the walls pressing both sides of his dress. That gave him the sensation of being trapped!

In vain Ronnie yanked again and again to request more slack so that he could fish without interruption. Pud would allow him a little more line and seconds later take it all back.

Growing exasperated, Ronnie slowly drew the rope as if he were descending into deeper water. He coiled this line, gripping it loosely with the same left hand that held the rope basket. Though the boat's movements at times snatched the line, it failed to disturb him at his work. He'd merely coil the rope again before Pud took up the slack. Ronnie realized it was dangerous to fool his tender, but with an overcautious one like Pud, it seemed to provide the only answer.

Working deeper and deeper into the crevasse, he filled and sent up four baskets. Then the fifth grew too heavy to drag farther, and he gave two tugs on the life line. After a pause, it descended, soon bringing down an empty basket. Before Ronnie could untie it, the empty rope container was torn from his hands and streaked past his vision plate. Most of the slack followed the basket—perhaps forty feet in all—and then the line began dropping at his feet.

Ronnie put his hands behind him to lean backward, the only way he could catch a glimpse of the upper part of the crevasse. One look was enough; he was stunned by what he saw. Overhead the walls closed to a thin gap, far more narrow than on the bottom where he worked. But for the chance that his life line was slack moments before, he'd now be imprisoned somewhere between the narrow walls! Possibly his line and hose might have parted as well! Intent upon fishing, he hadn't realized what foolhardy chances he was taking!

When the empty basket reappeared, he tied the one he'd filled above it, and twice pulled the line. The moment the two baskets started upward, Ronnie began retracing his steps to reach a wider part of the crevasse. That was hazardous, as his slack line might become fouled. Better take that chance, though, than remain in a place where a sudden drag might have fatal consequences!

When the undersea canyon opened overhead, and the light above was more turquoise than blue, he felt safe. He allowed Pud sufficient time to dump the abalones into the after-hatch and return to his post before signalling for an ascent. Ronnie was conscious, in doing it, of how similar it felt to pulling a bell-rope. As a swinging bell yielded, so with a tender's hands. He had half-expected resistance, the sign that his life line had snagged.

Pud may have been confused by events above, or perhaps he thought Ronnie had forgotten to remove the empty basket. His reply was two, not three jerks! Ronnie was startled to see the line rippling down, bringing with it the empty rope container. Already shaken, and faced by a slack line for the second time within minutes, Ronnie's teeth began chattering. Annoyed by the blunder, he repeated his message.

Perhaps Pud thought it an emergency signal, for he wasted no time in answering. Rapidly he took up slack, and then without pause started raising his diver from the depths. Ronnie did not breathe freely, however, until the dark walls slipped beneath him and he could see fronds of kelp undulating in the clear green water.

He exercised until he reached the surface. He found it harder than before to grasp the ladder and climb the rungs. For minutes after Pud removed his helmet, he leaned on deck, breathing heavily. But with the quick recovery power of youth, he was soon standing on the ladder, feeling only pleasantly tired. Smiling slightly, he described his narrow escape in the crevasse.

There were lines of strain around Pud's mouth when he finished his account. And Bill, usually of an equable temperament, was plainly angry.

"I thought you had better sense!" he exploded. "Not even a veteran abalone diver takes chances in a place like that when it's this stormy!"

"I learned my lesson," Ronnie admitted.

"I hope so," Bill snapped. "Remember this, Ronnie. There are old divers and bold divers—*but no old, bold divers!*"

Bill glanced at the tally-board bolted to the railing before him. By moving matches in holes in the board, he kept count of the number of abalones Pud emptied into the hold.

"Twenty-two dozen and two, Ronnie," he reported now, some of the edge gone from his voice. "About twenty dozen more than I expected you to take the first time. Shall we shove off before it gets worse?"

A shrill, gusty wind was making the seas run before it, driving the frosted combers high onto the beach below China Charlie's. Blacktop Rock was living up to its name, for the breakers surging far up its sides left only the dark dome exposed. Between the rock and the *Sea Spray,* the *Bubbles* was wildly plunging. Even under full throttle, Ken Carlson had difficulty holding the boat near the rising boil off the port side, and Hammerhead was weaving in an effort to maintain balance.

Apparently the old tender received a signal at that moment. Hastily he tied an empty basket to the life line, and rapidly paid out the light rope. When he brought up a heavy basket, he couldn't hoist it aboard. Carlson left the wheel to help. The boat was swept backward on a swell as they dragged the basket aboard. Carlson hurriedly climbed to the cabin to shift the gear-lever into forward position, but the boat still lost headway, until every foot of Marsh's life line and air-hose had been paid out. Before they parted, however, Carlson took advantage of a surging ground swell to regain his former position beside his diver's rising bubbles.

"See what we've been up against?" asked Bill. "You'd better let Pud help you aboard, Ronnie."

"How has Marsh done this past hour?" Ronnie asked.

"Not as well as you," Bill said. "But he was up for a rest."

"Well, if he's still able to fish," Ronnie declared grimly, "so can I. Give my helmet the old one-two, Pud."

"I should have known this would happen when we started fishing beside Marsh's boat!" Pud wailed. "Have a heart, Ronnie!"

"You're like your father," Bill said. "He never knew when to stop, either! You've done mighty well for a beginner, Ronnie. Let's head for Seal Cove while we've a chance to get there."

"You know as well as I do, Bill," Ronnie said, "that there's only a hundred days a year when a deep-sea diver can work off this coast. It might be a week before we can fish again. And Mr. Romano allowed me only a month to show what I can do."

"All right," Bill reluctantly agreed. "But I'm going to make sure you don't go back to that crevasse!"

He spun the wheel, turning northward. The boat pitched and rolled, almost out of control. After sailing a hundred yards, Bill stopped.

Ronnie went down through thick masses of kelp on his third dive, and found the bottom a mass of tumbled boulders. It was strenuous work clambering over the slanting, slippery rocks, and fighting against the tangle of hold-fasts. The currents had grown stronger, too, so that he was flung from some rocks and battered against others. Yet here and there, he discovered an abalone.

His second basket had gone up, and he was waiting for Pud to resume his duties when he was startled by a distinct beat, like the muffled ringing of a bell. His nerves grew jumpy at hearing the bell-like beat a second . . . a third time. Panic shot through Ronnie, for he was unable to imagine what caused the notes.

Grasping the life line, he yanked three times. Each pull drew down more line. Thinking at first that Pud had allowed too much slack, he quickly changed his mind when the rope continued to glide steadily downward. Pud was still aft, dumping the last basket of abalones in the hatch, and the line lay unattended on deck! The end was never secured to anything because the coil must be passed over and under the hose numerous times while a diver was below. And now his sharp tugs had started it peeling off! Nothing would stop the whole rope from sliding overboard unless Bill observed what was happening or Pud reached the forward deck in time!

Badly shaken at sight of the line rippling through the water, Ronnie felt even more disturbed when he heard the pulsing beat of sound a fourth . . . then a fifth time.

Should he unbuckle and kick off his shoes, close his exhaust valve, and pop up? But he had no clear idea how long he had been below. If he'd been down any length of time, and he probably had been, popping up might bring on the bends!

Still the line flowed through the water! Why didn't Bill notice what was happening?

The bell-like sound continued. Ronnie's nerves quivered with each beat. He was conscious of the perspiration streaming down his face. What made the sound—a submarine's bell, a ship off-course? Neither answer seemed plausible. And it couldn't be his own boat, for the *Sea Spray* had no bell. Having visited the *Bubbles* before it belonged to Marsh, he was sure it had none, either.

To his intense relief, the line ceased flowing through the water, and began rapidly ascending. The heap of rope at his feet grew smaller. And as the last of it left the sea floor, Ronnie grasped it, and gave a signal no tender could misunderstand.

Seconds later he was raised from the bottom and began exercising as he glided through the kelp. But he was shaking as he flexed arms and legs. He still heard the rhythmic beat of the bell . . . *if it was a bell.*

The seas tossed him violently when he reached the surface. Pud had to climb partway down the ladder to give him a hand before he could get his feet through the first rungs.

Ronnie was astonished, when his helmet was removed, to discover how much worse conditions were than when he'd gone below. The wind now fluted wrathfully, knifing the tops from the swells to fill the air with flying spray.

Marsh was aboard his boat, sitting on the edge of the after-hatch while Hammerhead removed his suit. Carlson had already started north, but against the adverse wind and sea, the *Bubbles* was losing headway. Her southeastward drift, unless Carlson could check it, might end in her destruction against Blacktop Rock or one of the exposed rocks impaling the waters farther off-shore.

Ronnie glanced about, but could see no other vessel. "Where's the boat that was ringing her bell?"

Pud looked blank. "You must be 'air-happy'!" he exclaimed. "I heard nothing like that!"

"You're not used to compressed air," shouted Bill. "Maybe that's why you've been hearing things." He stared somberly at the plunging *Bubbles.* "Marsh isn't going to make it, and neither are we. And I doubt if we could work southward through those rocks without being smashed up."

"Could we put the boat on the beach?"

Bill looked dubiously at the great foaming combers pounding high up the black gravel and sand below China Charlie's. "I don't know," he shouted, "but we've got to try it."

"Give me time to remove Ronnie's dress," pleaded Pud. "If

we're swamped while he's in this gear, he won't stand a chance."

"Hurry, then!" advised Bill. "We're drifting too fast for safety."

Ronnie clambered aboard, with Pud's help, and slowly made his way aft as the *Sea Spray* rolled and pitched in the heavy swells. His nerves were still taut from the bell-like beat he had heard, and despite what Pud and Bill had said, he was sure his senses had not deceived him. But now, listening to the thunder of the breakers, he knew that the pulsing beat heard underwater was the least of his worries. One-tenth of the abalone boats were lost every year. If he lost the *Sea Spray*, he and Mardie and Skip would be in far worse straits than if he'd never tried to become an abalone diver!

5.

THE PHANTOM LIFEBOAT

Pud worked with frantic haste, unscrewing the bolts from the breastplate and collar-strips, gripping the sleeves so that Ronnie could pull his hands through the tight cuffs, jerking off the heavy shoes. As he undressed his diver, his eyes kept darting toward the huge rollers pounding the beach, or at Marsh's boat drifting past. The *Bubbles*, with an engine of less horsepower than their own, was losing headway, and the faces of her crew were growing anxious.

Ronnie was equally disturbed. Several times, while Pud was busily employed, Ronnie's heart had faltered at hearing the *Sea Spray's* motor sputter. He feared that it might stop before he was free of his encumbering suit. And so it was with intense relief that he at last peeled it off, pushed it back under the deck, and replaced the hatch cover.

Bill, awaiting this moment, promptly swung the bow toward the beach. The boat climbed on a swell, then dropped with a smashing impact that made her timbers creak. The seas broke green over her prow, seething across the deck in a milky sheet. Stocky legs braced as he stood spinning the wheel, Bill fought a side-drift that threatened to make the boat broach.

"Let go our stern anchor, Pud," Ronnie shouted. "We've got

to keep her headed toward shore. I'll try to make it forward and see if we still have a mooring line."

Watching his chance, he worked along the starboard side. As he edged past the cabin, Bill shouted at him to be careful. Ronnie nodded. He was but halfway across the forward deck, however, when the *Sea Spray* plunged her bow under the first breaker. Hearing the hissing roar, Ronnie flung himself flat. Though water gushed over him, he kept a firm grip on the hatch cover and avoided being washed overboard.

As the boat rose, shaking like a wet dog, Ronnie crawled to the bow and grasped the mooring line. Most of it was trailing alongside. The *Sea Spray* trembled as another breaker rode under her. Once more Ronnie took a ducking. By fast work, he drew the rope aboard and started to coil it. This was done before the next sea curled over him. Blinking salt water from his eyes, he peered forward. A few more yards and they'd be through the breakers!

But at that moment the boat's engine coughed and sputtered—then stopped! The *Sea Spray* started to slide out on a back-wash.

Wasting not a split-second, Ronnie grasped his coil of line tightly, put a foot on the bow, and sprang. Splashing into water reaching to his arm-pits, he heard a breaker cracking behind him and ducked. He was tumbled heels over head toward the beach. Gasping for breath, he staggered erect, only to be flung from his feet by the next comber. Dazed and shaken, he tried again to rise. Another roller promptly flattened him.

Thrusting dignity aside, he crawled on all fours the remainder of the way to the beach before attempting to stand.

Looking back, he saw Bill turning the wheel hard over in an effort to prevent the boat, with her dead motor, from sweeping broadside. Pud was cautiously creeping forward past the cabin.

Ronnie dashed up the graveled strand, and braced the mooring line around a boulder. But he lacked the strength to hold it. The strain made the rope creak, and inch by inch it slipped away from him, allowing the *Sea Spray* to swing more and more into the throat of the thundering combers. If she broached under such conditions, she would surely swamp!

Pud had now reached the bow, and he recognized the danger. He jumped overboard, grasping the mooring line as he struck with a tremendous splash. But he, no more than Ronnie, could keep his feet! Half pulling himself along the line, half floundering as the swells roared over him, Pud gained the beach. Dripping water like a sieve, he lumbered up to help by adding his impressive weight and strength to the line.

Even with both of them pulling, however, they had a hard time taking up the rope. But slowly the *Sea Spray's* bow swung around, until she was perpendicular with the shore. Ronnie and Pud continued to exert themselves, using the lifting power of the larger combers to draw the little boat higher and higher onto the beach.

"I guess that's the best we can do, Pud," Ronnie decided, and made the rope fast around the big rock. "She won't broach now unless her anchor drags. In that case, we can take up slack on her stern line."

Bill left the wheel, and dropped to the after-deck. Removing the hatch-cover, he pulled out two life lines. Securing these to the stern towing-bitt, he cast one to Ronnie, the other to Pud. Grasping his idea, they made the light ropes fast around the rocks to port and starboard. Pinioned in four directions, the boat was not likely to swing broadside or suffer any damage.

But now Ronnie saw that the *Bubbles* was pointing into the breakers, several hundred yards to the south.

"Let's give them a hand, Pud," Ronnie suggested.

"Call if you need me," Bill yelled as they started off. "I'll be working on the engine."

They had just reached the place where the *Bubbles* was headed when there was a raucous grinding at her stern. Hammerhead ran aft, then uttered a high-pitched wail.

"*We're on a rock!*"

A hissing breaker lifted the *Bubbles* and she slipped off, but her propeller rasped and clanked.

"Keep her turning if you can, Carlson," Marsh shouted, running forward.

He picked up the mooring line, which had been coiled around the towing-bitt. Preparing to get it ashore, he noticed for the first time that help was already at hand.

"Cast it to me!" called Ronnie.

The rope came spinning. Ronnie caught the end and ran up the gravel slope to bend it around the nearest rock. Hammerhead had let the hook splash overboard, and now he snubbed the anchor line as the boat plunged through the breakers. At a ponderous gait, Pud hurried up to assist Ronnie. And when the *Bubbles* was in the surf, Marsh and Carlson splashed ashore and helped pull the boat higher on the strand. Approving of Bill's idea, they secured lines to either side to hold her in a rigid embrace. But her stern lay in deeper water than

Ronnie's boat, the pitch of the shoreline being steeper at that point.

Marsh promptly climbed aboard his boat, collected tools, and despite the surf breaking shoulder high over him, started to work on his damaged propeller. Hammerhead and Carlson stood by, gripping his belt so that he would not be hurled against the hull.

"Anything we can do?" Ronnie shouted.

Marsh raised his damp head. "No. We just bent the blades a little when we struck that rock, but they'll soon be straightened. We could sure use a fire, though, when we finish."

As Ronnie turned away, Hammerhead suddenly cackled. "Marsh dived today until he was hearing bells!"

Ronnie swung around with a start. "*You* heard that too, Marsh? A sort of muffled, regular beat, as though a bell were ringing underwater?"

Marsh straightened up abruptly. "That describes it exactly! So you heard it, too?"

"Did I! It scared me worse than the sting ray that shook me up."

"I practically jumped out of my suit, too," Marsh admitted. "What could it be?"

"You've got me there. But there must be a logical explanation."

Hammerhead had been staring from Marsh to Ronnie, as if wondering whether he were hearing right. Now he piped, "Sure there's an explanation! You both dived too long in heavy seas. Carlson and I didn't hear anything!"

Knowing that nothing he could say would convince the old tender, Ronnie shrugged and walked off with Pud to collect driftwood. They accumulated a large pile and laid a fire, ready to be lighted when the crew of the *Bubbles* finished their repair job.

As Ronnie placed the last stick, Pud clutched his arm, and whispered, "Am I dreaming?"

Ronnie whirled around. Jogging along the beach toward them was a figure that appeared to have been lifted bodily from China. It was a Chinese in a straw coolie hat, a pajama-like suit of quilted cotton, and slippers that flapped on the man's bare, bony feet. Balanced on his shoulder was a long bamboo pole, with baskets suspended from either end. When the man reached them, Ronnie saw that the baskets were filled with wet seaweed.

Curious as to what use it could be put to, Ronnie asked, "What do you do with it?"

The brown Oriental face lighted with a smile, but the man answered in his own tongue, his sing-song words meaning nothing to Ronnie. The Chinese turned, jogged up a zigzag trail hewn in the cliff, and disappeared.

"Bill can't use us as mechanics, Pud," Ronnie observed. "Let's go up there and see China Charlie. Dad used to know him."

They climbed the steep trail to the unpainted old building wedged into the break in the cliff. It was an *L*-shaped structure, the smaller part apparently serving as a house, while the larger portion was a warehouse. Through the open door of the latter, Ronnie saw dried seaweed stacked to the roof. The weathered building protected two sides of a cobble-stoned patio. The remaining two sides were sheltered from the wind by low, unmortared rock walls. Perched on the south wall was a decaying lifeboat, serving as a flower-box for geraniums.

The Chinese Ronnie had spoken to, as well as another dressed like him, were spreading wet seaweed over the cobbles to dry. Supervising them was a plump little Chinese man in a brown business suit. His close-cropped, salt-and-pepper hair suggested a venerable age which was contradicted by a broad face as smooth as brown velvet. The rotund little man smiled guardedly and nodded when Ronnie asked if he were China Charlie.

"This is my friend Pud Dart," Ronnie explained. "I'm Ronnie Nordhoff. I think my father used to run his boat in here sometimes to see you."

China Charlie nodded vigorously, his face instantly radiating warmth. "Velly glad meet son of fliend. Sometime you flather bling abalone. Make good talk. He is good health?"

Ronnie's eyes smarted. "Eleven days ago, Charlie, a crazy driver passed on a curve, striking Dad's car head-on. Mom and Dad were—" His voice broke, and he made a helpless gesture.

China Charlie's plump hands quivered slightly. Two tears rolled down his smooth brown cheeks. For a long time he stared in silence at the two men laying seaweed on the cobbles.

"Velly solly, Lonnie. No 'Melican man so good fliend you flather." Hesitating, he glanced up shyly, asking, "You like clup tea, yess?"

"We're pretty wet," Ronnie admitted. "We'd enjoy it."

China Charlie shouted in Chinese. Ronnie was surprised to hear a mellow voice answer from the house, "Yes, Grandfather."

While they waited, Ronnie asked about the seaweed, but

China Charlie found it difficult to explain in English. *"Chee-choi,"* he said, groping for words. "Velly good. Chinese eat much *chee-choi.*"

In a few minutes a pretty Chinese girl, dressed like a bobby-soxer, appeared with a tray. She smiled at Ronnie, but it was several moments before he could place her.

"Pud," he exclaimed, "look who's here! It's Dorothy Kwan who was in our class at Seal Cove High!"

The puzzled look left Pud's face, and he grinned sheepishly. "I thought I knew you. But I didn't expect to find you here, Dorothy."

The girl's dark eyes twinkled. "I'm visiting my grandfather."

"Why does your grandfather collect this *chee-choi?"* Ronnie asked.

"I believe it's the seaweed you call purple laver," the girl explained, setting the tray on the wall and starting to fill the three small, round cups with tea. "Grandfather used to ship tons of it to China to use with soup and meats. Now, with troubled conditions there, he sells what he can to Chinese restaurants in this country."

She handed the cups to her grandfather, Ronnie and Pud. And while they sipped the hot liquid, she explained that the Chinese never left the growth of this seaweed to chance. For centuries her people had known when *chee-choi* would release its seed-like spores into the sea. Shortly before that time, her grandfather would prepare for a good crop by having his helpers use blow-torches to burn all other marine plants from the rocks for miles along the coast. Thus the spores would not only have more places on which to lodge, but also more space in which the plants could grow.

After she finished speaking, Ronnie asked, "Where did your grandfather get that old lifeboat, Dorothy?"

She smiled. "When I was a little girl, you could still make out the name *Southland Star* on it," she began.

Her grandfather interrupted her explanation with a few brusque Chinese words.

Dorothy's head dropped, and without glancing up, she said apologetically to Ronnie and Pud, "You will excuse me, please." She turned, and with quick steps disappeared into the house.

China Charlie smiled blandly, as if nothing had happened, and continued to sip his tea with noisy, sucking sounds. His face had emptied of expression, however, and a film seemed to have slid over his eyes. When he asked Ronnie and Pud if they would have a second cup, his voice was polite but devoid of warmth.

"No thank you, sir," Ronnie said, feeling distinctly uncomfortable. "I guess we'd better get back to our boat."

They started down the trail, but halfway to the bottom, Ronnie paused. Absently he gazed down upon Marsh, Hammerhead, Carlson and Bill, who stood around a crackling driftwood fire that was sending up swirling showers of sparks.

"Pud," he said slowly, "why was China Charlie so upset when Dorothy mentioned the *Southland Star?* Seems to me I've heard of that ship."

"Maybe you heard Dad mention her," said Pud. "Years ago, when he was just a deputy, he served under an old sheriff who had worked on the case."

"*Case!*" Ronnie echoed. "Was there a mystery about her?"

"When a schooner carrying over half a million in gold disappears, that's a whale of a mystery!"

"Where'd the gold come from, Pud?"

"Some California miners chartered the *Southland Star* to bring back the gold they'd taken in the Klondike in '98. I believe the schooner was bound for San Pedro, but when she was somewhere off Santa Barbara a storm overtook her—"

"She was seen sinking, Pud?"

"Well, no, she wasn't," Pud admitted. "No one saw her after she passed Monterey. But a miner drifted into Santa Barbara Bay clinging to a hatch-cover that had washed overboard. He was speechless from shock and exposure, and died a few hours later, without having thrown any light at all on the mysterious disappearance of the vessel and his shipmates."

"Didn't anyone look for the gold?"

"You bet they did! Dad said the owners of the schooner and relatives of the miners raised money to hire a commercial diver. For weeks he explored the coastal waters off Santa Barbara and to the north, but he never found anything."

"Well, how did China Charlie happen to have one of the *Southland Star's* lifeboats if she sank miles to the south?"

Pud shook his head. "That's too steep for me. I didn't know even one had been found."

"China Charlie must know something he's not telling," Ronnie declared. "What is he hiding? Why did he send Dorothy into the house when she started talking about the schooner's lifeboat?"

"Right now, Ronnie, I'd rather get dry than solve mysteries. Let's toast ourselves."

When they reached the fire, Ronnie asked if any of the

others had heard of the schooner and her gold.

"Papers were full of it, fifty odd years ago, when I was a kid," said Hammerhead. "I've heard lots of theories, and I have my own. If the crew of a fishing boat was having hard luck, and turned pirates—"

"*Pirates!*" Marsh laughed. "Hammerhead, your imagination's too good!"

Hammerhead looked injured, and would say no more.

Though the sudden squall blew over quickly, the black clouds rolling overhead suggested that the brief flurry was but the prelude to a more severe storm. With each crew helping the other, they pushed the two boats off the beach while there was still water under their keels to float them. Marsh set sail for the north, hoping to reach Seal Cove before harsh weather would make that impossible.

Bill stepped behind the wheel, and then stared thoughtfully at the *Bubbles*, rolling and plunging as she fought her way along the coast.

"Ronnie," he said slowly, "our engine may hold out long enough to get us home. But the wind's shifted to a nor'westerly now, and we'll be bucking adverse seas for quite a spell. If we should have another breakdown—"

"Why not sail south to Morro Bay?" Ronnie suggested. "We'll have the wind with us."

"What will we do with our abalones?"

"Maybe Shumaker will buy them."

"That's an idea!" And Bill looked relieved.

Rounding Blacktop Rock proved hazardous, for there was only a narrow passage on the seaward side. Chugging through the gap, swept first one way, then the other, Ronnie thought they might fetch up against the big rock to port or the smaller ones to starboard.

Once Blacktop fell astern, however, they had nothing to fear. Choppy seas slowed their progress, without causing any real difficulty. The moderate cliffs rising from the water slipped by, their place taken by low bluffs and sandy beach. And then, nearly two hours after leaving China Charlie's, they saw black breakwaters, surmounted by the towering mass of the great rock that dominated Morro Bay.

Presently the *Sea Spray* glided past the sheltering breakwater, past Morro Rock, and across the bay to a cement quay on the eastern side. Bill nosed between the moored abalone boats, and Ronnie secured their line to the ladder.

Climbing to the cement platform, he turned left toward an open door of the little sheet-iron abalone plant. From within, he heard hissing, splashing sounds. Through the foggy atmosphere, he saw Shumaker hosing off the cleaning and packing tables and slicing machine with live steam.

Walking up to the stocky little diver, Ronnie shouted, "Could you use twenty-eight dozen abalones, Mr. Shumaker?"

To his surprise, Shumaker shook his head.

"But," Ronnie faltered, remembering that there were now no other plants operating in Morro Bay, "weren't you trying to expand your business?"

Shumaker walked over to turn off the steam valve. Returning, he looked up at Ronnie, hostility in his dark eyes.

"Buying your catch will help you to keep limping along," he stated bluntly. "It will merely delay the day when you go broke, and I can buy your plant."

That Shumaker had been jealous of Thor Nordhoff, Ronnie was well aware. Year after year the abalone fishermen had elected Ronnie's father as their leader; and rejected Shumaker with little more than a scattered handful of votes. But not until now did Ronnie clearly realize that the stocky little diver intended to continue his feud with the son of the man he had so bitterly envied.

Saying nothing, but flushed with anger, Ronnie was turning away when a thought came to him. "Do you know anything about the *Southland Star*, Mr. Shumaker?"

The little man gave an unmistakable start of surprise. His dark eyes shadowed as they scrutinized Ronnie.

"Why should I?" he asked brusquely. "Many ships pass Morro Bay."

"This was a schooner, carrying gold, and lost in '98."

"Oh, that one." And Shumaker's attempted show of indifference was somehow unconvincing. "Yes, I've heard the stories."

With another guarded glance at Ronnie, he turned through an open door to his office overlooking the water. Ronnie watched him drop his heavy body into a swivel chair and pick up a paper from the desk. The sheet shook badly in his hand.

Mention of the *Southland Star* had plainly disturbed Shumaker. But why that should be so, Ronnie could not understand.

Leaving the plant, he dropped down the ladder and jumped aboard his boat. Bill detected the annoyance in his face, and asked, "Anything wrong?"

"Shumaker won't buy my abalones. He's hoping I'll go

broke!"

"But I never heard of a plant owner who wouldn't accommodate another operator in an emergency!" Bill declared indignantly.

"Does that mean we must dump our catch outside the bay?" Pud demanded.

"No!" cried Ronnie, reaching a quick decision. "Move over to the pier, Bill. I'm going uptown and call Skip."

They sailed along the bay shore and moored the boat. Ronnie walked to the nearest drugstore to phone his brother. Skip promised to find someone to drive the truck.

It was dark when the old vehicle rumbled along the pier an hour later. Walking up to the cab, Ronnie was horrified to see a small trim figure with golden hair—Pud's younger sister!

"Ginger, I don't know what Skip could be thinking of to call you!"

The girl's pert face had the expression of one sorely tried. "Hurry up and load those smelly shellfish," she said impatiently. "I haven't had dinner yet."

While waiting, the three boys had raised their catch with winch and hopper. Now they tossed the abalones, two at a time, into the truck. After this was done, Ronnie scanned the sea beyond the breakwater. A piping wind still feathered the darkened ocean, but a few stars twinkled through breaks in the clouds.

"If this storm blows over, Bill," he said, "start north at daybreak. I'll meet you at China Charlie's."

Swinging behind the wheel, he drove through town, and on along the bare, wind-swept highway skirting the coast.

"You're a good scout to help out, Ginger," Ronnie said, breaking the long silence. "But I didn't know you could drive this thing."

"Last summer, when I kept your father's books, I learned to move the truck around the yard when it was in the way." She added tartly, "Not that I dreamed of making it my profession!"

Feeling her annoyance justified, Ronnie grimly promised himself that he'd speak to his brother. But to Ginger, he said, "I should have told Skip to round up a crew to help process this catch."

"I tried to call some of the people who worked for your father, but some had left town and the others were out. However, I persuaded the Camerons to stand by. They're already bored with retirement, and would like to do something useful."

"Have they ever processed abalones?" he asked in surprise.

"Have you?" countered Ginger, her voice faintly edged.

He said nothing rather than risk another argument.

"Of course," she went on, "I told them they'd be smarter to work for Marsh. He'll still be in business next week."

For a moment he took his eyes from the winding road unrolling before the headlights. "Do you always have to give me the Ronnie Nordhoff treatment?" he asked bitterly. "Can't we ever be friends?"

When she remained silent, he glanced her way. Her lovely face usually had a decisive quality, making her seem older than her years. But now Ginger looked appealingly youthful as she sat too erect, too tense, staring straight ahead. Was it the reflection of the dashlight, or were her eyes glistening?

He couldn't be sure.

He barely caught her reply, "It wouldn't work. You know Dad."

The words puzzled Ronnie. Once before, when she'd been angry with him, Ginger had implied that he was like Sheriff Dart. Knowing that she was devoted to her father, Ronnie might have taken it as a compliment except for her tone. But, now that he thought of it, he recalled occasions when both Ginger and her mother had shown impatience with Seal Cove's beloved and respected sheriff.

Martin Dart was the largest man in the village, and despite his weathered brown face and graying hair and mustache, he gave the impression of a boy made up for a male lead in a school play. Having seen the well-worn college scrapbook kept in the sheriff's office, Ronnie realized that the elder Dart must have held more offices and won more letters than any other man at the University of California in his day. Newspapers still occasionally referred to Martin Dart's great punting, his long passes, his 93-yard run for a touchdown against Stanford. He was still active in alumni affairs, and the townspeople were tolerant about his absences at Cal games and class reunions. Prominent men—lawyers, engineers, corporation presidents, and even judges—still stopped at Seal Cove to talk with the sheriff about their college days.

Following his graduation in the early 'twenties, Martin Dart had studied law for a time, then had tried many different jobs before becoming a deputy. Later, when he became sheriff of Seal Cove, there were people who thought him too easy-going for a law-enforcement officer. Then one day a robber rushed from the Seal Cove Bank, bumped into the sheriff, and was quickly disarmed and handcuffed. The confederate fled, but was captured minutes afterward when discovered unconscious in his wrecked car. The sheriff's critics claimed that in struggling with the first bank-robber, Dart had stumbled and fallen on the man, knocking him breathless. They also contended that the second robber would have escaped had he taken the turn at the bridge at more moderate speed. But these detractors were quickly silenced; to the townspeople of Seal Cove, their sheriff was a hero.

It was the only occasion when Sheriff Dart was called upon to prove his fitness for office. There was neither crime nor juvenile delinquency in Seal Cove. Sheriff Dart seemed to sense when a boy was having troubles, in a way few adults could, and he soon had that boy interested in hunting or fishing, playing baseball, basketball or football, or even photography. Sometimes, when serving a paper, the sheriff would stop to watch football practice, and he was delighted when the coach would say, "Sheriff, would you mind showing these dubs how to kick a ball?" The sheriff could still punt fifty or sixty yards, or make a forty-foot pass, straight as an arrow. But the light would fade from his face when he returned to his car to continue his distasteful duties.

"Every kid in Seal Cove is crazy about your dad," Ronnie now said to Ginger. "Except for arresting an occasional speeder, he rarely has to enforce the law because he prevents it from being broken."

Ginger sighed. "Check," she said.

"But what's wrong with that? I think your father's a fine man."

"So do I," she said, "but—oh, you wouldn't understand!"

She was right—he was so puzzled by her attitude that he had temporarily forgotten about the *Southland Star's* lifeboat.

It was not until they were approaching his home that Ginger spoke again, "Drive me down to the pier, will you, Ronnie? I left my car there when I picked up the truck."

He drove through town and at the cove parking space came to a stop beside her roadster. Finding some waste, he dried off the leather seat before Ginger took her place behind the wheel. He thanked her, and was turning away when she called.

He walked back, asking, "Well?"

"I have a bookkeeping job at Morro Bay in the morning," she explained. "It won't be much out of my way to drop you at China Charlie's, if you can be ready at seven."

"Good," he said. "It looks calm enough to fish tomorrow."

"Another thing, Ronnie." She avoided his eyes, and her hands tightened on the wheel. "Don't blame Skip. I—I happened to be at your home when you phoned. Skip didn't know who might be best to call, and—well, I told him I'd drive the truck to Morro Bay."

His mouth parted in astonishment. Before he could think of anything to say, Ginger shifted rapidly through the gears and was gone. Ronnie stared after the vanishing car in bewilderment. Why had Ginger acted like a girl imposed upon if she'd volunteered to drive the truck? And why had she helped out at all, when she disapproved of him as she did?

Girls! thought Ronnie with despair. *How can anyone understand them?*

Driving home, he left the truck backed up to the door of the abalone plant, so that he could unload and start processing his catch after eating. Mr. O'Malley greeted him at the kitchen door, and while he was stroking the setter's glossy head, he noticed with surprise that the kitchen was clean and warm.

The radio was broadcasting a popular tune. Mardie and Skip came from the living room. Ronnie was relieved to see that both children were reasonably neat, although Skip's hair, as usual, needed combing.

"Take any abalones?" Skip asked eagerly.

Ronnie gave Skip a brief account of the day's fishing, and then asked, "Have you kids eaten?"

"Ginger fixed us a swell dinner," Skip declared. "She left yours in the oven to keep warm."

Mardie's eyes glowed as she raised two flaxen pigtails to show him the two blue ribbons on the ends. "Look what Ginger gave me, Ronnie."

With an abstracted nod, Ronnie walked over to the stove to verify what Skip had said. He stared in perplexity at the heaped plate in the warm oven. Now why would Ginger go to so much trouble on their account, and at the same time make it pointedly clear that she disapproved of Ronnie?

"Ginger was awful worried when you didn't get back," Skip observed.

"She was worried about Pud," said Ronnie, carrying the plate over to the enameled table.

"I don't think so," said Mardie gravely. "She didn't mention him."

"Ginger's real nice," said Skip. "Why don't you ever take her to the Saturday square-dances?"

"Because she prefers to go with Marsh Marple," said Ronnie impatiently. "Now suppose you kids go in and listen to the radio and let me eat in peace."

The Camerons dropped in as he was finishing his meal. They looked much alike, for they both wore gold-rimmed spectacles, and the whiteness of their hair contrasted with their rosy complexions and plump, unlined faces.

"I'm afraid we're in for a stiff session," Ronnie said, pushing back his plate. He told them what his father had paid his employees, and something about the work. "I'd let the processing go until morning," he concluded, "except that I plan to fish again tomorrow."

"We don't mind," said Mr. Cameron cheerfully. "Mother and I can sleep late. We're retired."

"All right," said Ronnie. "Let's get started."

They walked out across the yard, and he pushed up the overhead door of the plant. Then he and Mr. Cameron shoveled the shellfish from the truck onto the first cleaning table, and, when it would hold no more, onto the cement floor.

Then, finding three rubber aprons for the Camerons and himself, he started to instruct his neighbors in the processing of abalones. The plant was arranged with a series of tables, each supplied with a sink. After turning on the faucets at each sink, Ronnie cut abalones from their shells, cleaned out the insides, and sliced off the black-and-orange suction foot with a razor-edged knife. Each rectangular piece of white meat, he then divided into four to eight fillets or "steaks" with the slicing machine. All these steps were comparatively simple, and the Camerons soon did the work as well as could be desired. Breaking down the tough muscular fibers of an abalone with mallet blows, however, was the crucial point in the processing. Only a man could swing the heavy wooden mallet for any length of time. And though Mr. Cameron was strong enough for the work, he was no judge of whether the fillet he pounded was sufficiently tender.

Again and again Ronnie would place a white steak on the pounding block, and deliver three sharp blows, turning the piece of shellfish each time. Usually the mallet would soften the muscular structure, but every so often Ronnie would point out a tough place where the mallet must be applied again. If his eye failed to detect the hard spot, he would feel it as he turned the slice in his fingers before tossing it to the packing table. Fred Cameron would then try to follow Ronnie's example. Splayed edges showed that he applied enough force, but if he missed a place because the three blows failed to overlap, he was unable to detect it.

"Why do you have to be so blamed particular, Ronnie?" Cameron finally complained.

"Because," Ronnie said, "Dad's *Seal Cove Abalones* have always maintained their reputation for being tender enough to cut with a fork. If properly processed and not overcooked, abalone is a dish fit for royalty—but any failure in the processing makes it tough as shoe leather."

Cameron kept trying, but with no better success. Ronnie began to doubt that the Camerons could ever do the work. He was at the point of trying to find some excuse to dismiss them without hurting their feelings when Mrs. Cameron pointed to a steak her husband had pounded.

"You missed one place, Fred."

After he delivered another blow, she picked up the steak, examining it critically with her fingers. "It feels tender now," she remarked, passing it to Ronnie.

Giving it a quick examination, he threw it to the packing table. "Maybe you have the eye and the hand for a packer," Ronnie cried, suddenly hopeful. "Try another."

Cameron pounded, and Mrs. Cameron passed three more steaks before she flipped one back to the pounding block. After that, she missed an occasional tough spot that Ronnie detected, but not many. She had a good eye, a sensitive hand like his mother. No amount of training would make Cameron a good judge of abalones, but it didn't matter so long as his wife was at the packing table, rejecting the steaks he failed to make tender.

"With a little practice, Mrs. Cameron, you'll do all right," Ronnie predicted. "Now, I'll show you how to pack."

He put a light box on the scales, quickly creased two sheets of waxed paper crosswise in the box, and carefully arranged the pounded steaks until the arrow pointed to five pounds. Folding the paper over the shellfish, he laid the slats on the box and nailed them into place.

It took hours to finish processing the abalones. Ronnie, already exhausted from the day's fishing, had to do the heaviest share of the work because of the Camerons' inexperience and need for constant direction. He could scarcely keep awake until the last box was nailed up and placed in the freeze room. And then, heavy-eyed from fatigue, he had to show Fred Cameron how to clean out the plant with hose and live steam.

Staggering wearily off to his room, Ronnie realized that Shumaker had been right in saying that the double duties of running an abalone plant and diving were too much for one man. But he'd been encouraged to discover how quickly the

Camerons had learned the different steps in the processing. They were intelligent, and he was sure that they could soon take charge.

Ronnie sat on his bed to take off his shoes. That was the last thing he remembered until he was awakened by the honking of a horn. Dazed with sleep, he sat up, surprised to find that he'd dropped off the previous night before he could undress. An impatient bleating outside brought him to his feet, and he walked sleepily into the bathroom to wash.

When he stepped outside in pea-jacket and blue knitted cap, Ginger sat primly at the wheel of her roadster. She looked as cute as a pixie in a green suit and green hat, with a perky green feather. But she'd apparently been sharpening her tongue for his benefit.

"Must you sleep all day?" she demanded. "I don't suppose you've even had breakfast!"

He jumped into the car, and as Ginger swished down the driveway, he murmured drowsily, "It's dangerous to eat before diving. That was a good dinner you—" His head nodded before he could finish.

The bumping of the car on a twisting dirt road awakened him. For a moment he could not understand how he happened to be on a rutted road above the ocean with Ginger. Then he gathered that they must have left the paved highway far behind and were climbing through the coastal hills. Rounding another turn in the road, he saw China Charlie's sprawling dwelling and Blacktop Rock, with the surf creaming about its base.

"I must have fallen asleep, Ginger."

"I practically suspected it," was her tart comment. "You're

the only boy I affect that way."

Ignoring her sarcasm, he scanned the Pacific, flecked here and there with spindrift. To the south he soon spied a small dot of a boat drawing a white V on the gray water.

"There's Pud and Bill! And it's not too rough for diving."

"Oh, Ronnie," she cried, her voice touched with anxiety, "won't you find some other work? Abalone diving is so dangerous!"

He glanced at her in surprise, wondering how she could be so impatient with him one moment and so concerned for his safety the next. Her green eyes were troubled, and she'd lost a little of her expression of pert self-assurance.

"Risks are the reason this game pays so well, Ginger."

"Oh, *you!*" she exclaimed with exasperation. "I should waste my breath!"

She stopped her car behind China Charlie's, and when Ronnie stepped out and tried to thank her for the lift, she raised her pointed chin and without a word left him. The angry grating of the gears, however, was a comment on her mood.

Ronnie watched a small dust cloud following the roadster up the hill. Then, shaking his head, he walked around the house and through a gate. China Charlie was alone, spreading damp seaweed over the cobbles of his patio. At Ronnie's request to cross the terrace to the trail, the Chinese beamed.

"All light. No tlouble."

Ronnie started around the edge of the patio and then halted abruptly. The decaying lifeboat that had stood on the south wall was gone. Geraniums that had been growing in it had been transplanted to a new flower-box which stood in its place!

"What happened to the lifeboat?" Ronnie cried in astonishment.

China Charlie looked blank. "Lifebloat?"

"Here," Ronnie said, pointing. "There was a lifeboat here yesterday!"

The old Chinese brightened. "Not lifebloat. G'laniums. China Charlie likee g'laniums. Velly plitty." He broke off one of the crimson flowers, and handed it to Ronnie. "Velly plitty," he repeated.

"But you—you've replaced the boat with a new flower box!" Ronnie blurted.

The brown face emptied of expression, then grew radiant again as the old man glanced toward the ocean and saw the *Sea Spray* drawing near Blacktop Rock. He pointed a plump finger.

"Bloat," he cried. "Come chop-chop. You catchum abalone?"

The pidgeon-English, quite unlike Charlie's usual speech, was not lost on Ronnie. The Chinese, the boy felt certain, understood perfectly well what he'd been asked. Apparently he hoped to convince Ronnie that what he'd seen was a fantasy of his imagination, a phantom lifeboat, not a real one from the *Southland Star*.

Still puzzled, Ronnie left the patio and started down the trail. And as he descended, he wondered what China Charlie really knew about the schooner lost so many years before with her golden treasure. Why was he concealing his knowledge? Did he hold the clue to one of the most baffling mysteries of the California coast?

6.

ATTACKED BY A
KILLER WHALE

THE *Sea Spray* had passed Blacktop Rock and was slowly chugging through the breakers when Ronnie reached the beach. He removed his shoes and socks and rolled up his dungarees before wading out to meet her. Pud leaned from the bow to relieve him of his footwear and help him aboard.

Bill promptly swung the gear-lever, and as the boat began to reverse, churning up foam astern, he shouted, "Get our first catch processed?"

Ronnie grinned wryly. "The Camerons and I finished up only a few hours ago. If I fall asleep on the bottom today, don't be alarmed."

Bill laughed. "Where will we fish?"

"I didn't find many abalones here on my last dive—and I don't care to hear that bell again! Let's try farther north, Bill."

Ronnie went aft, removed the hatch-cover, and selected his gear. Pud started to dress him for diving as the little boat glided along the coast. After sailing about a mile, Bill shifted into neutral and dropped from the cabin. He rummaged through the equipment until he located a lead-weighted line. He sent the lead splashing overboard. His lips moved mutely as he counted the ribbon-markers sliding through his hands.

"Forty feet," he reported. "How's that, Ronnie?"

"Good enough to start with, but I may go deeper."

Soon Ronnie was climbing down the ladder. Having proved himself the previous day, he felt confident that by nightfall there would be a respectable haul of shellfish on his boat.

After beginning his descent, he found that the currents were now comparatively mild. Even more reassuring was the fact that he could hear nothing in the undersea silence except the roar of his air. He'd dreaded the possibility of once more hearing the bell-like beat—a sound as disturbing as it was mysterious.

Approaching the last ten feet of his dive, however, he was plagued by an even more serious problem. The brightness of the water abruptly changed to a milky murk. At first he thought his breath must have condensed on his face-plate. Quickly he recognized his mistake. The sea was saturated with particles of sand stirred up by the recent storm. Sunlight striking down from above backlighted this silt as though trying to penetrate a lifting fog. Upon reaching bottom, he could see scarcely two feet in any direction.

How could he find abalones in this opaque murk? It seemed hopeless, until he recalled that his father had at times worked by feel when pressed for money. Well, he could at least try it!

Blundering slowly along, and worried lest he step into a hole he might fail to see in time, Ronnie soon bumped into a large boulder. Feeling around the rock, his fingers detected a place where it sloped inward near the bottom. He slid his bar along this surface until it met resistance. With a hasty movement, he pried downward. But the shell slipped off the point of his abalone-bar. By stooping, he made out the oval form of a shellfish. But it had clamped tightly to the rock. Probing, he failed to find any space large enough to work his bar under the abalone's fortress.

A miss! he thought. *I'll have to move faster!*

On his next try, he was successful—but the shellfish was below legal size. Ronnie kept on. Sometimes he pried off chitons or gastropods in their large, whorled shells; once he loosened an angry lobster from its lodging place. Yet at intervals he would take a red abalone eight inches or larger in diameter. After what seemed ages, he had collected enough shellfish to send up his first container.

With the empty basket he'd removed from the line, he stumbled on, until he almost fell over a rock reaching to his leather belt. He groped for an opening beneath it where an abalone might be hidden.

Suddenly the opalescent water grew darker. Ronnie raised his head and through his vision plate saw a vague, swiftly moving shadow gliding across the rock. In an effort to escape whatever danger threatened him, he crouched. A moment later a glistening black and white body, possibly thirty feet in length, streaked swiftly into view and vanished. It had come so close that Ronnie could have touched it.

There was no ledge under which he might duck, no crevasse into which he might slip for protection. He leaned against the rock where he'd been searching for abalones, his heart pounding heavily. If the monster attacked again, he hoped it might mistake him for part of the rock. After what seemed an endless wait, Ronnie caught a movement to one side. Glancing from his side plate, he saw the beast again . . . saw its rounded jaw and partly opened mouth, armed with rows of vicious conical teeth.

Only once before had Ronnie ever seen the terrifying creature that had charged swiftly through the water. That had been in a natural-history book, and though the illustration had given him but a faint idea of the monster's size, it now enabled him to identify his attacker. It was a killer whale, the most predatory creature in the sea!

His rising air bubbles, carrying the scent of man, must have attracted it. But they were difficult to follow in cloudy water. The sand in suspension, the silt stirred up by the storm, had saved Ronnie! Perhaps if he remained where he was, pressed against the rock, the killer whale would be unable to find him, and swim away. But if it continued its search, it might blunder upon and part his air-hose!

Staying here is my only hope! thought Ronnie.

He had scarcely reached this decision when his life line grew taut. Then he was lifted from the bottom! Pud must have seen the killer whale from the boat, and hoped to pull him up in time to save his life. Regardless of how good his intentions, it was a mistake that only a beginning line-tender would make.

Ronnie shook with fright, knowing that a diver in clear water would be easy prey to such a monster. In desperation, he reached upward and backward to tap his life line. Pud could not have failed to feel the signal. But perhaps he thought that Ronnie had not yet seen the killer whale. He continued to haul up the line.

Then, as if emerging from a fog, Ronnie was drawn into clear, sunlit water. Never had he seen the sun's rays with such a feeling of despair!

Tapping his line now seemed futile. Since he was in transparent green water, the killer whale must see him. But where was it? If the air bubbles had first attracted the great dolphin, it might be somewhere above him, circling the rising stream of small, silvery globes.

Starting to reach for his knife, Ronnie's hand dropped limply. Of what use was a sharp blade against a monster with such formidable teeth? A wound might discourage a shark, but it would probably only infuriate this even more predatory beast!

Into his mind flashed a story his father had told him of seeing a gray whale swim ashore and strand itself to die rather than endure further assaults by a pack of killer whales. Ronnie recalled his father saying that these largest members of the dolphin family could destroy any creature in the sea except the sperm whale.

Danger had made Ronnie's senses grow unusually acute. As he glided upward, he noticed even the small, vividly banded yellow and brown snails clinging to the swaying blades of kelp. He was sharply conscious of the roaring air, the trembling of his hands, the unsteady beating of his heart.

Suddenly, through his oval plate, he saw the brilliantly marked body of the killer whale, glossy black and white in color, its dorsal fin rising from its back almost to the height of a man. Though it was less than eight feet away, the impetus of its dive carried it past the boy. But as it streaked by, its powerful tail beat the water. Ronnie felt the rippling currents against his dress. The killer whale, having seen him, was swerving in its dive! Moments later it would be ascending, fins and flukes sculling the water to drive it upward for a slashing attack!

Ronnie believed himself still many yards from the surface. So it came as a shock to see the bottom of the boat passing by his vision plate. An instant later a sheet of liquid silver slipped across the glass. Then he was bobbing alongside the *Sea Spray*. There might still be a chance to save himself!

With a feeling of panic, his eyes sought the ladder. Where was it? Had Pud pulled it aboard? Peering through his side plate, he located the bow. The sickening realization swept over him that he had come up on the starboard side. The ladder was suspended off the port beam! How could it have happened?

Before he could think of any way to climb aboard, two hands grasped his and he was roughly pulled over the side. Pud unscrewed his helmet with a quick twist. Ronnie's perspiring face was bathed by a cool, salty breeze. He lay on the hatch, drawing air into his lungs with deep, shaken gasps that sounded almost like convulsive sobs.

"That was too close!" Bill muttered hoarsely.

"Next time we sail, I'm bringing my gun!" Pud declared fiercely.

These words were so startling, coming from Pud, that Ronnie boosted himself on his elbows and looked up. He had to smile slightly. For Pud's broad face, usually so childlike and gentle, was flushed with anger.

He was staring to port, and following the direction of his

glance, Ronnie saw a black dorsal fin cleaving the water only a few yards off the port side. The killer whale broke the surface, glistening briefly in the the dazzling sunlight, and then a rolling motion plunged its distinctively marked black and white body from view, leaving only its great flukes exposed. Presently they also slipped from sight. Where they had been was a patch of roiled water that was swiftly washed out by a shimmering swell.

Ronnie shivered. "You crazy coot!" he admonished Pud. "Why did you pull me up? That thing might have killed me!"

"It would have finished you for sure if I hadn't hauled you up!" Pud protested, in a voice hoarse with strain.

"But I was safely hidden in ten feet of silt!"

"*What* silt!" Pud demanded heatedly.

"The storm stirred up sand!" declared Ronnie angrily. "I was well hidden in it until you drew me up into clear water."

"Well, how could I know that!" exploded Pud.

"*Bong!*" yelled Bill. "Both fighters go into your corners!"

Ronnie glanced up and saw his boat-operator grinning sheepishly.

"We made an awful bobble," Bill went on, "and it was all my fault. I'd been on your father's boat long enough, Ronnie, to know that a storm usually stirs up silt. But I'd forgotten."

Pud whose broad, plump face was still strained, now tried to explain what had happened.

"I'm to blame, too," he admitted. "I should have been watching the surface as well as your line, Ronnie. But I slipped up on that and the first time I noticed the killer whale, it was off to port, circling your rising air bubbles as it went down. We were sure it had failed to get you when it came up and made another dive. Bill said that if it missed again, we'd move your line and air-hose around the stern and pull you up the starboard side while it was coming up to port. And that's what we did—but we were almost too slow!"

"But you didn't give me a signal!" Ronnie protested.

"I was too rattled to think of that."

Never one to dwell long on past mistakes, Ronnie laughed shakily.

"Well, we're bound to make a few mistakes while we're learning. But we'd better agree to one thing to avoid anything like this again. Signal next time, Pud, and don't pull me up until I answer. For all you know, I might be hidden under a ledge or in a cavern—a much safer place than dangling temptingly on a life line!"

Pud grinned. "Anything to oblige."

"Another thing we'd better settle, Pud. Yesterday I touched bottom, but didn't report, because I planned to go deeper . . . if I could find the crevasse where I'd been fishing on my previous dive."

"I remember, Ronnie. I let you down too fast. Next time I'll keep the line taut until I feel a single tug."

There was a frown on Bill's homely face as he glanced at the metallic sky and the ominous cloudbank to the westward.

"She's puffing out there," he said. "We'd better get home."

The seas grew heavier and heavier as the little boat sailed northward. The *Sea Spray* was rolling almost onto her beam ends before she could fight her way to protection behind the hooked arm of land that partially enclosed the cove. Bill ran alongside the pier. Ronnie sprang to the loading platform, hurried up the stairs, and after starting the winch, lowered the hopper. Pud and Bill loaded the small catch of abalones into it. The winch raised the big, black bucket, and Ronnie pulled it over the railing and let it drop.

Pud then joined Ronnie, while Bill made the public skiff fast to the stern of the *Sea Spray* and sailed out into the bay to moor her.

"I'll go for the truck," Pud volunteered.

By hitch-hiking a ride, he was back by the time Bill had rowed to the landing platform. When the shellfish were in the truck, Ronnie backed it off the rickety old pier, and started along the main street toward the village. But after driving a short distance, he stopped in front of a small, square cottage on the outskirts.

"I'm curious about what sort of a plant Marsh has set up," he explained. "Take the truck to my place, Bill. And tell Skip I'll be along soon, if you see him."

Bill looked at the dingy old sedan parked before the house. "That's not Marsh's car, Ronnie. He must still be out fishing. Wasn't that his old wreck parked at the pier?"

"Maybe I can look at his plant, anyway. Someone is here."

He walked down the driveway to a large woodshed. From the entrance, he saw that it was somewhat better than the usual "woodshed operation" by which a few of the abalone fishermen added the profits of processing to the value of their shellfish. There was a sink, a small cleaning table, a pounding block, an excellent nine-foot freeze cabinet, and, in a wall rack, several razor-sharp knives.

A large but rather flabby-looking man stood before the block, carelessly pounding abalone steaks with a mallet.

Something about the sullen mouth beneath the man's ill-kempt brown mustache stirred Ronnie's memory.

"Aren't you Luis Ruisant?" he inquired. "Seems as if I've seen you working in another abalone plant."

"I've worked in all of them," Ruisant retorted sourly.

Picking up a pile of white fillets, he washed them at the sink, and tossed them into a square box standing on a scales. Ronnie walked over to look at the steaks. He felt a prickling of anger. The hard muscle fibers of the uppermost one had not been broken down. Without a word, he flipped it to the pounding block, following it with three others.

"What are you doing?" Ruisant snapped.

"What are *you* doing?" Ronnie lashed back.

Ruisant's dark eyes met Ronnie's briefly, and then dropped. Sullenly he struck each fillet several hard blows to splay the edges.

"Who'd know the difference?" he demanded.

"The customer."

"A lot I care about him!"

Ronnie was nettled. "Look here, Ruisant. It's men like you who turn many of our customers against one of the world's finest seafoods by putting out tough steaks. I could excuse you if you didn't know any better. But you've been in this game a long time, you say."

"Who asked your advice, Nordhoff?"

"You'll get it regardless! You're hurting every one of us who fishes for abalones. And if I know anything about Marsh, he won't stand for slipshod processing, either!"

Ronnie was turning toward the door when Ruisant called, "I forgot, Nordhoff. Marsh needs two more boxes to complete an order. Can do?"

"He has his nerve!" Ronnie muttered indignantly. "He's taken my father's crew, and probably some of our customers as well. And now he wants help in supplying restaurants that formerly bought from us. Well, I'll lend a hand this one time!"

Pulling off his jacket, Ronnie helped the man finish processing the shellfish. Then Ruisant drove him to the Nordhoff plant. Ronnie pushed up the overhead door, and went into the freeze room for two boxes of fillets.

"Charge it to Marsh?" he asked, as he handed over the purchase.

"No," said Ruisant, passing over a ten-dollar bill and some small change. He drove from the yard as if in a great hurry.

Ronnie prepared and ate a hearty lunch. And then, without help, he processed the small catch, packing it away in boxes for sharp-freeze treatment. Dressing in his best suit after cleaning up, he set out to find buyers.

Orrie Shumaker, he discovered, had taken most of the Nordhoff plant's larger customers, while Marsh had agreed to supply some of the smaller ones. Several cafe and restaurant owners confessed that Shumaker had warned them Ronnie would fail as a diver and would therefore be unable to make regular deliveries. Which may have explained why he failed to obtain a single order that day.

When stormy weather prevented him from fishing the following morning, he visited other eating places which served seafood, but with no better results.

Not until shortly before noon on the third day did he receive an order. It came from the small Sunset Cafe, nearing completion in a notch in the hills north of Morro Bay. The proprietor bought only sixty pounds of steaks, but after so many unsuccessful calls, it raised Ronnie's sagging hopes. He delivered twelve boxes of abalone early that same afternoon.

As he walked back to his truck, a dingy old sedan hummed southward along the highway. Luis Ruisant was at the wheel. Briefly his eyes flickered toward Ronnie, but he gave no sign of recognition.

Shortly after Mardie and Skip left for school the following morning, Ronnie heard a horn bleating in the yard and stepped outside. In her roadster sat the redheaded Dart girl, clad in her green suit and perky green hat.

"I have several hours of bookkeeping to do in San Luis Obispo," she explained. "Anything I can get for you there, Ronnie?"

"Wait a sec, Ginger, and I'll go along. I need some rubber aprons, a spare life line and other gear."

When Ginger had finished her work and Ronnie completed his shopping, they started back. It was noon when they drove through Morro Bay.

"Let's stop for lunch with my first customer," Ronnie suggested, as they left the town behind. "I'd like to see how he's doing."

The next bend in the road brought them to the Sunset Cafe. It was set in a gap in the high, golden hills. The kitchen had been placed against the base of one slope to give the western windows an unobstructed view of the ocean through the small valley. Though a sign announced that the cafe was open, a scaffolding still stood along one side where painters were applying a second coat of white, and the roof had yet to receive its initial treatment.

Ginger parked her roadster, and Ronnie followed her into a small lounge furnished with a cashier's stand and three comfortable chairs. The moment they were inside, they could hear a loudly complaining voice.

"I'm poisoned, I tell you! You'll pay for this if I recover!"

Ronnie and Ginger stepped to the dining room entrance. The fuzzy-haired little owner of the cafe, Diego Antonio, was trying to pacify a patron at a center table. Antonio's broad back concealed the guest.

"Please, please," he begged. "You disturb my other guests. Please, sir, come to the kitchen, and I will do what I can."

Diners stared at the man in alarm as he shouted, "You can't serve spoiled abalone . . . and not pay for it!"

"*Spoiled!*" faltered Ronnie, looking at Ginger. "But those were the abalones I took the first day I fished. And they were processed and put in the freeze room that same night!"

"You didn't tarry on the way here?" whispered Ginger.

"Of course not! The boxes were frozen solid when I delivered them."

Antonio was still urging his guests not to upset the other patrons. Reluctantly the complaining man at last arose, and with both hands holding his abdomen and his face expressive of severe agony, he staggered toward the kitchen. Only when Antonio stepped aside to push back one of the swinging doors, however, did Ronnie see the man's face.

It was Luis Ruisant!

Ronnie himself was too sick with despair to see anything significant in the man's presence in the Sunset Cafe. It was of Ruisant's illness, and its disastrous consequences, that he was thinking. Stories of what was now happening would spread until not a cafe within a hundred miles would buy any shellfish from the Nordhoff plant. Ronnie knew he would be finished as a processor. Without both the plant's profits and what he could earn from fishing, he'd never repay his father's debts! He'd lose their home, the plant, even the boat! He felt as if his world were crumbling beneath him.

But Ginger, strangely enough, appeared quite unruffled. She glanced up inquiringly with cool, green eyes.

"Your shellfish never made that man sick. Who is he, Ronnie?"

"Luis Ruisant. He works in Marsh's plant."

"*Ah-ha!*" cried Ginger, as if that explained everything. "Did you ever know an abalone processor who would eat any?"

"Dad wouldn't, I know. He saw too many of them."

"Kitchens," observed the girl, "simply fascinate me."

And seizing Ronnie's arm, she pulled him toward the swinging doors. Beyond them, they found Ruisant doubled up in a chair and moaning. A cook, a waitress and Diego Antonio regarded him with concern.

"If you won't let me call a doctor," the little Italian was saying anxiously, "let me settle for what you consider fair."

Raising troubled eyes, the proprietor saw Ronnie. "It was you," he cried accusingly, "it was *you* who sold me bad fish!"

"Abalones," said Ginger coolly, "don't spoil if processed within thirty-six hours, and Ronnie processed the ones this man ate the same day they were taken."

Ruisant straightened in his chair. On his dark, sullen face was a trapped expression as he peered toward the side door.

"Relax," Ginger advised him. Turning to Antonio, she said calmly, "Before making any settlement, Mr. Antonio, you'd better call my father, Sheriff Dart. He knows how to handle such cases. It might also be a good idea to ask a doctor to bring a stomach pump. Though Mr. Ruisant will find it a trying experience, we can discover whether he was really poisoned."

Ronnie stared at Ginger with admiration, feeling as if a weight had been suddenly lifted from his shoulders. He was sure she'd guessed correctly. For Ruisant had stiffened, his face showing alarm.

"Do you mean," demanded Antonio excitedly, "that this man was *pretending* he was poisoned to make me pay damages?"

"That's exactly what I mean," said Ginger quietly.

Minutes before Ruisant had looked like a man breathing his last. Now he made a remarkable recovery. Crying hoarsely, "You won't use any stomach pump on me!" he sprang to his feet, charging toward the door with such speed that he upset the cook.

For three years Ginger had been cheer-leader of Seal Cove High, and in this emergency she recalled her training. "Hold that line!" she shouted at Ronnie.

Having responded to that appeal in many a football game, Ronnie didn't fail now. His knees pumped to give him momentum. And, after covering several yards, he launched his rangy body in a flying tackle. His shoulders struck above Ruisant's knees. With no holding penalties to bother him, Ronnie's long arms encircled Ruisant's legs in a tight embrace. Kettles rattled on the stove when they went down together.

Anyone who believed Ronnie was only a happy-go-lucky boy would have been startled by the stern expression of his face when he arose. Though much lighter than Ruisant, he hoped that the man on the floor had *not* had enough. He felt cheated when Ruisant pushed himself to a sitting posture, groaning as he rubbed a bloody nose; all fight had been knocked from his flabby body.

"I won't tell you anything," he muttered sullenly.

"That may be what you think," said Ginger. "Mr. Antonio, will you please put in those calls?"

"Wait, Mr. Antonio!" And Ruisant's tone of abject surrender stopped the little Italian midway to the swinging doors. "I'll do what you say."

"First you'll sign a confession, with these people as witnesses," Antonio cried angrily. "Then you'll go out and inform my guests just what you've done."

"You can tell them," growled Ruisant.

"All right. I call Sheriff Dart," said Antonio, starting once more toward the doors.

"You win!" snapped Ruisant. "Bring me a paper. I'll sign the confession first."

After the statement was drawn, and witnessed by everyone in the kitchen, Antonio stared at it for several moments. Then with a lift of his brows and a shrug, he handed it to Ronnie. After the proprietor and the cook left for the dining room to make the conspirator fulfil the second condition, Ronnie and Ginger read the statement.

To whom it may concern:

My employer, Marsh Marple, paid me to pretend I was poisoned by abalone served by Diego Antonio and supplied by the Nordhoff plant. Marple asked me to do this because he hoped to get the business of the Sunset Cafe himself. I hereby admit I suffered no ill effects whatsoever from said abalone.

                                                 Luis Ruisant

Ginger looked shocked. "It's not true!"

"I guess it's true, all right," Ronnie said grimly. "Ruisant was working in Marsh's plant. I saw him there."

"But Marsh is never underhanded!"

"I've never known him to be—until now," Ronnie muttered. "However, he warned me that it might be his turn to come out on top. If this is the way he intends to do it—"

"Marsh would rather lose out than win this way," Ginger protested. "I don't care who Ruisant is working for; he never put on this act for Marsh! There's something else behind this, Ronnie."

"I can guess what you mean," he said bitterly. "You love to go square-dancing with 'Eager-Beaver' Marple!"

Her eyes blazed like two emeralds. "Oh, you—you—!"

"I'm going to have a show-down with Marsh!" he interrupted.

They were still arguing when the cook and Antonio returned. The little Italian rubbed his plump hands together, beaming at Ronnie and Ginger.

"The guests," he said chuckling, "they don't like what this Ruisant do to me. Several were waiting to pay their bills, but when he explain, they return to their tables. And what they say to this fellow, I am too much the gentleman to repeat."

He smiled warmly at the boy and girl, quite unaware that they'd been quarreling. "To you both, I am most grateful," he cried. "You save me much money. You save my reputation. You are my guests, and I hope you will order my best luncheon."

"That's kind of you, Mr. Antonio," said Ronnie. "But I didn't intend—"

"No, no," broke in the Italian, taking Ginger's arm. "I will hear of nothing else. This is my pleasure."

He escorted them to a window table, where they could look through the deep-yellow walls of the gorge at the ocean, sparkling far below. Neither Ronnie nor Ginger had much appetite; they were exceedingly cool to each other, when they spoke at all.

Antonio, true to his word, refused to accept anything for the meal, and he followed them out to the roadster.

"Can you deliver another hundred pounds of abalone on Friday?" he asked Ronnie, as they were leaving.

"It will be here," Ronnie promised, with a grin.

Ginger drove several miles before renewing their argument. "I'm sure Ruisant wasn't telling the truth," she insisted. "Doing a thing like that isn't Marsh's way."

"I've always thought of him as a square shooter," Ronnie admitted. "But let's drop it now, Ginger. I'm going to give Marsh a chance to explain his side—but his story had better be good!"

Ginger dropped him at his door a short time later. Her smart green suit somehow did not seem to fit her troubled face. "Ronnie, why do we always bristle at each other?"

He felt it safer to step out before answering. "Because you're so stubborn!"

"I am not," she cried indignantly. "You'll find I'm right about Marsh!" Shifting gears to forestall a reply, she sped away.

Walking toward the house, he wondered again at Ginger's puzzling attitude. She'd been kind enough to give him a lift to town. Without hesitation, she'd gone to his defense against Ruisant. Yet when it was an issue between Marsh and himself, she'd placed herself squarely on the latter's side.

Shaking his head, Ronnie opened the door in time to hear the phone ring. Hurrying into the living room, he lifted the receiver, and heard the deep, assured voice of Walter Bonnell.

"We're making up the Inn's dinner menu, Ronnie," said the manager. "If you can deliver fifty pounds of steaks, we'll put abalones on the card."

"I'll be right up with them, Mr. Bonnell."

He went to the plant, and brought out ten boxes with his father's decorative *Seal Cove Abalone* labels. Then, as an after-thought, he returned to the freeze room for another box. Packed by the Camerons and himself, it bore only a typed label reading *Red Abalone Steaks—5 pounds net weight.*

Loading the eleven boxes in the truck, Ronnie climbed in and drove eastward several blocks before turning southward to cross the bridge spanning San Pasqual Creek. A winding road ascended the ridge, and at the top a driveway led to the Seal Cove Inn. Colonial in design, it was surrounded by a maze of paths leading through the graceful radiata pines and the beds of blooming roses. The Inn stood on the brink of the ridge, looking down upon the fertile green valley and the tree-bordered creek, and from its upper windows guests could see the cove and a wide sweep of the Pacific beyond.

Ronnie parked at the side service entrance, and with five

---

boxes of frozen abalones under each arm, walked to the kitchen door. The big French chef Henri saw him coming and opened the screened door of the service porch. Henri had twinkling dark eyes, plump cheeks, and a wisp of a black mustache beneath his prominent nose.

"*Voila!*" he cried, beaming. "The abalones—specialty of the Inn!" And then he frowned. "But with your father no longer to supply us, it is a new specialty we must find, no?"

"I'm diving and processing now," Ronnie informed the chef.

Henri sighed and shook his head. "*M'sieu* Shumaker and this young *M'sieu* Marple, they bring boxes for me to try. But, no—it is not the abalones of perfection that Henri make the specialty of the Inn! Every fillet of your father's, it is perfect, yes?"

Walter Bonnel walked into the kitchen before Ronnie could reply. Seeing them on the service porch, the manager came to shake Ronnie's hand with a firmness that spoke of his understanding and sympathy. He was a handsome, well-knit man with prematurely white hair and a face that radiated the good health resulting from his earlier years as a college athlete.

"Bill Ballard tells me you've been diving in spite of the rough seas we've been having. How'd you like it, Ronnie?"

"Fine—except for a killer whale." And he briefly described his narrow escape. Then, sobering, he added, "I brought a box of my first pack, Mr. Bonnell. Have you time to look at it?"

"Bring it in," said Bonnell, after a slight hesitation. But it was not the older brother of the boys of Seal Cove speaking now; it was the manager of an inn famous for its food. "We're pretty particular, though," Bonnell added, as if preparing Ronnie for disappointment.

Ronnie's knees felt wobbly as he went out for the box he had packed. An order from the Seal Cove Inn would help him recover some of his father's former customers. But he was well aware of how small was the chance of pleasing the critical French chef or Walter Bonnell. Upon his return, he held up the box for inspection.

"You see I have only a typed label, Mr. Bonnell. Dad's brand stood for top quality in abalones, and I won't use it until I'm sure I can produce as good a pack."

"Wise idea," said the manager, his voice still reserved.

Henri's dark eyes expressed their doubt as Ronnie took a small crowbar from a hook and pried off the slats. Bonnell lifted out the first white fillet, pressed the splayed edges, carefully felt of the center portion, and turned it over for a critical look. Without comment, he passed it to the French chef, who examined it with even greater care. They scrutinized every steak in the box in the same way.

"Who helped you process this?" Bonnell asked abruptly.

"The Camerons, a retired couple living next door to us."

"*Hmmmm.* Have they had much experience in an abalone plant?"

"N-none, sir," Ronnie faltered, fearing something was wrong.

"I suppose you instructed them. But you never had much experience yourself, Ronnie."

"That's what people think, Mr. Bonnell. But plenty of times when Dad was out fishing and Mom was short-handed, she'd ask me to help out. We never said anything to Dad. He didn't want me to work in the plant, maybe because he was afraid I'd quit school as he did."

"*Hmmmm!*" murmured Bonnell, looking questioningly at Henri.

The chef shrugged. "It is the cooking that tells, *M'sieu.*"

He placed a flat iron griddle on the range and then prepared a batter of bread crumbs and egg. Into this batter Henri dipped six slices of abalone. Then, when butter was sputtering on the griddle, he added the steaks. No one knew better than Henri that fish should not be over-cooked. He allowed only time for the steaks to lose their transparent appearance, no more, before flipping them over. And in perhaps two minutes both sides were done. He dropped them onto a serving platter.

Taking two forks, Henri frowned as he handed one to Walter Bonnell. The two men began cutting the steaks into small pieces with their forks—the acid test for abalones. After several minutes, the chef found a little resistance to his fork. He hissed disparagingly.

"Come on—be fair, Henri!" Bonnell advised. "Thor Nordhoff's steaks were never *that* tender. Remember, this is not halibut."

Henri pressed a little harder and the slice fell apart. When he finished his division without once resorting to a blade, the chef put a piece into his mouth. Slowly he began chewing, a far-away expression in his eyes. Eagerly then, he took a second—a third—and a fourth piece. Then, with a sigh, he laid down his fork.

"*M'sieu,* what a chef you have! The abalones are as tender as a mother's arms. Still will they be the specialty of the Inn!"

So relieved was Ronnie that he wondered whether his knees would support him. Bonnell grinned at him, and went over to the sink to wash and dry his hands. Then he gave Ronnie's shoulders a hard, friendly squeeze.

"You've done it, Ronnie!" he said, sounding as pleased as though it were a personal triumph. "Your mother never let you get away with anything when you were working for her, did she?"

"She sure didn't!"

"Lucky for you," said Bonnell. "You can't deceive Henri when it comes to food. You can safely use your father's labels if your pack wins our chef's approval. Come out to the office. I'll have the bookkeeper give you a check now. You might need some ready cash."

While Ronnie stood at the desk looking around the spacious lobby, with its bright drapes and upholstered furniture covered with flowered chintz slip-covers, Bonnell went into a back office. Ronnie heard him dictating, though he couldn't catch the words. The manager came out and talked until a stenographer appeared with a check and a letter. Signing both, he passed them to Ronnie.

It was with astonishment that the boy read:

Dear Ronnie:

We have given your pack a critical examination and are so well satisfied that abalones will remain a specialty on our menus.

You may regard this as an order for a minimum of one hundred pounds of your steaks weekly until further notice, with such additional amounts as we will indicate from time to time.

> *Sincerely,*
> *Walter Bonnell, Manager*
> *SEAL COVE INN.*

"Thank you, Mr. Bonnell," Ronnie cried gratefully. "But you didn't need to bother dictating this. Your word is good enough for me."

"Yes, I know," said Bonnell. "But having known that generous dad of yours, I suspect his affairs may be in a muddle. My letter may help you at the bank."

Though the check was in Ronnie's name, and he was somewhat short of money, he knew he couldn't keep it. The payment was for abalones packed by his parents, and they were the backing for his father's loans. So he went directly to the bank. Seeing Mr. Romano at his desk, he passed through the swinging gates and laid both the check and the letter before the banker.

Joseph Romano glanced up with a start, then leaned back in his chair, smiling slightly as he studied the papers. He appeared as pleased by the evidence of good faith as by the order. Drawing up a form, he wrote out a receipt for $50.

Then he rose, squeezed Ronnie's arm, and accompanied him to the counter. Ronnie was nevertheless vaguely disappointed, for it was unlike Romano not to ask about his fishing experiences.

This omission was explained when he said, "Matt Ballard tells me you're a natural diver, Ronnie. Glad you persuaded me to give you a chance. How are you fixed for cash?"

"I'm holding out so far."

"Well, don't pinch yourself on necessities, even if it takes a little longer to clear up the loans. Maybe some day you'll have accounts to carry, or fishermen supplying your plant, eh?"

"Land's end!" cried Ronnie, lapsing into his father's vernacular. "Haven't I enough to worry about already?"

The banker's dark eyes twinkled. "These things may come sooner than you expect. And remember: We will carry you as long as you do your part. Good luck!"

Ronnie felt an encouraging glow as he left the bank and crossed the street to his truck. Then the edge was suddenly taken from his pleasure. He remembered Luis Ruisant's effort to injure his business.

"I'm going to have a reckoning with Marsh right now!" he decided.

7.

SQUEEZE PLAY IN THE DEPTHS

PREPARED for a warm discussion, Ronnie felt let down when he reached the little box-like cottage on the outskirts of town. Marsh's car was not parked before the house, and the window blinds were drawn. Nevertheless, Ronnie stepped from his truck and knocked. Receiving no answer, he walked to the back, only to find the woodshed abalone plant padlocked.

Returning to the truck, he was startled when a shiny sedan, approaching from the north, suddenly swerved toward him, its siren wailing. As it came to an abrupt stop beside him, Ronnie saw the sheriff at the wheel. Martin Dart pushed his worn stetson from his weathered brown face, looking boyishly pleased.

"Got my new gas buggy today," he said. "Scared you, didn't I?"

"Sure," Ronnie admitted with a grin. "Sheriff, did Pud mention seeing the *Southland Star's* lifeboat at China Charlie's?"

The sheriff rubbed his gray mustache. "He said Charlie had replaced it with a new flower box."

"Maybe he'd tell you why. It might be a clue to the disappearance of the *Southland Star*."

The sheriff looked bored. "I've got enough to do without digging up old cases."

"Pud tell you about the undersea bell Marsh and I heard?"

"Many fishermen believe the waters around Blacktop Rock are 'spooked,'" said the sheriff indifferently. "I don't pay much attention."

Ronnie was disappointed at this lack of interest. For the first time he noticed that the sheriff had become so portly that his big body rested against the wheel. And then the boy observed something else. There was an odd discrepancy between Martin Dart's forceful face and his eyes, which were listless and devoid of purpose.

"Pud says you'll make a good diver, Ronnie," went on the sheriff. "I'm kind of sorry in a way. You might have made a big name for yourself as a college athlete."

"Can't afford it, Sheriff. I've got to take care of Mardie and Skip."

"I've still got influence with Cal alumni," said Martin Dart. "Say the word, and I'll try to arrange a scholarship."

"I'm not much of a student. And I couldn't work my way through college and pay off Dad's debts."

"Too bad," said the sheriff. "Add a little weight, and you might have made All-American."

For several moments Martin Dart sat brooding, and then a remarkable change came over him. His eyes glowed with sudden excitement.

"Howie Thorgenson dropped in yesterday. He's a big name in the construction world today, but back in the 'twenties, we were sophomore backs on the Cal squad. He reminded me of a punt I made that broke up a tie game in the closing minutes. I recovered a fumble—"

And for half an hour the sheriff described the game, from the opening kick-off to his winning punt over the cross-bar. But for the first time Ronnie found himself growing impatient with one of Sheriff Dart's stories. It seemed to him that a law-enforcement officer should be more interested in a fresh clue to the mysterious disappearance of the *Southland Star* than in a football game played twenty-odd years before.

"Those were the days," concluded the sheriff. With a deep sigh, he added, "But I suppose I'd better get back to the office."

The boy was relieved when the sheriff's sedan glided away. "The old wind-bag," he muttered, and instantly felt ashamed of his disloyalty to Seal Cove's popular sheriff.

Still, there was something about this visit which had left Ronnie with a feeling of irritation. Why would the sheriff think that making All-American was more important than supporting Mardie and Skip? Why was he always giving his long-winded accounts of bygone games? And why did Ginger think that he, Ronnie, was like her father?

The comparison now annoyed Ronnie, although he could not quite understand why. He wished Ginger would explain what she meant. But past experience had taught him that she would not. She was too loyal to her father for that. Somehow, he must find the answer himself. And when he did, Ronnie suspected that he would have the key to Ginger's puzzling attitude toward him. He'd learn what it was that she disapproved of in Ronnie Nordhoff. It was that simple . . . and that confusing!

Driving home Ronnie pondered over the problem, without finding any satisfactory clue. He had scarcely parked the truck behind the house before Mrs. Cameron stepped from her back door and came hurrying toward him. Her smile was a little troubled.

"Oh, I'm glad you got home, Ronnie. I wanted to talk to you about . . . well, something disturbing. Miss Prindle called with a petition she's circulating to . . . to put Skip and Mardie in an orphanage. I sent her hustling, you may be sure, but I'm worried for fear someone may listen to her."

Ronnie's heart gave a heavy lurch. Burdened with other worries, he'd forgotten Miss Prindle's threat to send his younger brother and sister to an orphanage.

"I'm diving now, Mrs. Cameron, and I can support Skip and Mardie."

"Oh, I know," said his neighbor. "But you are pretty young to be caring for two children. Regular meals, and things like that."

Ronnie groaned. "I can't afford to hire anyone just yet."

"I know you can't, Ronnie," Mrs. Cameron said stoutly. "And I don't like that old busy-body butting in when you're trying to do your best! I don't think Miss Prindle could convince anyone that Skip and Mardie weren't well cared for if you'd let them eat with us when you're away fishing. I'd only charge you for the food; I have to fix my husband's meals anyway."

Ronnie's eyes smarted. He knew he had a staunch friend. He said, "Didn't Dad call you Aunt Nelly when he lived in Morro Bay?"

Her lips parted. "Why yes, he did. But—"

"May I call you *Mother* Nelly?"

Her face brightened with a kindly radiance. "Of course you may, Ronnie. Does that mean you'll trust me to keep an eye on Skip and Mardie?"

"I'd sure be grateful if you would. But I'm not kidding myself that that will keep Miss Prindle quiet. To prevent her from winning any support, I must convince the townspeople that I intend to stick to abalone fishing and processing. Few of them believe that yet."

Mrs. Cameron smiled. "I do," she said. Surprisingly, she added, "And Ginger is hoping."

Ronnie didn't debate the point. As he went into the house, however, he reflected on how little his neighbor understood Ginger. What would "Mother" Nelly Cameron think if she'd seen the girl exposing Ruisant's shabby trick, and then defending Marsh, who employed the man? How could you explain Ginger's bewildering changes of loyalties?

Ronnie called Bill and Pud, asking them to meet him at six the next morning, for he thought the sea might be growing calm enough for fishing. He begged them to be prompt because he intended to have a talk with Marsh before they sailed.

Bill and Pud were on time. As they were stowing away lunches, spare clothing and Pud's rifle in the back of the truck, however, a stranger drove up behind the house. He appeared to be about forty—a deeply-tanned man in a long-billed flyer's cap, pea-jacket and dungarees. He scrutinized the three boys, and then walked up to Ronnie, extending his hand.

"You look like you might be Thor Nordhoff's son. I'm Jim

135

Griffiths. You won't remember me, but I used to supply your father, years back."

"Glad to know you," said Ronnie. "Where've you been fishing?"

"Out of Morro. For Shumaker. But his count and mine disagreed once too often. I sailed into the cove last night, and I'd like to go out today, if you'll take my catch. You operating?"

Ronnie nodded. "Yes. But only my own abalones so far. However, I'll take all the reds you bring in. Operations have been stalled for a while. My parents were killed in an accident, and most of the fishermen pulled out of here, thinking I wouldn't reopen."

"I was sorry to hear about that accident. I was a fool ever to move to Morro Bay. Your father played square; never a short count." He hesitated, then asked cautiously, "What are you paying?"

"My father's last price. Six dollars a dozen."

"Fair enough." Griffiths paused, and looked embarrassed as he said, "I hate to ask this, but I've had some bad experiences with Shumaker." He cleared his throat and said doggedly, *"Can you pay?"*

"To be honest with you, Griffiths, *I* can't."

The fisherman looked at him inquiringly.

"But you'll get your money," Ronnie continued. "The Inn is taking my pack. The bank has promised backing. Talk to Mr. Romano if you have any doubts on that score."

"You talk straight enough for me," said Griffiths. "I'll be in with some abalones tonight."

"Load them on this truck if you get in before I do."

———

"I get you," said Griffiths. And with a wave of his hand, he returned to his car and drove off.

Ronnie had a buoyant feeling as he drove to the cove. He now had another fisherman supplying his plant; maybe in time there would be others. The largest share of his father's income had come from processing the abalones taken by others, and Ronnie knew it was that end he must build upon if he were to clear up the loans at the bank. But when he reached the pier, he realized that the delay caused by Griffiths' visit had made him miss Marsh. The *Bubbles* was already well out in the cove. A minute later she rounded the spit and turned northward.

"We'll follow her," Ronnie declared tersely. "I want to talk to Marsh about that business at the Sunset Cafe."

They soon had their gear and lunches aboard the *Sea Spray*. When they sailed from the cove, the *Bubbles* was several miles to the north, rolling gently on the dazzling blue and silver swells.

They followed her mile after mile, while the coast changed from white sand beaches and bare, wind-swept shorelines to low, rocky bluffs, with timbered hills soaring in green waves beyond.

At last they saw Marsh's boat draw into the lee of a rounded cluster of high rocks, offshore from the cliff where the Piedras Blancas Lighthouse stood. Swells burst like white plumes over the seaward side of the rocks and, rushing on, foamed between them and the cliffs. It was this restless clash of water that had prompted an imaginative Spanish explorer of early days to name the landmark "White Rocks."

"Marsh is dressing for a dive," Bill called.

"I doubt if it's smooth enough, even today," answered Ronnie. "But I'd better start getting into my gear. Come on, Pud, give me a hand."

Approaching Piedras Blancas, they could hear the boom and hiss of the seas, the hoarse barking of the sea-lions on the rocks. Marsh was already below, and Ken Carlson was finding it difficult to keep the swooping boat near the boil of his air bubbles. Swells surging between the great boulders swept her toward the bluff. Seething backwashes drove the plunging, rolling craft toward the rocks.

Bull sea-lions, weaving their heads, roared defiance each time the boat drew close, while the more timid cows, disturbed by the popping air-compressor, flopped along ledges to dive or slither into the sea. Several cows, attracted by the rising bubbles, circled Marsh's life line and air-hose in swift descents.

"Looks too risky to me," said Ronnie. "If Marsh doesn't come up by the time I'm dressed, so that I can talk to him, I won't wait. We'll try farther north."

It did not surprise him when Hammerhead Halvorson pulled up a basket of abalones so heavy that Carlson had to leave the wheel to help pull it aboard. Ronnie's father had claimed that shellfish were always plentiful at Piedras Blancas—for the diver willing to take risks.

Carlson clambered over the rail to grasp the wheel, while Hammerhead dragged the basket aft. Before he could dump the catch into the hatch, however, the rotund boat-operator shouted. Hammerhead had to run forward to take up slack in the life line and air-hose.

The *Bubbles* was borne toward the rocks by a ground swell.

Even in reverse, she could not resist its sweep, and struck with a jarring impact that almost hurled Hammerhead overboard. Momentarily his thin shoulders hung precariously over the side. Then, by wriggling, he wormed his body across the deck. Though he staggered erect, he looked dazed.

Meanwhile the air-hose uncoiled as the boat slid toward the cliffs, leaving slack when the next backwash carried it toward the rocks. Hammerhead saw that the hose must be his first concern. It stretched beneath the boat, and should be coiled. The life line, for some reason, slanted downward toward the side of Piedras Blancas.

Abalone fishermen generally conceded that there was no better line-tender than Hammerhead, but even the best man can be badly shaken up by a hard fall. Though he tried to draw in the hose rapidly, his movements were slower than usual. And suddenly bubbles clouded the water alongside the boat. Hammerhead's pale-blue eyes went wide with fright. Swiftly he whipped the hose upward. A severed end came into view!

"The propeller cut Marsh's hose!" he cried shrilly.

Ronnie was dressed now. Anxiously he watched the old tender give three jerks on Marsh's line before starting to draw it in hand over hand. Only a few yards had been hauled aboard when the line resisted his pull. Hammerhead exerted himself until his jaw muscles stood out like white cords in his thin face. He could not free the line!

"It's fouled, Carlson!" he shouted hoarsely. "You've got to help me!"

It was no time for an operator to leave the wheel. With no other choice, however, Carlson eased his heavy body over the rail and dropped to the deck with a *thump*. Even with his strength added to Hammerhead's, the line would not budge.

Ronnie's nerves were so taut now that he jumped when Bill started the air-compressor. The popping broke his frozen inertia. He climbed from the hatch, steadied himself, and then kicked the diving ladder overboard. It rose and fell on the heavy swells, creaking against its supporting side-brace, until he had worked forward and slid over the side to stand on the rungs.

"Give us some room, Carlson," he shouted. "I'll go down between your boat and the rock and try to free Marsh's line . . . Pud, quick—my helmet!"

Pud's broad face was drawn with the strain. "Ronnie, we might cut your line or hose! Bill can't control our boat, either!"

"I've got to risk it!" shouted Ronnie, forgetting for the moment his quarrel with Marsh. "He has only enough air to remain alive for five minutes!"

Ronnie was chilled with panic as he looked at the churning currents around the rocks. Seaward swells warring with the backwashes from the cliffs created rips and small whirlpools that moved swiftly in one direction or another, then vanished.

This was no place for a novice, with only the experience of four dives behind him! Unless he tried to do what he could, however, Ronnie knew that Marsh would strangle in his dress. There was no one else to attempt the rescue!

Ken Carlson was now working the *Bubbles* away from Piedras Blancas, while Hammerhead paid out Marsh's life line. When there was enough space between Marsh's boat and the rocks, Bill let the *Sea Spray* glide into the opening on a roaring wash. Ronnie thought for several terrifying moments that he'd be crushed against the rock. Intent on his own danger, he failed to see a bull sea-lion, poised for a dive. Its bark, close to Ronnie's ear, gave the boy a bad start.

He glanced up, and the sea-lion roared. Ronnie looked down once more through the rippling water. Marsh's life line led toward the rock. It must have snagged in a crack, perhaps when the *Bubbles* struck Piedras Blancas.

No air bubbles were rising. Had Marsh lost enough air to be squeezed? Or had he closed his valve promptly when air ceased flowing into his helmet? It must have taken fully sixty seconds for Bill to maneuver into position. Now, if Marsh had been lucky enough to retain his air, he had only enough to keep alive possibly four minutes!

Pud was holding the copper helmet. The moment the *Sea Spray* slipped away from the rocks, he eased it over Ronnie's head. He gave it a quarter-turn to lock it on, then snapped the air-hose to the back of Ronnie's belt. To save time, Ronnie flung himself from the ladder in a sidewise, twisting motion he had seen Shumaker use at Blacktop. He landed with a splash. Pud let him sink swiftly for a few yards before bringing him to a stop.

Now, where was Marsh's line? Ronnie looked first from his front, then from his side vision plates. A dark body glided by his left porthole, grazing his shoulder. Ronnie was startled until he realized it must be the sea-lion that had barked at him. Well, he could forget it! Though sea-lions were often curious, they rarely attacked divers. The important thing was to find the other life line!

Strong currents swept Ronnie against something hard.

Reaching down, he was relieved to feel a rope. Ronnie signalled Pud to give him slack, and then pulled himself toward Piedras Blancas along Marsh's line. The rock was bearded with masses of kelp and other marine plants; here and there half-buried sea-urchins or reddish abalone shells were visible.

Presently, reaching a broken bulge jutting out from Piedras Blancas, Ronnie saw where Marsh's life line was wedged. He gave a tug on his line to warn Pud to stay his descent. Coming to a quick stop, he groped with his feet until his cleated shoes located a small slanting ledge, several feet below the bulge. The ledge was partially covered with kelp and slippery as ice, but at least it gave him something to brace against. Before he could pull on the fouled life line, however, he was dragged upward by the plunging boat. Made overcautious by his concern, Pud was keeping the life line too taut. Impatiently Ronnie snapped repeatedly at the rope to request more slack.

Masses of sea plants, the weaving spines of sea-urchins and numerous abalones slipped past his vision plate as the boat sat in the trough, allowing him to descend. And at the same time Pud responded to his urgent signals by giving him so much slack that Ronnie would have passed Marsh's line had he not grasped it quickly as he descended.

Scarcely had he taken a firm hold on it when he was struck from behind and hurled against the bulge of rock. Such was the force of the impact that Ronnie thought for a moment the constellations were bursting before his eyes. Slightly stunned, he had to wait several moments until his vision cleared enough to see the darting shadowplay of light across the rock. He realized then that he'd been attacked a second time by a sea-lion, probably the one that had grazed his shoulder earlier. Its intentions were clearly hostile!

But knowing that Marsh would soon strangle for lack of air, Ronnie forced himself to ignore this danger. He found footing on the same slippery ledge and tugged on the snagged life line. It wouldn't give! Remembering his abalone-bar then, Ronnie wedged its point into the crack to pry away the rope. His heart-beat quickened when the bar gave slightly. Another hard wrench—and the line came free!

Clinging to it, Ronnie swung away from the rocks until he was suspended beneath the *Bubbles*. He jerked the line upward three times to signal Marsh. Then he repeated the signal to tell Hammerhead, on the other end, to take up his diver. A surge of relief washed over Ronnie when he felt three downward tugs—Marsh repeating his signal!

From his side plate, Ronnie caught a streak of movement, and turned his head in time to see a dark form diving toward him. He released Marsh's line, and his own line still being slack, he sank rapidly. Though he escaped the full force of the sea-lion's assault, he felt a jarring blow as it passed over him. Swallowing and blowing to adjust to the changing pressure, Ronnie glanced from front and side plates until he could once more locate the sea-lion. It was circling for another attack!

In that unlucky moment, Ronnie took up the last of the slack Pud had allowed him. His line jerked him to an abrupt halt, leaving him dangling helplessly. There wasn't even time to draw his knife. The bull was streaking toward him like a torpedo. Ronnie clenched his teeth, his heart quaking. The impact might make him lose consciousness, might even rip his dress!

Before this could happen, something black darted upward between Ronnie and his attacker. The bull swerved in fright, then disappeared in pursuit of the intruder. A split-second later, a life line and hose flashed past Ronnie. The black thing which had saved him, he realized now, was Marsh popping up.

The reprieve left Ronnie feeling weak. And before he could recover he was horrified to see the great rock once more slipping past. What was happening? He'd given Pud no signal to pay out line!

Penetrating even the roar of his inflowing air came a sharp crack, followed seconds later by two similar reports. The three claps resembled shots. *Why, they were shots!* Ronnie realized that Pud must be trying to put a bullet into the sealion before it could injure or kill Marsh. To meet this emergency, Pud must temporarily have abandoned the life line!

Hardly had this alarming explanation of the sounds come to Ronnie when he landed on rocks made treacherously slippery by sea grasses. A current like a mountain torrent bore him seaward before he could find firm footing. With foreboding he recalled his father telling of the dropoff on the western side of Piedras Blancas. If he sank into that abyss before he had time to build a sufficient cushion of air to resist the squeeze of pressure, he'd be crushed like a snail's shell beneath a heavy boot!

Stumbling and slipping, Ronnie fought the thrust of the current. Abruptly the force driving him toward disaster was withdrawn with the coming of a seaward current. Taking advantage of this brief respite, he shoved his cross-cleats hard against the slippery, uneven bottom and sculled with swimming motions until he reached the base of the rock, and could bury one hand in kelp. With the other, he tugged on his line. But, still untended, it rippled loosely through the water.

Pud would soon take up the slack—but by then, it might be too late. Ronnie's only hope seemed to lie in "popping up" as Marsh had done. Swiftly he screwed his monel valve to prevent the escape of air. He unbuckled both shoes. With his knife, he slashed the cord supporting the lead weight from his breastplate, and felt it drop away. Before he could cut away the lead weight on his shoulders, however, a ground swell started another powerful eastward current.

The kelp he gripped tore from the rock. Ronnie was almost lifted from the bottom by the strong surge. Then there were no longer rocks underfoot. He sank into an abyss where the pale sunlight faded into darkness below him. With the violence of desperation, he kicked, and the heavy shoes slipped from his feet. He pawed the water with frantic strokes, trying to slow his descent until the increased air in his dress would bring him into static balance.

But it was Pud, taking up slack on the life line, who really stopped his swift plunge. Pud hauled his diver upward only a few feet, however, when Ronnie's air took charge.

Without shoes or one heavy lead weight, in a dress fast-filling with air, Ronnie needed to rise only a short distance before he was far more buoyant than necessary to withstand the pressure of the surrounding water. He shot upward like a rocket. Rocks, kelp and several sea-lions streaked by in a confused blur. Momentum lifted him half out of the sea when he surfaced. His feet, now having nothing to hold them down, rose to leave him spread-eagled in his greatly inflated suit. Probing behind his eyes and in his ears were excruciating waves of pain from the abrupt decrease in pressure.

Repeatedly he bumped his monel valve to bleed air from the bulging dress before it burst from internal strain. Soon it resumed its normal size. But only after swallowing and blowing numerous times could he clear his blocked ears. When they popped, the relief was so marked that Ronnie nearly fainted.

Pud and Bill quickly hauled him aboard, removed his dress, and helped him into his sleeping bag. They were fearful that Ronnie's quick ascent might bring on bends, though that was unlikely, after such a short dive. Pud poured two cups of coffee, and after Ronnie had drunk the second, he felt the warmth beginning to seep through his body. He lay on his back, relaxed and drowsy. He felt no pain, the sign that nitrogen bubbles might be forming at his joints. And within half an hour, he had such a feeling of well-being that he was certain there would be no ill-effects from the experience.

Rolling over, he saw the *Bubbles* nearby, pitching as the big swells surged beneath her. Marsh lay in his bag on the afterdeck, heavy-eyed with fatigue.

"How are you feeling?" Ronnie asked.

"Pooped," Marsh answered wearily. Steadily he stared at Ronnie for several breaths before adding bitterly, "I should be grateful, but I'd rather owe my life to any other fisherman!"

His edged voice surprised and angered Ronnie, who felt an apology was due him after what had happened at the Sunset Cafe.

"For that matter, Marsh," Ronnie retorted with warmth, "I didn't free your line because of any great admiration for you. The truth is, I don't like your methods—"

"I think even less of yours!" cut in Marsh.

"Pipe down!" cried old Hammerhead shrilly. "You're lucky to be alive. Maybe one or both of you will have the bends before we can reach Seal Cove."

Ronnie glanced at the gentle, glistening swells beyond the rocks. Slowly an idea took form. Certain portions of the coastal waters known to be rich in abalones were seldom fished because of treacherous currents. During dead calms the currents lost their strength, and the little abalone boats struck out for these places usually avoided, sure of good catches. Might this not be one of those rare opportunities? Ronnie thought it was, and he knew just where he'd like to try his luck.

"I don't need a doctor!" he cried suddenly. "I have a hunch it's mild enough for diving off the San Simeon Coast."

The magic name brought Marsh upright. Pensively he studied the seas and breakers to north and south of Piedras Blancas.

"Much as I hate to admit it," he growled, "you could be right. I'm sailing north, too!"

"No, you're not!" protested Hammerhead. "You're going to a doctor!"

They were still warmly debating the point when Bill chugged out to open sea. A short time later Ronnie looked aft at the high, round lighthouse, dazzling white against the deep blue sky. A movement to the west of the cliffs caught his eye, and he shifted his gaze in time to see the *Bubbles* appear as she rounded Piedras Blancas. Apparently Marsh had convinced Carlson and Hammerhead that he was no longer in any danger of having the bends!

Ronnie rolled on his side and watched the rugged shoreline glide southward. The great rocks that at first dotted coastal waters were replaced by the soaring San Simeon cliffs. Raw scars, high above the sea, showed where a highway had been carved from rock and shale. The high domes of the mountains surmounting it were tufted with trees. And in places where the precipitous slopes were cleft by deep gorges, streams tumbled in small, white-water cataracts to the Pacific, glistening mirror-like under a warm sun. Only a thin line of breakers lapped lazily against rock-girt cliffs that were normally pounded by thundering combers. Ronnie knew that his hunch had been good.

Offshore from the highway bridge that spanned Mill Creek were three Monterey boats that had sailed south to take advantage of the calm. A husky tender on one was lowering an empty rope basket on a life line. When, after a short pause, it bobbed twice, he drew up the rope and hauled aboard a dripping basket of abalones.

"How's fishing?" Bill called.

The tender grinned. "Twenty dozen, not counting what I have here."

"Who have you got down?"

"Madman Morley," answered the tender.

Bill's face lighted with amusement as he turned toward Ronnie, now pulling up his diving dress.

"I met that character once when I was your dad's operator, Ronnie. Morley got his nickname because of the chances he took when he was younger. But after some close calls, he's become more cautious."

Bill sailed farther northward and then left the engine idling while he went forward to cast off the sounding lead.

"Seven fathoms," he reported. "Will this kelp give you trouble?"

Ronnie was now dressed for diving. When he stood up, he saw that the boat drifted through a bed of the giant kelp his father had usually called by its scientific name, *macrocystis pyrifera*. It was the world's largest plant, for its stalk and blades would reach more than half the length of the tallest redwood tree. Many small air bladders kept it afloat, making the kelp so buoyant that its holdfasts would at times raise great boulders from the bottom and sail to sea with them. Curiosity overcame Ronnie's faint sense of uneasiness about diving where marine plants grew thickly. There was a challenge in giant kelp. For moments he stared at the scimitar-shaped blades. Because they grew from only one side of the stalk, they suggested wind-blown trees as they weaved in the clear green water.

"You'll have to keep my line clear with your kelp-knife, Pud," Ronnie cried abruptly. "But I'd like to see what it's like down there."

Pud directed a troubled glance at the long-poled kelp-knife. "I'll try not to cut your hose. But I don't like this stuff."

When Ronnie's helmet was locked on and he had lowered himself from the ladder, he glided through weaving fronds and stalks that formed a canopy overhead, filtering the sun's rays to create a green twilight. It was what divers called a "kelp jungle," the ocean's closest parallel to the "bush" of tropical Africa, or South America or Borneo.

But Ronnie quickly perceived that a marine "forest" had its own distinctive features. Even here the magic of sea lighting was not entirely lost. There was the play of shadows and the subtle change of subdued colors. And through the emerald gloom came brief blazes of silver or ghostly blue, where fish were caught in fleeting darts of sunlight. Another difference in the submarine jungle was the kelp stalks, weaving in response to the currents like the trees in an enchanted woods.

He landed in a chaos of great boulders, heaped in wild disorder, as if flung there haphazardly by some giant. And again he felt the kinship with earthly jungles in the giant holdfasts of the kelp, entwined about the rocks for anchorage, and resembling the vines and roots in a tropical swamp. These rootlike snarls trapped his feet when he tried to work through the great stones, so that he stumbled and tripped time and again. The big stalks also hindered his progress, growing so thickly in places that he had to bend double to squirm through. In the dim light they loomed about him like the trunks of saplings, but their solid appearance was deceiving. Grasping them for support when he lost his balance, Ronnie discovered that they gave freely with his weight. Though sorely handicapped by the kelp, he was still able to pry an occasional large abalone from the under sides of a rock.

His basket soon became too heavy to drag farther. When about to send it up, Ronnie had the misfortune to step into a snarl of creepers. Giving an impatient wrench to free himself, he pulled off his cast-iron shoe. His foot, no longer held down, was instantly hoisted by the air in the lower part of his dress.

Tottering on one leg, he tried to force the other down. But even when he used both hands, he succeeded in pushing his errant limb down only a few feet before he started to lose balance. Then he'd have to scull the water to remain erect. Through his vision plate his leg could be seen like that of a high kicker frozen in position.

At last, after many futile efforts, Ronnie paused to deliberate. Should he signal Pud to pull him up? But if he ascended, might he not rise feet first? How, then, could he climb aboard?

Bending slightly forward, he peered through his oval glass at the basket of abalones he'd dropped. Nearly two hundred pounds, it must weigh, and while it was considerably lighter than that in water, it might still help him if he could find a way to attach it to his ankle.

Ronnie thought a moment, and then squatted to make it easier to maintain balance. Twice he tugged on his line. While Pud was lowering an empty container, Ronnie recovered his shoe and placed it where his foot might fall if he could force it down.

Removing the basket, he secured the filled one to his life line. Then, after a moment of consideration, he passed the slack end of the rope over his ankle, and reeved it through the mesh of the bag. When he drew in line the basket of shellfish did not budge but his foot slowly descended to within a few inches of the shoe. He stopped, puzzled as to how to get it on.

At length he saw a way that might work. Lashing the rope to his extended limb, he used it for leverage when he staggered upright. Like the board on a teeter-totter, the movement brought his foot down, though not quite enough. Pressing on his knee depressed it even further. He was able to wriggle his toes under the tire casing top of the shoe, and it was driven firmly on when he stepped down hard.

Seconds later the life line was freed, and he signalled Pud to take up the basket of abalones. After it ascended, Ronnie was so exhausted that he wondered whether it was worthwhile to fish in a place where conditions were so trying for a diver.

Spying a gleam of sunlight off to seaward, he stumbled wearily on over the rocks, hoping he might be heading toward more open water where there would be less kelp. As he clambered over the treacherous boulders, he kept his eyes on the bright streak ahead. Drawing nearer, however, he realized that the golden shaft of sunlight struck down through only a small window in the canopy of kelp fronds. Though disheartened by the discovery, Ronnie worked slowly on toward the yellow beam for want of any better goal.

Presently he came to a trough, and cautiously lowered himself down the side of a rock. The subdued light revealed a bed of lacy red seaweed, rippling in the strong current flowing along the depression. He was buffeted about when he tried to pry shellfish from under the rocks. Half a dozen nevertheless went into his basket. Then, flung sidewise by the underwater stream, his helmet collided with a rock, and he decided that fishing there was too hazardous.

Pushing hard with his cleats, he forced himself seaward, hoping to find the bright gleam once more. After progressing several hundred feet, the channel divided, and the current was no longer so strong. He groped his way around a rock. With startling suddenness, the gloom vanished and the water ahead blazed golden.

Within a few yards, walking became easier. He failed to understand why until he tried to halt upon reaching the brink of a deep hole where the sun shaft lanced down to create a yellow pool of light. Ronnie was alarmed to discover that he'd blundered into another current which was driving him forward. He pawed the water with hard, pushing strokes to avoid being swept into the pit.

An octopus or a moray eel might inhabit the hole! The depression in the sea floor might also be deep enough to squeeze a diver. But it was in such pockets that his father had always found fishing the best. The brightness below was strongly tempting after the twilight murk of the kelp jungle.

"I'm going to take a chance," Ronnie decided.

His warning jerk on the line brought a quick answer. Pud was alert! Ronnie screwed his monel valve several turns, reducing the escape of air. He might need a strong cushion of pressure in his dress to avoid a squeeze. And then, abandoning all resistance to the current, he let it sweep him over the edge. Slowly he began sinking into the submarine well, down into the pit of radiant golden light.

8

GINGER ANSWERS AN SOS

A DIVER soon grows accustomed to certain conditions of his work. Gliding downward into the sunlit hole in the ocean floor, Ronnie was scarcely more aware of the thunderous roaring of his air than a motorist of a purring engine. Blowing and swallowing to equalize the changing pressure now seemed as natural as breathing deeply after violent exercise. But one condition of deep-sea diving, he suspected, would forever remain strange and fascinating to an earthling in rubber dress and copper helmet. That was the weird and dreamlike beauty of the world beneath the sea.

Concerned though he was about what he might find in the pocket, Ronnie could still, with a portion of his mind, experience a feeling of wonder at the brilliant colors passing before his vision-plate. Sea plants and small marine animals of so many hues clustered on the walls slipping by that they looked like a lapidary's display of dazzling gems. Sprinkled through the variegated array were larger animals: sea urchins, scarlet and orange starfish, spiny lobsters, crabs and abalones in their rough reddish shells.

His passage seemed long, but in reality he descended perhaps no more than twenty feet before his shoes struck the bottom. Swiftly Ronnie looked about, his hand on his life line. He was prepared to order Pud to pull him up if he saw any predatory creature. There was not even a crack in the walls, however, that might hide an enemy.

He was about to begin work when a great ugly fish swam up to his front plate and nuzzled his grill. Magnified by the water, it seemed as large as a shark. In a moment Ronnie realized it must be much smaller than it appeared, and his alarm subsided. It was only a capazoni, better known on that coast as a "bullhead"—quite harmless, and often referred to as "the diver's pet." To test stories he'd heard, Ronnie probed in the sea growth until he found a marine worm. When he raised it slowly, the bullhead accepted the tidbit with a kind of grave dignity.

It hovered nearby as Ronnie glanced about. Everywhere, on the walls, beneath jutting ledges, and half-buried in aquatic plants, were abalones. This was luck! He'd discovered a pocket never visited by any other diver! Each time he pried off a shellfish, his ugly friend would swim up in a leisurely way to seize small worms and tiny crustaceans brought to light. Ronnie began to enjoy the companionship and he understood now why his father and other divers spoke warmly of their "pets." The bullhead made him feel less lonely.

The soft golden light made it easy to see shellfish. He filled his first basket without moving from where he stood. Four more followed it before Ronnie ascended.

Pud relieved him of his helmet, and then counted the abalones in the last container as he cast them into the hatch. "Two dozen and eight, Bill!"

Bill moved matches on the tally-board, and then grinned

broadly. "Fifteen dozen and six—ninety-three dollars on that dive, Ronnie!"

"Boy, oh, boy!" Pud exulted. "If the weather will only stay calm, we'll all get rich."

"I won't," Ronnie said, with a tired smile. "But maybe I can whittle down some bank loans."

After a short rest on the ladder, Ronnie returned to the same hole to take six additional baskets of abalones. On his third dive, he stripped the pocket of every remaining shellfish of legal size by gathering seven more containers. The bullhead had remained with him all this time, and as a farewell present, Ronnie found a few choice worms for his pet before ascending. When his helmet was removed, he saw that there were now six small boats fishing below the cliffs.

"It's a shame wasting time sailing back with our haul when it's this mild on the San Simeon," he observed with regret.

"No way to avoid it," said Bill. "Abalones must be processed within thirty-six hours."

"The fishermen should have a pick-up boat," Pud lamented. "Then when the weather's this good, they wouldn't lose precious time transporting their catches."

"Dad considered that, Pud, but a pick-up boat would cost probably $10,000. It wouldn't pay." Ronnie gave a start. "*Uh-uh!*"

"What's on your mind?" asked Bill curiously.

Ronnie didn't answer. His eyes strayed to the lacy surf breaking lightly against the base of the high cliffs. Then he studied the combers rolling in languid white streamers along the beach south of Mill Creek. In silence he surveyed the rough tracks running parallel to the streambed and disappearing under the high span of the highway bridge. He and Pud and Bill had camped below the arch, and while the road was not good, it was passable.

Maybe a pick-up boat wasn't necessary! But the idea taking shape in his mind would require money—a considerable amount, at that! Where would he get it? He remembered Mr. Romano's promise, and wondered how far the banker would go in backing him.

"Give me a hand, Pud," Ronnie cried. "I'm getting out of my rig. Think you could land near the creek, Bill?"

"Sure. If the beach is steep enough."

"Get going then, pal."

Ronnie had his diving dress removed and a note written by the time Bill nudged the bow of the boat against the sandy beach. He sprang ashore, and gave the *Sea Spray* a push.

"Better anchor, Bill. It may be a while before I'm back."

"Why so mysterious?" asked Bill. "What's up?"

"Maybe nothing," said Ronnie. "But we'll see."

He walked up the tracks leading under the bridge and turned right to reach the highway. Then he sat down to wait. Twenty minutes passed before a sedan with fishing rods strapped on top appeared. He hailed the car, and when it came to a stop, he saw that the men inside were dressed like sports fishermen.

Ronnie walked up and handed the driver the note he'd written and a dollar bill. "Would you be good enough to buy a post-office envelope at Seal Cove, and mail this special delivery? The name of the girl it's going to is here on the outside of the letter."

The man glanced at his wrist-watch. "Guess we'll be there

before the post-office closes. Glad to help out."

Ronnie walked back under the highway bridge to the beach, and when Bill chugged in, he scrambled aboard, and stood thoughtfully gazing about. The sun was a low blaze of red in the west, and the smooth sea was marcelled with unbroken, opalescent swells. Most of the divers were still fishing, but several stood resting on their ladders. When Ronnie located the *Bubbles*, he was disappointed to see Hammerhead drawing his line slowly upward and then releasing it, as was his habit. Marsh was still below. No chance to speak to him until he finished his trick on the bottom!

"Might as well be 'scratching' while I'm waiting for him to come up," Ronnie observed.

"You've had enough today," cautioned Bill.

"It's not often this calm here," said Ronnie. "Got to make the most of it! But see if you can find a place where I won't have to struggle with kelp."

Bill cruised until he located clear water, relatively free of kelp. As soon as Ronnie was dressed, he went down. By working around the bases of big rocks, and in the depressions between them, he gathered three more baskets. But as the light was then growing dim, he decided to call a halt to fishing. The moment his helmet was off, he looked for the *Bubbles*.

"Where's Marsh's boat?" he asked.

"Sailed south while you were down," answered Pud. "I guess he's going to process his catch this evening, and return during the night."

"Rugged program," said Bill. "But he won't lose fishing time."

He sailed closer to the Mill Creek beach before shutting off the engine and letting go the anchor. Then he broke out a hand line and sent the sinker splashing overboard.

"I'd better get busy," he said, "if we're going to have fresh fish for supper."

Pud helped Ronnie aft, and while the plump tender unbuckled the plates and pulled off the dress, Bill jigged for fish. He was rewarded with half a dozen perch and groupers, and one sole, hooked by the tail. Bill dumped several cans of mixed vegetables into a pot and lighted the butane stove. Then he cleaned the fish, and soon had them sputtering in the frying pan.

When he loaded their plates, Pud tried a large piece of golden brown fish and then some vegetables. Uttering a deep sigh of contentment, he settled down to his favorite pastime. Ronnie, however, was hardly aware of what he ate. Absently he watched the sea turning mauve in the purpling dusk, and the small boats rolling gently in the light swells. There appeared to be more craft than before his last dive, and now he counted them. Fourteen in all!

"Wouldn't surprise me, Bill," he observed, "if a quarter of the abalone fleet was here tomorrow morning."

"And the boats will be pulling out by late afternoon," said Bill.

A secret smile lighted Ronnie's face as he thought of the letter he'd written. He hoped Bill would be wrong.

They washed the dishes, and then Pud and Bill spread out their sleeping bags on deck. Ronnie continued to watch the highway, where the lights of an occasional car bobbed along but never paused.

"Want to stay up a while?" asked Pud.

Ronnie looked at the cliffs looming above them, like a black cardboard stage set against the star-powdered sky.

"I don't feel like sacking in yet," Ronnie said, but for the first time doubt had crept into his voice.

Maybe he should have written the note to one of the Camerons, he thought. They were older, and might have more influence with Mr. Romano.

When another half hour passed, Ronnie decided it was useless to wait up any longer. In low spirits, he tossed his bag onto the cabin, and climbed up to spread it out.

Even the appearance of a pair of headlights swinging around a bend to the south failed to cheer him. So many cars had raised his hopes, only to dash them again when they sped by. But when these lights approached the bridge, they left the highway, vanished briefly, and reappeared beneath the arch, rising and falling as a vehicle descended the rough tracks beside the creek. They turned south then, and above the lapping of surf Ronnie heard the faint crunch of gravel as the machine drove onto the upper part of the beach.

"There's my truck!" he cried jubilantly. "Head for the beach, Bill!"

"Why didn't you say so?" asked Bill, who had unlaced his shoes. "Planning to move our catches by land, and remain here?"

"That's not all I've planned!" Ronnie exclaimed.

As soon as Bill had the engine started, Ronnie heaved up the anchor. The little boat chugged up to the beach. Three figures stood awaiting them beyond the white fringed surf.

"Well, what do you know!" exclaimed Pud. "Isn't that my

---

kid sister?"

"It's Ginger, all right," said Ronnie. "But I didn't dream she'd come along."

He ran forward to cast a line to one of the two tall boys beside her. When they shouted greetings, Ronnie recognized the voices of Eddie Raybold and Rickie Dore. Both were high-school classmates who had worked summers at the Nordhoff plant with such energy and willingness that Ronnie's father had hoped to find permanent places for them. They were lanky six-footers, but otherwise differed greatly in appearance. Eddie was a tow-head; Rickie, quite dark. They were inseparable companions, but bickered constantly, so that strangers sometimes imagined they were about to come to blows.

Yelling insults at each other, Eddie and Rickie pulled the boat up onto the sand so that Ronnie could jump ashore dry-shod. He grinned at the tall boys, and asked, "Still at it?" But when he turned to Ginger—a trim little figure in green slacks and a green sweater that matched her scarf—his cheeks grew warm and he didn't know what to say.

"The name is Miss Dart," she explained crisply.

"Golly, Ginger," he said in embarrassment, "I didn't mean to put you to all this trouble, coming up here and everything."

"I'm amazed you'd think of that," said Ginger. "Shall we broadcast this, or have a private conference?"

He saw the papers in her hand and wondered whether they bore good or bad news. He said, "Just a minute, fellows," and walked along the beach until the girl stopped. When she looked up at him, he was surprised to find no hint of the annoyance her voice had suggested. Even in the starlight, there was no mistaking the excitement in Ginger's pert face.

"Would Mr. Romano loan me enough to buy the catches of these fishermen?" he asked anxiously.

"The post-master delivered your note on his way home," she said, breathless with some half-suppressed emotion. "I went immediately to see Mr. Romano, knowing he'd turn you down. But of all the crazy things—*he said he'd back your plan!*"

Ronnie's knees shook at hearing her words. So the banker would stand behind him, advancing hundreds, perhaps thousands of dollars against abalones he was not sure he could sell! True, frozen fillets were no great risk; they would keep indefinitely, and the bank could, if necessary, recover its loan by placing the entire pack with another processor, if Ronnie failed to dispose of it. For all that, Ronnie knew that Mr. Romano would not have given the bank's support if he had not believed that the new operator of the Nordhoff plant could put out a first-class pack. Walter Bonnell's letter had convinced him of that! And the banker, thought Ronnie, must consider his proposed plan a sound one.

Now the question that troubled the boy was whether the fishermen would sell their catches to anyone as young as himself.

"Mr. Romano went down with me to open the bank and fill out some forms," Ginger went on. "I brought a pen, and I'll show you where to sign away your life."

"You think I'm silly to tackle anything this big?"

"Insane!" corrected Ginger. "But I've always suspected it."

Angrily he snatched her pen. "I'll show you! You've always wanted me to fail!"

Her reaction was so swift, so unexpected, that Ronnie had no idea of her intention until her arm shot out. He felt the sharp sting of her small hand on his face.

"You take that back, Ronnie Nordhoff!" she cried tempestuously. "It's not true!"

More astonished by the slap than her burst of fury, he said grimly, "Spitfire, if you were my sister, I'd be tempted to turn you over my knee!"

"Do you take back those words?" she demanded with warmth. "Do you think I'd be here, trying to help, if I didn't want you to make good?"

"I guess not," he said slowly. "But honest, Ginger, I can't make you out. You're such a good scout part of the time, and the remainder you give me the Ronnie Nordhoff treatment."

Her eyes dropped. Even in the uncertain light, he thought her face was working, and he was sure there was a glint of tears on her cheeks.

"Oh!" she cried impatiently. "How like a man!"

"It will take one to put this over! But maybe you're right in thinking I'm out of my depth in attempting it."

"You know I didn't *really* mean that!" She paused, blinked several times, and quickly added, "I want to do everything I can to help."

More confused than ever, Ronnie peered anxiously at the girl, and said apologetically. "Look, Ginger, I don't want to make a nuisance of myself. I sent you that SOS because you're such a smart cookie with figures. It seemed to me you could handle these arrangements better than the Camerons."

"And so I can. I'd be simply furious if you'd called anyone else!"

Becoming suddenly businesslike, Ginger drew a small flashlight from her pocket, turning its beam on the top form.

"This is the loan agreement, but there are a number of other papers to sign. It's awfully complicated, Ronnie. Because you're a minor—that is, under legal age for making contracts—Mr. Romano has to approve of everything as your guardian and the executor of your father's estate. Then, as if he were a completely different person, he has to pass on his previous acts in his role as manager of the bank. But that part needn't worry you. The point is that Mr. Romano is allowing you almost unlimited credit for the purchase of abalones from the fishermen here. He can close down your credit at any time, however, and all payments to these men must go through the bank. Another thing: the loan he's granting you is a lien against the steaks you pack."

Ronnie looked bewildered. "What does he mean by *lien?*"

"It just means that the boxes of abalones in your freeze room are security for the loan. The bank can take them if you fail to pay."

"I'm almost afraid to sign, Ginger!"

"Not you!" said Ginger. "Or you wouldn't have dreamed up this crazy, wonderful idea. It will either break you, or make you!"

"Well, I'm already in debt over my neck," he grumbled. After carefully reading the first form, he scrawled his signature opposite a check-mark the banker had made.

When he had signed the last paper, Ginger explained how the payments were to be taken care of by the bank. Then they walked back to the truck. Eddie and Rickie had already unloaded a dory and several boxes of provisions which Ronnie, in his letter, had requested Ginger to send up to Mill Creek.

"Let's see if I can buy some abalones," Ronnie said to the two boys.

"Better hang a horseshoe around Eddie's neck," suggested Rickie. "He'd jinx a four-leaf clover."

"Look who's talking!" hooted Eddie. "Old 'Hoodoo' Dore himself."

Ronnie helped his new employees to launch the dory. Eddie told Ronnie and Rickie to get in, and then, disregarding soaked shoes and dungarees, he pushed the boat through the surf.

"What are these for?" Rickie asked, picking up an oar. "Oh, I get it!"

Seeing Eddie was scrambling over the bow, he applied the flat of the oar, none too gently, to the seat of his friend's pants.

"Let me at him!" bellowed Eddie. "There's going to be a slight case of disaster in this boat!"

"Cut it out, you two!" admonished Ronnie, suppressing a grin.

He took the oars and rowed until the dory lay alongside a boat moored not far off the beach. The crew were strangers to him. The largest of the three, who had a certain air of authority, looked as though he might be the diver. He was a man of powerful build, and his bare, freckled arms were knotted and muscular. There was nothing attractive about his face, with its heavy, almost coarse features, and florid coloring.

Nevertheless Ronnie smiled good naturedly as he introduced himself and explained his plan to buy any abalones the fishermen would sell him. While he spoke, he was uncomfortably aware of the big man's sharp scrutiny. The stern, blood-shot eyes were neither hostile nor friendly. They were calculating.

"I'm Les Blaizdall," the man declared, when Ronnie finished, "I did take some abalones farther south, but I don't know if I can sell them to you."

"You're tied up with another processor?"

Blaizdall hesitated. "Yes—in a way."

"It's up to you," said Ronnie, hiding his disappointment. "But if you have no contract, you can sell to anyone. I expect to be trucking from here all night, Mr. Blaizdall, so if you change your mind there's plenty of time to let me know."

"Okay, kid, I'll think about it."

Ronnie rowed a short distance, then rested on his oars, wondering which boat to try next. On a nearby craft, he saw the tender Bill had spoken to at the time of their arrival on the San Simeon. He turned that way, shipping his port oar as he glided alongside. Of the three fishermen eating their dinners from paper plates on the afterdeck, only one was old enough to be the fabulous "Madman" Morley. And he failed to fit Ronnie's mental picture of the colorful Monterey diver. The older man was small and inconspicuous in appearance, but his round and grizzled face had an expression of puckish good humor.

"Are you Mr. Morley?" Ronnie asked doubtfully.

"I'm Morley," said the little man, turning to his mates with a humorous grin. "But do you guys think I rate a *Mister?*"

Ronnie knew Morley by reputation. More than that, abalone fishermen had been visiting in his home for as long as he could remember. He knew how to take a ribbing, and return measure for measure.

"Look, Morley, I'm trucking my catch down to my plant at Seal Cove so I can stay here and fish while it stays calm. I'm keeping this dory here so I can anchor my boat and set up a comfortable camp on shore. I'd like to buy your abalones while you're here, if you have any in your hatches that aren't undersized."

Morley seemed delighted at the dig. "How much are you paying, you pirate?"

"Six a dozen to the other fishermen, but I thought I could talk you into taking five. And fifty cents off that for hauling."

"No, you don't!" yelled Morley, his small, brown eyes twinkling with amusement. "I'd demand six if I were dumb enough to fall for your game. But I wasn't born yesterday! What would I get in return for my catches, eh? Promises?"

Ronnie glanced at Eddie and Rickie. "Does the man expect cash!"

"He's out of luck," said Eddie.

"Offer him an I.O.U.," suggested Rickie.

"That's probably all I'll get," said Morley. "What is this deal you think I might tumble for?"

"Talk to the girl on shore," advised Ronnie. "She brought up papers from the Seal Cove Bank. They don't know me too well, I guess, because they're backing me, and issuing checks every Saturday for the abalones any of you fellows will deliver to me up to Friday night. Eddie or Rickie will bring up the payments. I'll remember to tear up your check, Morley."

"Don't let me catch you at it," said Morley, turning to his mates. "The kid speaks our language. What do you guys think?"

"What is there to think about?" asked the husky tender. "Why live cramped up here on this boat when we could live in plush on shore, Madman? It would cost far more in lost time transporting our catches to Monterey than paying the kid's hauling charges. Only trouble is, we didn't bring enough provisions to stay here more than two days."

"The boys brought up some grub, and more will be along every night," explained Ronnie. "We can split costs, and I'll deduct it from your payments."

"And probably overcharge us, too," said Morley. The good humor in his face was replaced by a puzzled expression. "Blamed if you don't remind me of someone I've known."

Ronnie chuckled. "Years ago you and my dad used to fish for Bill Pierce. Remember the time the two of you slipped up on a Jap diver and cracked rocks together near his helmet so that he'd think his air-compressor was blowing up?"

"I got it!" And Morley grinned broadly. "Why didn't you say you were Thor Nordhoff's son! Better start ferrying my catch ashore. I'm going into camp."

With three in the dory, they couldn't take many abalones ashore that trip. Eddie and Rickie took turns rowing out for the shellfish after that. As the last of Morley's haul was loaded in the truck, Ronnie wrote out a receipt in a note-book Ginger had brought, and then rowed out to deliver it.

The little diver glanced at the paper, tucking it into his pocket as he stepped into the dory. "For a wonder, it agrees with our tally!"

Ronnie grinned at the husky tender, who was settling himself on the stern thwart. "I knew Morley couldn't count well enough to know the difference if I docked him three dozen."

"You robber!" wailed Morley. "You're worse than Shumaker!"

When the dory touched the sand, the fishermen stepped out with their sleeping bags and a few cooking utensils, and walked over to find level spots beside the stream. Apparently in no mood to retire, they gathered pieces of driftwood from the beach and built a fire.

Ronnie found Ginger at the truck, and asked her to come and explain matters. She walked with him to the fire. Morley asked a few questions, examined her papers, and then returned them, shaking his head.

"Who'd think a bank would trust a kid your age, Nordhoff!"

"You're making the same mistake," Ronnie said with a grin.

"Ain't it the truth!" Morley paused, glancing at Bill and Pud, who had just come ashore in the dory to join them at the fire. "Better go out and talk to the other boys, Nordhoff," he went on. "You might find them as simple as I am."

Ronnie relieved Rickie of the oars, and rowed out to another nearby fishing boat. The men were watching the flames in their leaping dance against the dark background of willows and sycamores.

"What's going on?" a fisherman asked Ronnie.

"That's Morley's crew," the boy explained. "They're selling me their catches and camping ashore while the good weather lasts. I'm hauling from here for anyone who doesn't think they can beat my fifty cents a dozen trucking charges."

"Let's hear about it," said the man, as if already half-convinced. And when Ronnie had given him the details, the fisherman remarked, "If it sounds all right to Morley, I'll go along with him."

At boat after boat, Ronnie discovered that little persuasion was necessary after he mentioned Morley's name. The daredevil antics that had earned Morley his nickname lay behind him. Sobering years of experience had given him judgment that the other fishermen respected. They followed his lead as they'd once followed that of Thor Nordhoff.

More and more men were rowed ashore to gather around the blazing pile of driftwood, until only Les Blaizdall and his two mates remained on their boat.

It was not until the last of the men were ashore that the ferrying of abalones began in earnest. When the first load was stowed away, Ronnie and Pud walked over to the truck with Ginger.

Eddie and Rickie were already bickering about who should drive.

"You'll take turns," Ronnie promptly decided. "And while one of you is making a trip in the truck, the other can be bringing abalones ashore in the dory. You take this load, Eddie. And see that you deliver Ginger safe at home before you drop your cargo at the plant."

He thanked Ginger for her trouble while she settled herself on the high seat beside Eddie. She sat very still for several moments, her eyes seeming quite large in the white blur of her face.

"Oh, Ronnie," she cried suddenly. "This is an awfully big thing you're attempting. I—I hope nothing goes wrong!"

Though he was already growing appalled at the size of the undertaking, Ronnie managed to laugh, and say, "Don't worry, Ginger."

As he returned to the fire, he was grateful when Pud gave his arm a reassuring squeeze. "That goes from both us Darts, Ronnie! Boy, I'm sure glad this isn't on my shoulders!"

Talk had been somewhat restrained while the girl was with them. But now the fishermen around the fire began to recount stories of close escapes at sea, or boisterous experiences ashore. Best of all the tales told, it seemed to Ronnie, were Madman Morley's accounts of the days over twenty years past when he and other young abalone fishermen had been fighting to break the Japanese abalone monopoly.

At last, one or two at a time, the fishermen disappeared to slip into their bags. Ronnie found a level spot between Pud and Bill. For a long while, however, he lay wakeful, listening to the deep breathing of the men, the crackling of the dying fire, the soft lapping of the surf, and the musical murmuring of the creek. As he thought of Morley's madcap experiences, an idea came to him.

Morley had sailed along every part of this coast for more than two decades. He must know China Charlie! The little diver might be the man who could explain how the old Chinese had come into possession of a lifeboat from the long-lost *Southland Star*. He must remember to ask Morley in the morning!

9.

A SPY IN FISHERMEN'S CAMP

THROUGHOUT the night, the unloading of abalones from the small craft continued. At intervals Ronnie was awakened by the click of oar-locks, or the grinding of gears as the truck set off for Seal Cove with another cargo of shellfish. But each time he dropped off to sleep again with an easy mind, remembering that Eddie and Rickie had never neglected their work in any way when employed by his father. He was sure they would follow instructions and keep an accurate count of each boat's haul.

In the early morning hours, however, his slumber was disturbed by a hand on his shoulder. Drowsily, Ronnie rolled over and opened heavy eyes. The glowing embers of the fire dimly lighted a florid face.

"It's Les Blaizdall," the man whispered hoarsely. "The boys are unloading your boat now. It seems foolish to waste time sailing my catches to Morro Bay if you'll buy them. How about it?"

"Tell one of the boys to take your haul," Ronnie murmured sleepily. "Are your men still aboard?"

"We might as well remain there tonight. Thanks, kid."

Gravel crunched under the big man's feet, but a few moments later he was back. "Mind if I borrow your flashlight? I haven't one aboard, and it will help in unloading."

Had he been more alert, Ronnie would have sensed something odd in the request. For both Eddie and Rickie had electric torches; and after the first load, they had beamed the truck's headlights on the boat from which they were discharging shellfish. But being only half-awake, Ronnie handed over the long, chromium flashlight—a four-battery one on which his father had scratched "Thor Nordhoff."

"Don't forget to return it."

"*I* wouldn't worry about that," said Blaizdall, giving the first word peculiar emphasis.

The incident left no more impression on Ronnie's mind than the fleeting fragment of a dream. Having several other flashlights on his boat, he thought no more of the one Blaizdall had borrowed—a forgetfulness he was later to regret. . . .

The next time he awakened, it was with a feeling of alarm, for he was moving back and forth through the air like a pendulum. Ronnie popped his head out and saw that Pud and Bill had grasped opposite ends of his sleeping bag and were swinging it in high arcs from side to side.

"Aim for the fire," cried Bill, "before letting it go."

"Say when," answered Pud.

"Let me out!" Ronnie protested, laughing.

They dropped him with a thump. He unzipped his bag and sat up. Most of the fishermen were gone. Those washing their faces at the stream were grinning, amused by the rough horse-play.

"You looked so peaceful," said Bill, his dark eyes crinkling, "that we hadn't the heart to disturb you until we'd eaten. Ready to fish?"

With a nod, Ronnie rose and stretched. Then, with soap and a towel, he walked over to the stream, splashed cold water on his face and scrubbed vigorously. As he dried his face, he looked out across the water. Morley was already below, and the *Bubbles* had sailed in from the south and was anchoring.

"Let's go out and talk to Marsh," Ronnie said grimly.

There was a delay after reaching their boat; they had to return the dory and push it ashore so that the fishermen on the beach could board their craft. When they drew out into deeper water, Marsh was down and Hammerhead was watching his foaming bubbles.

"Let's fish close by," Ronnie called to Bill. "Sooner or later, we'll both be up at the same time."

Bill sailed out to clear water beyond a kelp bed. Ronnie glided downward through sixty feet of bright water on his first dive. The ocean floor slanted sharply seaward where he landed. Tilted at every angle about him were great slab-like boulders. Luxuriant algae—sea plants—on the rocks bowed first in one direction, then in another, in the relatively strong currents. Bracing against the water movements was trying. To escape their buffeting force while he fished, he worked along a narrow trough flanked with high stony barriers and found himself well sheltered. Here, where abalone divers seldom had a chance to venture, there were shellfish under every slanting surface, in each rocky pocket.

In perhaps no more than ten minutes his rope bag was filled and he exchanged it for an empty one. Six more were sent up on his life line before Ronnie began to feel the effects of climbing over the rough bottom while breathing warm compressed air. He gave Pud a signal and started vigorous flexing exercises as he was drawn slowly upward through the flashing green water.

When he broke the surface, he pulled himself over to the ladder. He clung to it for several minutes, bobbing on the long, glistening swells, before he could summon enough strength to climb. After Pud slipped off his helmet, he lay with his face pressed against the cool deck.

"You took seventeen dozen and ten that dive, Ronnie," Bill reported. "And in only an hour and a quarter, too!"

Heartened to learn he'd done so well, Ronnie did some quick mental arithmetic. Why, his diver's half share and his sixth share as boat owner would amount to nearly seventy dollars! This was a good game when weather conditions were right! He straightened up, and was surprised to see that no other boat was near their own.

"Where's Marsh?" he asked.

"Conditions were too rugged where he was diving," said Pud. "He sailed southward about a mile."

"Want to follow him?" inquired Bill.

Ronnie hesitated, then shook his head. "Fishing is good here—if you can get protection from the currents. I'll talk to him when I knock off for the day."

"Hammerhead isn't keen about this day and night routine," Pud observed. "He'd rather sell their abalones to you than make the two-way trip to Seal Cove every night. He claims that Marsh is so sore at you that he'd rather dump his catches than let you have them."

"Sore at me?" Ronnie snapped. "It's *my* reputation he tried to ruin at the Sunset Cafe! What's gotten into him?"

"I wouldn't know," said Bill. "But he'd hardly speak to us."

Ronnie vowed that he'd get to the bottom of the trouble that day. Once more, however, he failed to do so. For, while making his last dive before the sun set, Marsh sailed southward past the *Sea Spray*. The same thing was to happen day after day, until Ronnie became convinced that Marsh was avoiding him. His strange behavior, however, was the only jarring note during that tranquil period on the San Simeon.

Ronnie took nearly seventy dozen abalones that day. And when he rowed ashore in the dory and compared notes with the fishermen preparing their dinners around the fire, he was overjoyed to learn that only Madman Morley had gathered more.

"You're lazy, Nordhoff," Morley railed good naturedly. "Letting an old man like me beat you by two dozen and six!"

"You probably bought someone else's catch to make your own look good, Morley," declared Ronnie, winking at Bill.

The little diver continued to make derogatory remarks about Ronnie as they sat eating around the fire, but every so often his eyes twinkled to show that it was all in fun. When plates had been washed in the stream and the fire built up, Ronnie approached the subject that had been on his mind all day.

"Morley," he said, "do you know anything about the sinking of the *Southland Star?*"

Les Blaizdall turned suddenly at the question. Ronnie was conscious not only of the big diver's sharp scrutiny, but of the searching glances of his crew as well. Blaizdall's lanky boat-operator, and his line-tender, a stocky, swarthy little man, exchanged secretive glances that the boy did not miss.

"Do I!" Morley exclaimed. "My old man was the commercial diver called in to find the *Star* off Santa Barbara!"

"Who hired him?" asked Ronnie, uncomfortably aware that the same three men were watching him with more than usual interest.

"The vessel's owners, and the heirs of the miners who had chartered the schooner," answered Morley. "They gave Pop a little money for expenses. It was to be deducted from the share he was to get of the half million in gold on the *Southland Star*. However, he worked months for nothing because he never found her."

"Was it true, Morley, that a miner was found clinging to a hatch-cover off Santa Barbara Bay?"

"That's the way Pop told it."

"Was that the only evidence that the schooner was lost near there?"

"Absolutely all, Nordhoff."

"Well, couldn't she have been lost farther north, and the survivor have been blown south by the storm?"

Morley cocked his brows, and then sat, like a thoughtful brown-faced gnome, pondering the question.

"Funny you'd ask that, Nordhoff. I've always figured that's what happened, but never before has anyone seen it my way. It's certain that a lifeboat did drift to the beach below China Charlie's three or four days after the dying miner was found to the south."

"Charlie wasn't living there then, was he?" asked Pud.

"He sure was," said Morley. "Fifty-odd years ago, when

the *Southland Star* vanished, he was a young man, just starting to collect seaweed to export to China. Couldn't speak a
word of English, so the authorities had to question him
through an interpreter. The experience gave Charlie a bad
scare. Knowing nothing of our laws, he was afraid he was
about to be hustled back to the Orient. He stuck to the story
that the lifeboat found below his place had been empty,
though, and after a time he was let alone. No one considered
it an important clue, anyhow. There had been nor'easterlys
for a day or so before the Chinee discovered the boat, and it
might have been blown up from the south."

The little diver poked at the fire for a minute, and then
continued. "I saw that lifeboat at Charlie's years ago. But I
suppose it's fallen apart with age by now."

"I saw it not many days ago," said Ronnie. "Charlie
wouldn't talk about it, and when I returned the next day, the
boat was gone. Could he be hiding something he knows about
the *Southland Star?*"

Morley chuckled and shook his head. "I doubt it. Even
after a half century here, Charlie has never learned much
about our ways. Chances are he was afraid you might revive
interest in the *Star*. And he wouldn't want to be questioned
a second time."

Morley might be right. But Ronnie still had a lingering
suspicion that the old Chinese knew more about the schooner's disappearance than he would admit.

He temporarily dismissed the problem, however, when
Eddie Raybold and Rickie Dore drove up in the truck to begin the night's work. The dory was soon bringing abalones
to the beach. Ronnie helped the two boys in transferring

them to the old vehicle.

When the first load was ready to move, Ronnie asked his helpers, "How are the Camerons making out with the processing?"

"Okay, I guess," said Eddie.

"How would *he* know?" scoffed Rickie. "He's dumping shellfish when he's in Seal Cove so he can get back here in a hurry."

"All right, you tell us how the Camerons are doing," Eddie jeered.

Rickie's dark face lighted. "When I'm at the plant, I'm busy unloading, too. But it looks as if everything is going swell."

"Wait a minute, Eddie," Ronnie said. "I'm going south this trip and see for myself."

Tired though he was from the day's diving, Ronnie hollowed out a place in the mound of shellfish, spread a tarpaulin, laid his sleeping bag on it and crawled in. Despite the swaying and lurching of the truck, Ronnie slept soundly until they halted in his own back yard.

The Camerons appeared relieved to see him.

Mrs. Cameron pointed to the steaks she was packing, and said anxiously, "I'm trying to be careful, Ronnie. But I'm so new at this, I wish you'd tell me whether I'm doing it properly."

"She's a terror," said Mr. Cameron good naturedly. "But I'm getting the hang of pounding now, and my wife doesn't make me do over so many steaks."

Ronnie washed his hands, and dumped out the white fillets from three open boxes. With quick, deft movements, he examined each slice before packing it once more. When finished, he nailed slats on the boxes and carried them into the deepfreeze room.

"I might as well have remained in camp, Mother Nelly," he said with a grin as he returned. "You have as good an eye and hand for this as Mom."

"Well, I feel better to have you look things over, anyway," said Mrs. Cameron with relief. "There were several other matters, too."

She told him of a convention at the Seal Cove Inn and Mr. Bonnell's order for two hundred pounds of abalones. Eddie had delivered them that morning, after he had finished hauling from the San Simeon.

Mr. Cameron's round, pink face brightened. "Word is getting around that the Inn is buying from you, Ronnie," he said. "Two of the town restaurants, The Elite and The Shell, placed small orders."

"Dad used to supply them," said Ronnie. "But Shumaker took over their business after the accident. Didn't they like his pack?"

"It isn't that exactly," explained Mrs. Cameron. "Shumaker is now rationing his customers."

"What for?" asked Ronnie. "From what I hear, Shumaker's freeze room is practically stocked to the roof!"

"That's what I've heard," said Mrs. Cameron.

Ronnie looked puzzled. "It doesn't make sense!"

"Don't be too sure of that," said Fred Cameron. "Looks to me as if Shumaker were up to something. He usually is!"

"Maybe you're right, Mr. Cameron," Ronnie said slowly. "Rumors are afloat that Shumaker has borrowed heavily at the Morro Bay Bank. If he's that hard pressed, why would he limit the amount of abalones his customers could buy? Could be that he's building up his stock with an idea of taking over the business of other plants if their supply falls low!"

Seeing a roadster parked at the side of the yard, Ronnie took his leave of the Camerons and entered the house.

Laughter drifted from the direction of the children's bedrooms, and he headed that way. Looking into Mardie's room, he saw his small sister in bed. Skip, in pajamas and dressing gown, sat on the opposite end. Both youngsters were laughing at something Ginger was telling them. The girl was in Mardie's small rocker, and she seemed little older than either child. The tenderness in her face was hard for Ronnie to reconcile with the competence of a girl who kept books for the shopkeepers in two communities.

Her gentle expression vanished when she observed his disheveled appearance. "Oh, Ronnie!" she protested. "Are you planning to stand in a corn field to frighten away the birds?"

"Aw, we've seen fishermen before," said Skip.

Mardie giggled. "Ginger's telling us the funniest story."

Skip nodded his tousled head. "About the time you got confused in a game and tackled Pud when he was carrying the ball."

"That's ancient history!" snorted Ronnie, flushing.

"Oh, is it?" asked Ginger, sounding strangely interested. "It happened only two years ago."

"My football days are past," he cried impatiently. "I have more serious things to think about."

Ginger glanced up quickly, a sudden suggestion of a smile puckering her mouth. There was a glowing quality in her green eyes that made Ronnie wonder how he could ever have imagined them cool.

"Could it be possible?" she asked, as if speaking to herself.

"Do you always have to talk in riddles?" Ronnie complained.

Ginger didn't answer, and she didn't quite smile. But there was something radiant in her face as she tucked the covers around Mardie and kissed her.

"Sweet dreams, my little friend," she said tenderly. And giving Skip a small push, she added, "Off to bed, my fine bucko!"

"Will you tell us more stories tomorrow?" Skip begged.

"I might," said Ginger, "if you're in bed in five seconds."

Skip went scampering.

Ginger hummed a rollicking tune as she walked briskly down the hall. Ronnie recognized the square-dance melody. He thought it was probably an air the redheaded girl had picked up when she was doing the old-fashioned figures at the Grange Hall with Marsh Marple. But why was Ginger so happy? Had he said or done anything to make her feel that way?

She continued to hum the gay lyric as they crossed the yard to her roadster. She settled herself on the seat and smiled.

"Mrs. Cameron is taking wonderful care of the children. But I like to drop in to be sure everything is all right. Mind, Ronnie?"

"Of course not. They like you."

"Did I mention that I'm working part-time for you at twenty dollars a month? May I?" And without awaiting an answer, Ginger rushed on, "From the slips the boys make

---

182

out, I'm keeping records of the abalones delivered by the different fishermen. Saturday morning I'll go to Mr. Romano and get their checks, minus deductions for their food."

"Eddie or Rickie can bring them up that night."

"Oh, I'll do that," said Ginger. "Might be papers to sign."

As she stepped on the starter, he asked, "What are you so cheerful about all of a sudden, Ginger?"

Amusement kindling in her green eyes, she released the brake. "Keep guessing, Ronnie," she advised, as she left him.

"Redheaded girls!" he muttered.

Ginger was as hard to understand as Shumaker's rationing of his customers, as Marsh's curious behavior, or China Charlie's unwillingness to discuss the lifeboat. Why was everything so confusing?

The truck had left for another load, so Ronnie decided to help his crew. Processing abalones was something a fellow could understand! Walking into the plant, he greeted three men the Camerons had hired. He removed a rubber apron from a peg, and took his place beside them at the cleaning tables. But while he cut the mollusks from their green mother-of-pearl shells, his mind was at work on several baffling mysteries.

It was Rickie Dore who appeared with the truck an hour later. Ronnie helped him unload, then tossed the tarp and his bag in back, and climbed up onto the high seat. Rickie drove slowly until he was through town. Then he began to highball northward at such speed that the old vehicle rattled and clattered.

"Did you see Shumaker pass you when you were coming south?" Rickie shouted above the racket.

"I was asleep."

"He dropped into camp and tried to buy the men's catches at seven a dozen. Pud and Bill were for throwing him out, and Eddie and I would have loved to help them! After all, the camp was your idea. But before we could do anything, Madman stopped him. I think he likes you, Ronnie."

"What did Morley do?"

"Simply asked Shumaker when he was going to pay for twenty-odd dozen that Madman Morley dropped off at Morro Bay several years ago when a storm caught him to the south. That stopped Shumaker cold because the men just hooted every time he tried to say any more. Finally he stalked off down the beach with Blaizdall."

Rickie nursed the truck through an S turn, and then continued.

"A minute before that I'd gone down to meet the dory because Eddie was bringing a load ashore. My shoe-lace broke, and I was leaning up against a big boulder, fixing it, when Shumaker came along with Blaizdall. I was hidden in the shadow of the rock. Not knowing anyone was around, Blaizdall whispered something about 'Nordhoff' and 'China Charlie.' The gravel made so much noise I couldn't catch all his words, but I did hear part of Shumaker's answer. He said, 'If he mentions Blacktop Rock or Charlie. . . .' "

"Meaning me?" Ronnie asked in astonishment.

"That would be my guess."

"Did you hear anything else?"

"No, because Eddie called me to come help him. The two men didn't say anything until they'd walked on a distance, and then I could hear a low muttering, but I couldn't make out their words. By then my shoe-lace was patched up and I ran down to give Eddie a hand."

"Why would Shumaker be asking about China Charlie and Blacktop?"

"You tell me!"

"Blaizdall must be spying for Shumaker!"

"That's what Eddie and I think. You'd better watch him, Ronnie!"

"I will. But I can't understand why Shumaker is so curious about my affairs. Was he still in camp when you left?"

"No. But he was still down the beach somewhere with Blaizdall."

Ronnie was tempted to suggest that Rickie drive faster on the chance that they might reach Mill Creek before Shumaker departed. But the level coastal highway lay behind, and the truck was now swinging around the narrow curves hewn from the rocky San Simeon palisades. If they struck a chuck-hole or a rock at high speed, there were few barriers to prevent them from plunging over the cliffs into the quick-silvered water a hundred or more feet below. Ronnie decided to curb his impatience.

When at last they passed under the Mill Creek Bridge and turned toward the beach, no other car was in sight. Eddie was unloading abalones from the dory, but he left his work at Ronnie's call.

"When did Shumaker leave, Eddie?" Ronnie asked.

"He pulled out shortly after Rickie left."

Ronnie nodded. Leaving the boys to carry on without him, he headed toward the glowing embers of the fire. Silently he crept between the sleeping men sprawled on the ground until he located Les Blaizdall. He was about to shake the man and demand an explanation of what had happened when he noticed something peculiar.

Blaizdall's heavy face, and the big, muscular hand exposed from the bag were twitching. Blaizdall's lips also moved, and at that moment his hoarse muttering changed to distinct words.

"I won't do it, I tell you!"

Though he uttered no more words, Blaizdall continued to mutter. From time to time his twitching would cease, and his florid face would contort with painful grimaces.

Ronnie suspected that the man slept with an uneasy conscience, but it seemed wiser not to disturb him. He might learn more by keeping a watchful eye on Les Blaizdall!

10.

DEAD ENGINE AND SHEERWATER CLIFFS

Whenever there was an opportunity during the next few days, whether in camp or when out fishing, Ronnie watched Les Blaizdall. He became convinced that there was a mystery about the big diver, some secret that weighed heavily on the man's mind.

Blaizdall was powerfully built, and should have experienced no difficulty in diving in the calm seas then prevailing along the San Simeon coast. Yet he would stand on his ladder for long periods, his face gray-blue with strain, his breathing labored. Time and again he'd shake his head when his tender Jim Vasco offered him his helmet. In contrast to his almost fearful reluctance to dive was Blaizdall's great energy when below. If he located a spot where abalones were plentiful, he would often send up a heavy basket of shellfish every ten minutes.

Ronnie suspected that there was little harmony between Blaizdall and his mates, a strange thing to find in a crew that had fished together for five years. The fact that an uncongenial crew would soon break up suggested that the trouble was of recent origin. Blaizdall either snapped at his operator, Link Taylor, and line-tender Jim Vasco, or ignored them completely.

The Saturday evening that Ginger brought up the first payments from the bank, Blaizdall appeared almost embarrassed as he accepted his check from Ronnie with a gruff, "Thanks, kid." Turning abruptly, he walked up the road, disappearing under the bridge as if headed toward the highway. Blaizdall was missing from the group that sat talking around the fire that night. Nor did he return by the time the others slipped into their bags.

Ronnie was finding life among the abalone fishermen too diverting to dwell long on the mystery surrounding Blaizdall. Every day saw some improvement in their camp. Boats would come in towing planks the men had spied on the beach, so that before long they were eating at a long, rough table. Rustic chairs were nailed together from pieces of driftwood. One night Madman Morley and his mates laid a rock fireplace. And not wishing to be outdone, Ronnie, Pud and Bill damned up the stream, creating a small pool in which everyone could take a dip before eating.

Ronnie's days were so full that he had no time to seek out Marsh and come to a settlement with him. The ideal conditions of windless days and smooth seas were making it possible to improve his diving technique. Under the pressure of his father's debts, he reacted as he had in high-school days to the Ronnie Nordhoff treatment. He fished with a dogged tenacity, refusing to quit until there was too little light below to see abalones. Only the seemingly tireless little Morley made more dives in a day or took larger catches.

Ronnie had little strength left for trips southward on the truck every second or third day, even though he often slept both ways. It worried him to see the boxes of abalones rising in the freeze room, to know that it meant his debt was mounting at the bank. But so long as the weather remained mild on the San Simeon, he could do nothing about finding a market for his pack. Soon he was forced to eliminate the trips to Seal Cove. They were too exhausting after a hard day of diving, and they no longer appeared necessary. He could find no fault with the way the Camerons and Ginger were doing their work.

Two weeks after the camp was established at Mill Creek, a breeze sprang up one morning, and within an hour the wind was wailing. Presently it was blowing spindrift across the seas in smoking flurries. By mid-afternoon breakers boomed along the cliffs, and curling ground swells, rolling back, tossed the abalone boats, dragging divers by their life lines. In this unequal struggle with the elements, one crew after another lost heart and sailed homeward with the day's haul. Les Blaizdall, one of the last to go, shouted a loud farewell and as he passed each boat, he announced boastfully that he had thirty-three dozen shellfish in his hatches.

"Let's quit," Pud begged, when Ronnie came up from a dive. "Bill can hardly keep the boat near your air boil."

"It may be a long time before we can fish here again," Ronnie answered.

His glance betrayed him when it strayed to the *Bubbles*, now rolling and pitching in a cloud of spray.

"So that's why you want to stay!" Bill guessed. "You think you can stick it longer than Marsh! Well, maybe you can—

if you don't care what happens!"

"He's been so unfriendly that I hate to let him get the idea he's the better diver. Why, he hasn't once visited our camp!"

"Your trucking operation gives you a real advantage in Seal Cove," Pud pointed out. "You have a big stock of fillets, and he hasn't. Do you expect a competitor to like it?"

"In high school, I always gave him a pat on the back if he was elected captain of a team or won an office. Now, if he wants to get huffy—" Breaking off abruptly, Ronnie said grimly, "Let's have my helmet, Pud."

Diving conditions grew worse as the day advanced. Finally only the *Bubbles* and the *Sea Spray* remained on the grounds. Ronnie always asked for his helmet each time he saw Hammerhead slip on Marsh's. And Marsh requested his when his rival prepared to dive. At dusk Pud and Hammerhead became so desperate that they ignored safe procedure, and by mutual consent pulled up their stubborn divers without warning.

Ronnie was indignant until he observed Marsh being helped aboard. Then he allowed Pud to guide him aft. He was so exhausted that he could hardly stand in his heavy gear.

"Anyway, Marsh didn't show me up," he growled.

"I wouldn't brag about having no better sense than he has," Pud said angrily. "You divers!"

The *Sea Spray* turned southward first. When Mill Creek slipped astern, there was only a wilderness of great rocks and sheerwater cliffs off to port.

Ronnie felt a catch at his heart when the engine coughed and sputtered. But each time it seemed about to stop, Bill nursed it through its spasm, so that the storm-buffeted boat would plunge on for a few minutes with steadily throbbing motor. The sputtering, however, became more frequent. It started whenever the bow was buried in a swell, or the boat trembled under the impacts of beam seas. Bill was forced to reduce speed, allowing the *Bubbles* to creep by, well off to seaward.

Her small riding light was dancing several miles to the southward when the *Sea Spray's* engine at length stopped. Bill left the wheel, dropped to the after-deck, and dived into the cabin. Ronnie pulled a flashlight from a bracket and switched it on so that he could see to work.

"I'm to blame for this!" Ronnie cried apologetically. "If I hadn't been so pig-headed—"

It was like Bill to be most cool in a crisis. "Forget it," he said. "Won't matter, anyway, if I can find the trouble."

A sea crashed to starboard with punishing force. The boat, creaking from strain, rolled so far to port that for several moments Ronnie thought she'd turn turtle. Bill bounced, and came down hard. A look of surprise swept over his homely face.

"Give me the light, Ronnie!"

Taking the flashlight, he turned the beam on the cabin's deck. Several thin streams were joining to make a small pool.

"That opened seams!" cried Bill. "We're taking water!"

"Get topside!" Ronnie yelled at Pud. "See if you can head her into the seas."

"Don't hope for too much," replied Pud, clambering onto the cabin.

Anxiously Ronnie gazed toward shore. It was too dark to make out anything except the blue-white flash of sea fire where the breakers lashed the base of the cliffs, several hundred yards away. Phosphorescence glowed in showers of silvery sparks all along the rock walls. Nowhere could he see the diminishing roll of breakers that might indicate a beach. Unless Bill started the engine without delay, the boat would fetch up against the rocky palisades and break up within minutes. And no swimmer could survive much longer!

With flashlight in one hand and wrench in the other, Bill sought the source of trouble. He squatted in water, and the inflow from opened seams might soon deepen the pool to the point where the motor would not run. But the cabin could not be pumped out until the engine was turning over. Ronnie was sick with remorse at having put his two best friends into such a hazardous position.

"Suppose our hook would hold?" Bill inquired with no trace of alarm.

"It might," said Ronnie, striding forward.

As he reached the end of the cabin, Pud grasped his intention, and shouted, "Watch you don't wash overboard!" '

Pud had brought the boat about with rudder alone. The seas were splintering over the bow and gushing across deck. Steadily the *Sea Spray* was being driven toward the cliffs.

Ronnie waited until there was an explosion of spray before dashing across the streaming deck. He got a grip on the towing bitt as the boat ducked her nose into a glittering silver swell. Water dealt him a brutal blow, but despite the wrenching it gave his hands and arms, he managed somehow to cling to the short post. Moments later he located the anchor and toppled it overboard. Most of the light line went with it; the remainder he dogged around the bitt. Brought up short into the seas, the boat shuddered from each impact. Yet the line withstood the first assault, the second, then the third. Ronnie was beginning to take hope when the line snapped like a thread.

Stunned with disappointment, he awaited his chance and scurried aft to the cabin. He clung to the operator's rail, watching the bluish-white fire glowing brighter as the boat drifted once more toward the cliffs. Bill would not have many minutes left in which to start the engine! Ronnie wished there were canvas and spars aboard so that he could rig up a sea-anchor; it might check their progress long enough for Bill to do his work. But with no such means at hand, Ronnie listened with chill foreboding to the thunderous boom and crash of the breakers, now almost deafening.

"Can you see whether she's coming toward us?" Pud shouted, pointing.

Ronnie looked quickly and saw a swinging light to the south. For minutes he couldn't decide whether it was approaching or receding. Then he became convinced that the shining spot was growing larger.

Marsh was coming to assist them! Observing their riding light moving eastward, he must have guessed they were in difficulties. But would he arrive before they were in the breakers, before they were being pounded against the sheer rock walls? There seemed small chance he would.

Fixing the engine appeared to be their last hope. Ronnie hurried aft to the cabin to see how Bill was making out. Squatting in a swishing pool of water, he still worked with sure, unhurried movements. Although he could not avoid hearing the mounting roar of the breakers, Bill spoke calmly.

"Found the trouble, Ronnie."

193

"Marsh is heading this way. But he probably won't reach us in time."

Bill nodded without glancing up.

Ronnie stepped outside and looked southward. The light at the top of the *Bubbles'* short mast was growing brighter. But every time his eyes shifted toward shore, the flashing glow of the marine bombardment along the palisades made a tremor dart down his spine. Back-washes from the cliffs clashed with the charging seas to raise a ghostly army of silvery waves. The cannonading of these opposing forces made a hideous din.

Presently the sparkling outline of the *Bubbles'* hull was visible. Not long after that Ken Carlson's broad figure was dimly illuminated by the swaying light above him. Where were Marsh and Hammerhead? Aft perhaps, making a line fast? Ronnie's heart pounded heavily as he looked at the black cliffs towering above the boat, then back at the little craft rising and falling as she sped toward them.

The *Sea Spray* was almost in the breakers before Marsh's boat swung alongside. Running the risk of being swept overboard by the seas gushing in green cascades over the bow, Ronnie clambered forward. At one moment the other boat, rising on a swell, loomed high above him; then it would drop away swiftly in a trough, almost hidden in the showers of bursting spray.

For a few brief instants the air cleared. On the *Bubbles'* rolling after-deck, Ronnie could distinguish the figures of Marsh and Hammerhead. The old tender was on his knees, bracing the young diver. Ronnie saw the latter's hand making a rapid movement. He flung out his arm, feeling sure that

Marsh was casting a line. Another sea exploded over the bow, blotting out Ronnie's view. At the same time he felt a sharp sting on his cheek, and grasped in desperation. His hand closed on a rope. Quickly he whipped it around the towing bitt.

Moments later Carlson headed westward, opening water slowly between the boats. He looked back as he took up slack. Upon him rested the responsibility for setting the *Sea Spray* in motion without placing too much strain on the line. The impact of a heavy sea on the after craft, however, was still a dread possibility that no amount of skill on Carlson's part could entirely avoid.

Ronnie held his breath when the rope jerked from the water, smoking as it was drawn taut. The *Sea Spray* snapped at her tether, her timbers shivering in resistance to the opposing stresses. Foam spread around the *Bubbles'* stern in her struggle to make headway. Then, with a lurch that jolted her, Ronnie felt his helpless boat sluggishly responding. His body grew tense. Would the line part? It did not, though again and again the tow-line jerked while taking up slack. Slowly the two little vessels gained momentum. The thunderous clash of the breakers faded away astern.

Ronnie shivered with relief when he heard the pulse of their engine once more. Seconds later the pump began its rhythmic throbbing. The tow-line dropped into the sea as they picked up speed. Ronnie freed the rope and cast it overboard before hurrying aft.

Bill grinned broadly as he stepped from the cabin. "Oh, for the life of a sailor!" he cried cheerfully.

Bill took over the wheel from Pud, and turned southward.

Ronnie was relieved when the *Bubbles* dropped astern. She cruised in their wake on the entire passage to Seal Cove, prepared to offer further assistance if needed. Ronnie was grateful to have help at hand, for he couldn't rid his mind of certain unpleasant statistics—one out of every ten abalone boats was lost yearly through different mishaps! At the same time, he hoped he would not have to trust his life a second time to a light tow-line. He didn't draw another easy breath until the sheltering arm of the cove broke the force of the heavy seas, and he could see the lights of the pier across a sheet of water that shimmered like black marble.

When they glided up to the pier, the boat-operators remained aboard to unload the abalones, but the other four fishermen climbed the stairs.

"I'll go for the truck," Pud offered. "You've had a rough day of diving, Ronnie."

"I'll tag along, Pud," said Hammerhead. "Luis Ruisant can bring the sedan, and I can get to bed. I'm tuckered out." Marsh had removed the back seat from his old sedan so that he could load it with shellfish by raising the lid of the luggage compartment.

Ronnie felt uncomfortable at finding himself alone with Marsh. For the other boy stared bleakly across the water. The withdrawn expression of his old-young face appeared to be a deliberate defense against any overtures of friendship.

Because he felt indebted to Marsh for saving their lives, however, Ronnie at length spoke. "I'm mighty grateful. So are Pud and Bill."

Marsh looked at him. His eyes and face were cold and remote.

"Skip it!" he said brusquely. "You pulled me out of a bad spot at Piedras Blancas. Now I've done as much for you. We're even. Let's let it go at that!"

When he faced out to sea again, as if to end the discussion, Ronnie's gratitude was washed out by a feeling of bristling antagonism.

"There are things I can't forget!" he snapped.

Marsh didn't turn. But after a long silence, he asked bluntly, "Such as?"

"You know what I mean!" Ronnie retorted sharply. "Why did you send Ruisant to the Sunset Cafe to order one of my abalone steaks and pretend it had poisoned him?"

Marsh wheeled around, his lips parting in astonishment. "That's not true, Ronnie! You know I wouldn't do such a thing!"

"Ruisant signed a confession. In it he said that he acted on your instructions. Besides, I have witnesses."

The strong lines of Marsh's face deepened. "No matter what Ruisant claims, I never ordered him to do that!" he burst out angrily. "But if I had, you'd be in no position to object, after slipping two boxes of spoiled abalones into my pack! I might have lost my best customer if I hadn't discovered them before they were delivered!"

Ronnie gave a start of surprise. "When did I ever have anything to do with your pack? I've never even had the chance!"

"You visited my plant," Marsh declared. "Ruisant told me so."

"I sure did," Ronnie went on warmly. "And I caught him putting out steaks you could hardly cut with a diver's knife. I told him what I thought of his shiftless processing, too!

When I was leaving, he said you were short two boxes to fill an order. He drove me back to my plant, and paid me for the ten pounds you needed."

"But I've never had to buy steaks! I've always had a small surplus beyond my customer's requirements."

"I sold Ruisant two boxes from my freeze room," Ronnie insisted. "I defy you to find a single spoiled steak there. If you found any bearing my labels that weren't good, Ruisant must have deliberately left them in the sun."

Convinced of Ronnie's sincerity, Marsh nodded.

"I caught him packing tough steaks myself. I should have been smart enough to guess he was behind this. I swear I knew nothing about that Sunset Cafe business until now, Ronnie. Ruisant has been trying to make us both think the other was guilty of pretty raw methods."

"What has he to gain from setting us against each other?"

"Nothing," said Marsh, shaking his head. "But someone else might have. When Ruisant gets here, I'm going to make him tell us who is behind this. I have a hunch what the answer will be. Ruisant has worked on and off for Shumaker the past few years."

Ronnie grinned faintly. "Well, I'm glad we talked this out, Marsh. I'd hate to think that you—"

"Me, too," Marsh interrupted. "You've rubbed my face in the dirt at times, and I've done the same to you. But it was always in a good, clean fight for something we both wanted."

The rattle of planks caught their attention. Approaching them was Marsh's old sedan. As it drew closer, they were clearly revealed in the headlights. Ruisant must have observed their stiff bodies, their stern faces, and knew that his game had been played to its end. Abruptly he stopped. Putting out his head to look behind, he grated the gears, and backed rapidly along the pier.

Before he could reach the shore end, however, Pud appeared in Ronnie's truck, blocking his way. Bringing the car to a halt with squealing brakes, Ruisant leaped out, dashed past the truck, and disappeared.

It was so dark that Marsh and Ronnie spent little time looking for the man. Ruisant apparently lay hidden in the bushes somewhere along the banks of San Pasqual Creek.

"Chances are," Marsh said, as they returned to the winch, "that we'll never see *him* again in Seal Cove. But I would like to know whether he was acting on Shumaker's orders."

"So would I," said Ronnie. "Are you processing tonight?"

"I'd rather get up early," said Marsh. "You can unload first."

As soon as his day's catch was on the truck, Ronnie drove off the pier so that Marsh could drive up to the winch. He and Pud had a short wait while Bill moored the *Sea Spray*.

Ronnie dropped his two crewmates at their homes, and then rolled on to park beside the plant. The Camerons greeted him warmly.

"We sent Eddie and Rickie up to the San Simeon earlier," Mrs. Cameron explained. "They came back with the dory, and the provisions you'd left in camp, and said that all the fishermen were gone."

"We were pretty much worried by the time Pud came for the truck," Mr. Cameron confessed. "Then we knew we'd be processing tonight, and called up two of our workers. They should be along any minute."

"I'm glad you won't need me," Ronnie said with relief.

Nelly Cameron's face was sympathetic. "We certainly won't. Get right to bed, Ronnie. You look terribly haggard."

Glad to escape additional work that night, he dragged himself wearily into the house. When he washed his face, he bumped his forehead on the faucet. He jerked upward at the impact, and grumbled to himself. But when he lowered his head again, he collided with the fixture a second time.

He straightened up, wondering what was wrong with his vision. Then he noticed his image in the mirror. It wavered, appearing to recede and draw nearer like a scene viewed through a binoculars being brought into focus. Try as he would, Ronnie could not make that haggard reflection of himself assume its proper perspective.

He began to grow uneasy. Was he losing his eyesight?

Then he realized what had happened. For too many hours, these past two weeks, he'd been subjected to the pressure of compressed air; for too many hours, he had looked at objects magnified by the water. Only his sight had so far suffered. If the good weather had lasted a little longer, however, he might have been troubled by faulty coordination as well. He recalled the time when his father, after weeks of steady diving, had tried repeatedly to put on his hat but always missed his head because he could not make his hand obey. But after a little rest from undersea work, his father could again focus his eyes and regain control over his movements. The same thing would probably be true in his own case.

When Ronnie crawled into bed a short time later, he thought: *I'll sleep late, and then drive to Morro Bay to see Shumaker.*

He had no way of knowing how greatly coming events would change those plans!

11.

THE VANISHED CREW

Ronnie's plans for a long sleep were interrupted in the morning by a repeated pounding on the door. Heavy-eyed, he sat up and looked at the clock on his dresser. Ten o'clock, if his blurred vision could be trusted.

Swinging out of bed, he slipped into his dressing gown, and walked down the hall to the kitchen. The raps began afresh when he paused to brush his rumpled red hair with his hands. Buttoning up his gown, he opened the door. To his astonishment, Sheriff Dart stood outside.

"Will you come in, Sheriff?"

The big man shook his head. His worn gray stetson was pushed back; despite his gray-tinged mustache and weathered brown face, he looked somehow like a troubled boy. Almost apologetically, he held out a long chromium-plated flashlight.

"Recognize this, Ronnie?"

Ronnie took the torch and turned it over until he saw the script on the handle.

"Yes. Dad scratched his name on it. I loaned it to Les Blaizdall on the San Simeon. I'd forgotten he didn't return it."

The sheriff shifted uneasily. "Anyone see you give it to

him?"

"N-no," faltered Ronnie, wondering why he was being questioned. "All the fishermen were asleep around the fire at the time. He woke me up."

"You're sleeping late this morning, Ronnie."

"Not as late as I hoped to." And he explained about the long hours of diving and the engine trouble the previous day.

"*Hmmm.* Did you process the abalones you brought back?"

"The Camerons did. Last night. Why, Sheriff?"

"You're sure they did?"

"I can soon find out."

Ronnie went to the 'phone in the living room and called his neighbor's number. When Mrs. Cameron answered, Ronnie inquired about the catch he'd brought home.

"Why, yes, Ronnie," she replied with a note of surprise. "We finished up every last one, and put the boxes in the freeze room. Is anything wrong?"

"I don't know," Ronnie admitted truthfully. "Sheriff Dart is here."

"Well, if he has anything to ask about our part, I'll be glad to talk to him. We didn't clean up until nearly midnight."

Thanking her, he returned to the kitchen to repeat what she had said. Sheriff Dart rubbed his chin. His face had the bewildered expression of a youngster faced with a problem too great for him.

"What is the trouble, Sheriff?" Ronnie asked.

"Come, and I'll show you."

He led the way out to the old truck. Heaped in the back was a mound of abalones! For several moments Ronnie stared at it in astonishment. Had the Camerons shirked their work?

That seemed unlikely; they had always been dependable. But where had these shellfish come from?

"Know anything about them, Ronnie?"

"No; I don't, Sheriff."

"Let's find out how many there are here."

The truck was already backed up to the plant. Ronnie began tossing abalones to the cleaning table, and the sheriff counted them.

"Thirty-three dozen," he reported, as the last one thumped the table. "That number mean anything to you?"

Ronnie frowned. "Well, I remember Les Blaizdall saying when he left the San Simeon yesterday that he had thirty-three dozen aboard."

"Exactly," said the sheriff regretfully. "I've already learned that from talking long-distance to several Monterey fishermen."

"You don't think these are Blaizdall's abalones?" Ronnie cried. "Does he claim I took his catch?"

"He claims nothing." And the sheriff added hesitantly, "He's . . . disappeared."

"*Disappeared!*" Ronnie echoed. "Maybe he was wrecked in the storm."

The sheriff shook his head. "China Charlie came to my house about seven, so excited that at first I could hardly understand him. A Chinaman gathering seaweeds for him had found a boat on the beach, but there was no one aboard. Charlie walked over the hills to the highway, and hitch-hiked a ride up here to report to me. He was afraid that if he didn't act at once, he might be in trouble with the law. Many years ago he'd had some difficulties for failing to say anything about a *Southland Star* lifeboat that had drifted in below his place."

"It's funny lightning would strike the same spot twice!"

"It didn't," said the sheriff. "This boat did not *drift*. It has an automatic pilot which steers when the crew leaves the wheel. The gadget was set, and it brought the boat ashore under its own power."

"The coast juts out to a point at Blacktop Rock," Ronnie suggested. "Maybe the men forgot about that when they set the pilot and turned in for a short nap."

"In that case," said Sheriff Dart, "they would come ashore when the boat ran aground."

"Didn't they?" Ronnie asked in surprise.

"No," replied Sheriff Dart. "When I drove back with Charlie, the only marks on the beach were made by the sandals of the Chinaman who discovered the boat. Your flashlight was aboard—"

"I explained that, Sheriff."

"Yes; but I have only your unsupported word. And there were other suspicious circumstances. Not a single abalone remained in the boat's holds. Nor could I find any sign of Blaizdall, or his mates, Link Taylor or Jim Vasco."

"You don't think *I* had anything to do with their disappearance?" Ronnie asked in alarm.

The sheriff shifted uncomfortably and glanced at the shellfish on the table. "I hate to think it, Ronnie. But where did these abalones come from?"

"I haven't the faintest idea! I was asleep shortly after the Camerons came over last night, and didn't wake up until you knocked."

"Trouble is, no one can verify that, can they?"

"No-o-o—" Ronnie faltered. "But how would I know Blaizdall hadn't reached Morro Bay? He left the San Simeon hours before I did."

"It's the duty of a law-enforcement officer to consider every possibility in a case as confusing as this one," said Sheriff Dart unhappily. "You could have drained gas from Blaizdall's tank the last night he was in fishing camp. It is conceivable that after telling the Camerons you were turning in, you actually set out alone to find Blaizdall, wherever his tank ran dry. Under the guise of friendship, you might have jumped aboard, and taken his men by surprise—"

"*I* am the one who would be surprised," Ronnie interrupted indignantly, "if I could, single handed, overcome three fishermen as strong as Blaizdall, Taylor and Vasco!"

"Unprepared men are in no position to defend themselves," observed the sheriff in a melancholy voice. "But to go on: You could have tied up these men and hidden them somewhere. Then, after loading Blaizdall's abalones onto the *Sea Spray*, you might have put gas in his tank, set his automatic pilot, and let his boat run ashore. There's another unpleasant possibility I must consider. These men could have fallen overboard if there was a struggle. I'm having Coast Guard planes search for anyone who might be afloat in life-jackets."

"Even if I could do all this, dog tired as I was, what possible reason would I have, Sheriff? I had nothing against Blaizdall!"

"Shumaker has been taking a lot of your father's former customers, hasn't he?"

"That's right. But what has he to do with this?"

"I talked with him a few minutes ago on the 'phone, and learned that Blaizdall sold his boat to Shumaker three weeks ago, but was being allowed to use her until she was fully paid for. Maybe you knew about that. Perhaps you're trying to get even with Shumaker for taking away your business by making it appear that he'd done this to avoid paying Blaizdall the balance on the boat. It was a private agreement of sale, Ronnie, and the craft is already licensed in Shumaker's name. *Now don't you think you'd better tell me where you're hiding those men?*"

Ronnie stared aghast at the sheriff, wondering if the man could believe his own preposterous theory. No; it was most unlikely! The sheriff must know his flimsy evidence would never stand up in court! The truth must be that he was completely at sea, and was fishing for information. Possibly he hoped to scare Ronnie enough to make the boy tell him anything that might help in the case. But the whole chain of reasoning seemed too involved for a simple man like Sheriff Dart, and suddenly Ronnie grew suspicious.

"Did Shumaker suggest I knew something about this, Sheriff?"

Martin Dart coughed and looked embarrassed. "He threw out a few hints," he admitted. "But I didn't take them seriously until I saw these abalones in your truck."

"So that's it!" Ronnie muttered. "Well, I don't know how the three men disappeared from their boat, Sheriff, but I believe you have struck a warm trail."

The sheriff looked puzzled. "Whose trail?"

"Shumaker's! He's casting suspicion on me to divert your attention from himself. He's up to something! Maybe he thinks that by keeping me in hot water, I'll be too busy defending myself to prevent him from carrying out his plans.

I think he's trying to organize a monopoly of the abalone industry."

"That won't hold water, Ronnie. Shumaker is in tight straits. And your theory doesn't explain how Blaizdall's catch got here."

"Perhaps Shumaker could explain that."

"I'll talk to him again. But we'd get farther, Ronnie, if you'd be frank with me. I'll help you all I can."

"I've told you all I know."

The sheriff's voice suddenly became brusque. "If you're going to be stubborn, I'll have to do my duty as I see it. Don't touch these shellfish! I must remove them to a San Luis Obispo cold storage plant to be kept as evidence."

Walking stiffly to his car, the sheriff drove away.

Ronnie stood thinking, while a feeling of uneasiness mounted within him. Oh, he knew that Sheriff Dart was a good man, an honest officer who would sift out what evidence he could uncover to the best of his ability. But could he meet this test? Ronnie had heard of law-enforcement officers paying their own way to the F.B.I. school in Washington, taking college science courses to learn more about crime-detection methods, or assembling small personal libraries on police work. Such officers stood a good chance of clearing an innocent person of suspicion.

But to Martin Dart the office of sheriff was a means of making his living, nothing more. He had no interest in the F.B.I. He cared nothing about the latest police procedures. Even the mention of scientific methods bored him. The only book that Ronnie had ever seen the sheriff examine was his album of college clippings!

And when the boy grasped the significance in that, Sheriff Dart's weakness was at last revealed to him. Where the ordinary college student regarded sports and offices as a preparation for life, Martin Dart had accepted his triumphs as "A Big Man on the Campus" as his greatest accomplishment.

After he was graduated, the ability to carry a football or shoot a basket brought no easy honors, no offices, no positions of prestige. And so, shrinking more and more from the world of reality, Martin Dart tried to relive the bright days of his youth. He attempted to revive the past by turning pages of yellowed clippings, by haunting University of California reunions and homecomings, by alumni activity to keep his memory alive in the minds of "old grads." Regardless of what changes the years had brought, he had at heart remained the young man he was upon graduation from college!

Was that why Ginger was impatient with her father? It must be!

Ronnie realized that it must also explain Ginger's puzzling attitude toward him. Seeing him become a popular figure in Seal Cove High, she feared that he might in time become "A Big Man on the Campus" and a misfit in later life, like her father. But Ronnie had faced an adult world in quite a different way than Sheriff Dart. He had severed his ties with the past and had tried to meet his new responsibilities.

Ginger must have sensed this change most strongly when he had spoken of his football days as "ancient history." And now that Ronnie understood her father better, he knew why the remark had pleased her. She knew Ronnie would grow up, as her father never had.

Ronnie would have been relieved at solving the secret of

Ginger's baffling moods had he not been so worried about what her father would do. Sheriff Dart would try, with the best of intentions, to discover why Blaizdall and his mates had disappeared. And it was almost equally certain that he would accomplish nothing. In the end, unless someone else cleared up the mystery, Ronnie would be under a cloud of suspicion that might hamper all his future business efforts.

It's up to me to prove I'm innocent! he thought.

When he went to glance into the freeze room, and saw boxes of abalones stacked almost to the ceiling, however, he saw that any attempt to clear his name must wait. Somehow he must find customers for this pack—and quickly, too! If he could sell it, he would reduce by a considerable amount the Nordhoff loans at the bank. But if he failed—well, he'd better put that thought behind him! What might happen then was too appalling to think about!

It was with a heavy heart, and without breakfast, that Ronnie set out an hour later to find new business. He was more successful than usual. Six of his father's former customers gave him orders; they were dissatisfied with Shumaker's pack, and with his recent system of rationing the amount they could buy. But the sales did little to raise Ronnie's spirits, for distorted stories about the thirty-three dozen abalones found in his truck were already circulating in the town. Several restaurant owners would not do business with him until the mystery was solved.

Since high winds prevented him from fishing, Ronnie spent the next two days canvassing seafood restaurants along the highway. By persistant effort, he garnered ten more customers. And by making an early start the following morning, he had filled all orders, and one-third of the accumulated pack in his freeze room was gone.

He drove to the Seal Cove Bank when this was done. And though it was late afternoon and the doors were locked, he was admitted. Mr. Romano listened in silence to his report.

When he finished, the banker said soberly, "The plant that puts out a really good pack, and can supply its customers, is sure to get business, Ronnie. That part has never worried me. But this other—"

He tossed a copy of the *Seal Cove Weekly* over the desk. Ronnie had seen the paper, which had gone on sale several hours earlier. Emblazoned across the front page was a headline in large type:

CREW OF SHUMAKER BOAT VANISHES

The story related the mysterious circumstances surrounding the disappearance of the crew from the Shumaker boat, and told of the Coast Guard's failure to find Blaizdall, Taylor or Vasco. Facts linking Ronnie to these three men were given in great detail. But, in fairness to him, several paragraphs were devoted to statements by Pud Dart, Bill Ballard, and the Camerons. Describing Ronnie's hard day, they had expressed strong doubts that anyone so exhausted could in any way be involved with the missing crew.

Mr. Romano's brown face was thoughtful as he stroked his iron-gray mustache. "This will hurt your trade, Ronnie."

"It already has," Ronnie admitted. "A few restaurant owners believe I know more than I've told Sheriff Dart. Others are equally sure that someone is trying to ruin my business; they know I wouldn't be fool enough to leave thirty-three dozen abalones in my truck if I'd taken them from Blaizdall's boat."

"So it is with the people who have talked to me," said the bank manager quietly. "Even though more than half believe you innocent, it is not good for business."

Ronnie was heartsick when he left the bank. His success in buying the catches of the fishermen on the San Simeon, his many new customers, brought no satisfaction while he was under suspicion. He saw Marsh Marple approaching, and turned away without speaking. So many people, for the past several days, had looked at him with cold and stony faces that Ronnie had come to dread fresh rebuffs. He heard footsteps following him, and was about to step into the truck when a hand grasped his arm. Ronnie swung around, inwardly bristling. In Marsh's rugged face, however, he saw nothing but sympathy.

"Ronnie, I'm mighty sorry about all this," he said soberly. "Ruisant tried to give our customers the idea that we both put out an inferior pack. Could he be behind your troubles?"

Ronnie deliberated, then shook his head. "He wouldn't know when Blaizdall was sailing south." After a pause, he added, "Has it struck you, Marsh, that a number of curious things have happened near Blacktop Rock? Shumaker saw an octopus, you and I heard an undersea bell ringing, China Charlie apparently destroyed a *Southland Star* lifeboat after I inquired about it—*and now this boat turns up there without a crew!*"

Marsh grinned. "Not getting superstitious, are you?"

"No," said Ronnie grimly. "*Suspicious!*"

Marsh frowned. "What are you getting at?"

"Is someone trying to make fishermen think the waters around Blacktop are bad luck, so they'll stay away?"

"*Hmmm.* I hadn't thought of that." Briefly Marsh considered the idea, before continuing gravely, "Someone planted those abalones in your truck to hurt your business. If you can think of any way to discover who he was, I'd like to help you expose him."

Ronnie was so touched by this unexpected loyalty that for several moments he couldn't trust himself to speak. "I'll remember that, Marsh. Thanks a lot."

Driving home, Ronnie tried to discern a pattern behind the mysterious chain of events that had occurred near Blacktop Rock. But he was still groping for possible connections between them when he brought the truck to a stop in his back yard.

Mrs. Cameron was closing the overhead door of the plant. Now she pushed it up again, picked up a newspaper from a cleaning table and walked over with it.

"Ronnie, I was wrapping up a box of abalones for a customer when I noticed an item that might interest you. Do you need any extra equipment?"

She handed him a day-old Los Angeles paper, opened to the classified advertising section. The ad she'd marked offered a diving dress and helmet for sale at a Newport Beach address. The seller's name was not given.

"That's funny," Ronnie observed. "Divers who are quitting usually have no trouble selling their gear to friends, if their price is right. Either this man has no friends here, or—" He broke off abruptly, struck by an odd notion.

"Or what?" asked Mrs. Cameron, smiling.

"Will you take care of things here, Mother Nelly?" he asked. "If the sheriff inquires about me, tell him I'll be back by noon tomorrow. And if I'm not—" He smiled faintly, but when he went on, his voice had a serious note: *"He might ask the Coast Guard to look for me, too."*

Anxiously she peered at the tall redhead. "Ronnie, hadn't you better tell me what you're planning?"

"I'm going to look up a diver who either has no friends in these parts or for some reason can't get in touch with them."

Tucking the paper under his arm, he climbed into the truck and started southward. He passed through Santa Barbara and Long Beach before the sun set.

It was dark when he reached Newport Beach. After stopping at a service station to ask directions, he turned into a district taken over by fish canning and packing plants and marine supply houses. The address he sought was a swordfish processing and storage plant, closed at this hour. However, there was an apartment above it, and the drawn blinds at the windows were edged with light.

Ronnie stepped from the truck, wondering how to reach the upstairs rooms. At the side of the building he discovered an outside stairs, with a landing at the top. He climbed slowly. If the man upon whom he was calling proved hostile, he'd need all his breath! Pausing before the door, he rapped sharply.

His heart pounded with slow, hard beats while he waited. No sound came from within. Again he knocked, more loudly. In a moment a creaking inside was followed by the thud of heavy footfalls.

A key scraped in the lock. The door opened a few inches.

And through the crack Ronnie saw a florid face with heavy features. Before the door could be slammed, Ronnie forced his foot into the opening.

"I'd like to speak to you, Mr. Blaizdall!" he said grimly.

Ronnie had hoped the classified ad would lead him to Les Blaizdall. But his first glimpse of the man had given him a confused feeling caused in part by anger, in part by relief. Blaizdall must have sensed this momentary unpreparedness, for his heavy body stiffened and his right knee bent suddenly backward. Barely in time, Ronnie realized that the big diver intended to kick his foot from the crack.

Football training made Ronnie react automatically. Hurling himself against the door, he caught Blaizdall off-balance, sending him staggering backward to land with a thump against the kitchen range. Blaizdall stood motionless as Ronnie stepped over the threshold, but his glance darted around the room. Once more football training enabled the boy to grasp the big diver's intentions. As a quarterback, he'd learned to watch for opponents to "telegraph" their next moves by a shift of eyes, the bracing of muscles before a play.

"You're probably fifty pounds heavier than I am," Ronnie observed. "You wouldn't look for a weapon unless something was wrong."

Blaizdall's embarrassed expression told Ronnie that he'd guessed correctly, and now the boy continued rapidly: "On the San Simeon diving exhausted you more than the other divers. I didn't suspect the trouble then, but I should have. What is it—*a bad heart?*"

The big man gave Ronnie a startled glance, then his eyes dropped and he nodded.

———

"My heart won't stand diving any longer. That's why I had to sell my boat to Shumaker. And advertise to dispose of my diving gear."

"I'm sorry about that," said Ronnie. "But it was a poor excuse for what you've done to me, Blaizdall! You must read the papers. Many people suspect I had something to do with the disappearance of you and your two men. Are they also safe?"

Blaizdall nodded morosely.

"Why did you do it? What have you against me?"

Anger flared briefly in Blaizdall's eyes. "Nothing—and that's the truth! Can't you imagine how cheap I felt up there on the San Simeon when I saw the fight you were making to save your father's business? Oh, I'll admit that at first it looked to me like pretty much of a make-shift operation. Two kids rowing our abalones ashore in a dory and taking them south in that wreck of a truck. And the pretty red-headed Dart girl, who looked as if she should still be in high school, bringing you papers to sign. But the point is you pulled it off. And you treated us so square in every way that I wished before I left there that I'd never seen Shumaker!"

"So *he* was behind this?"

For several moments Blaizdall hesitated; then he spoke brusquely: "Close the door and come in, Nordhoff. It will be easier to face myself in the mirror mornings if I tell you what's been on my mind."

Knowing it might be a trap, Ronnie was wary as he followed the man into a small living room. But no one else was there, and Blaizdall acted like a friendly host, turning on several more lights before he dropped into a deep chair. He indicated the diving gear lying on the floor under the back windows.

"I've always figured I could 'scratch' for abalones any time I needed money, Nordhoff. So I spent freely, never saving a cent. The doctor's verdict of a fatal stroke if I kept on diving made me desperate. I had to sell my boat, and the only buyer I could find was Shumaker. He could pay only part down; worse than that, he tied strings to the deal. I sure would have balked at his terms if I hadn't been nearly broke and sick."

Blaizdall's heavy face shadowed. For a short while he sat silent, clasping and unclasping his hands between his knees.

"In short, Nordhoff, Shumaker wanted my help in causing you some trouble. Even though I didn't know you then, even though I had to sell my boat, I told him I wasn't that kind of a guy and walked out. Then, a couple of days later, while resting on the ladder and feeling terrible, my heart gave me another bad jolt. I sure thought I was finished. Vasco and Taylor urged me to accept Shumaker's terms. We had some hot words about that, and then they let it slip out that Shumaker had promised them some mighty fancy jobs when he got control of the industry. When we got back to Morro Bay, I tried to sell my boat with no funny business on my part, but Shumaker wouldn't agree. So I consented to a transfer of title, but I had a lawyer draw up the papers. I didn't trust Shumaker!"

"What did he want you to do?" Ronnie asked.

"First of all, he asked me to report it if you asked any questions about Blacktop Rock or China Charlie. Then he wanted me to borrow something that could be identified as yours without out Bill Ballard or Pud Dart knowing about it. I asked you to loan me your flashlight."

"You announced to everyone before leaving the San Simeon how many abalones you had," Ronnie said. "That was to establish the fact that you had thirty-three dozen aboard?"

Blaizdall bobbed his head once, his eyes downcast.

"For days I've been trying to figure out what happened," Ronnie said soberly. "My present theory is that both you and Shumaker agreed to sail when it grew stormy. After you met at sea, he took your abalones and crew aboard, and then put your boat on automatic pilot so that she would run ashore below China Charlie's. Probably Shumaker had a truck waiting at the Seal Cove pier to pick up the shellfish. It slipped into my yard in the early morning hours and your catch was dumped into my old van. The kids and I were sleeping too soundly to be awakened."

"I had nothing to do with planting the abalones in your truck and I hadn't been told about that part of the plan beforehand," Blaizdall cried angrily. "When I learned what Shumaker intended to do, I tried to stop him. He and I would have come to blows if the other four men hadn't seized me and tied me up with a life line."

"Why has Shumaker taken such a dislike to me?" Ronnie asked.

Blaizdall shrugged. "That's anyone's guess. It might go back to this: Year after year he ran for leader of the abalone fishermen, and every time your father won hands down. Maybe you've inherited Shumaker's resentment for all those defeats. But I believe there's more to it than that. You can't talk to him without feeling that he has some mighty ambitious plans. Crazy as it sounds, I'm sure he's confident that he'll soon control the abalone industry."

"I've heard rumors about that. But how could he do it? Doesn't he owe everyone who will trust him?"

"Yes—including me," said Blaizdall with a wry grin. "But he acts like a man expecting big money from somewhere. If that's not true, why would he promise my boat-operator the job of managing your plant when he takes it over? And why would he offer to let my tender take over a Monterey plant?"

"I don't understand it," Ronnie admitted. After a thoughtful pause, he added, "Blaizdall, your disappearance has done me plenty of harm. Will you make a statement to the police of what you've done?"

Blaizdall seemed about to refuse. Then, clearly reluctant, he arose.

"You'll have only my unsupported word," he pointed out. "My crew won't verify a thing I say; they want those jobs Shumaker promised them. I'll probably make trouble for myself, but . . . I'll do it."

He clapped on his long-billed flyer's cap, and together they went down to the truck and drove to the Newport Beach police station. Blaizdall explained to the white-haired desk sergeant why he was there. The officer called a man in uniform to take his statement. When it was typed, Blaizdall initialed each page and signed his name to the confession.

"Nordhoff," the sergeant said, peering over his glasses at Ronnie, "you're the one who has suffered from this man's actions. Do you want to prefer charges?"

"No," said Ronnie. "Blaizdall has been very helpful."

"I'll grant you that," said the sergeant. "But he has still failed to clear up one point." Turning to the big diver, he asked, "What had Shumaker to gain from his actions?"

Blaizdall shook his head. "You'll have to learn that from him, if he'll tell you anything. His reasons are as much a mystery to me as to you, Sergeant."

12.

THE BELL REVEALS ITS SECRET

Ronnie drove northward to Santa Barbara, and stopped for the night at a motel. But he was on his way early; it was still two hours short of noon when the old truck rattled into Morro Bay.

Morning sunlight glistened on the sheltered water. Beyond the massive bulk of Morro Rock, however, the running seas were frosted with spindrift. Since conditions appeared too harsh for diving, Ronnie thought Shumaker might be found at his headquarters. So he continued down the main street until but two blocks from the bay, and then turned southward.

Shumaker's small plant was on the east shore. It stood on a cement quay, and on the edge of this platform was a winch for raising shellfish from the hatches of abalone boats. A truck was being loaded on the quay. Ronnie parked and walked toward it. He failed to recognize the large man wheeling a cart stacked with boxes of steaks from the open plant until the worker glanced up. Then he was looking into the slack, discontented face of Luis Ruisant!

Ruisant's sullen mouth parted. An unpleasant memory of Ronnie's flying tackle at the Sunset Cafe must have risen in his mind. For suddenly he sprinted across the quay, swung over the edge, and disappeared down the ladder.

It took Ronnie a little longer to recover from his surprise, and when he reached the western side of the platform, Ruisant was scrambling from one to another of the small craft moored below. At the same time he was shouting at the crew of an abalone boat getting under way to take him aboard. Glancing upward, and seeing Ronnie, Ruisant clambered aboard a barge which had previously been screened from the boy's view by the plant. He ran the length of this barge and sprang to the forward deck of the little boat as it chugged alongside.

Ripples winged away astern as she continued northward, apparently headed for another mooring. Ronnie knew he could meet her by driving along the bay to the pier where she would tie up. But there now seemed no point in doing so. Ruisant's flight was a clear admission of guilt! No words could say more plainly that his attempts to hurt Marsh's and Ronnie's businesses were made while in the pay of Shumaker.

Ronnie stared curiously at the barge, wondering where it fitted into Shumaker's plans. Since Shumaker was strict in permitting only abalone boats to moor at his quay, the barge must be one he'd rented or purchased. It was of the light type used for dredging operations on the mud flats or river channels around San Francisco Bay. Instead of the usual scoop suspended from the winch, however, it had a grapple—a mechanical adaptation of a human hand that could grasp and raise objects from under water.

Of what possible use could such a piece of machinery be to the owner of an abalone plant?

Ronnie was still staring wonderingly at the grapple when

221

Orrie Shumaker stepped from his small office. Fishermen often referred to the little diver as "Mr. Five-By-Five," or "The Barrel Who Walks Like a Man," and the bright morning sunlight seemed to emphasize Shumaker's shortness and the great breadth of his shoulders to make these unflattering comparisons appear strangely appropriate. His brown face was hostile as he glanced up from beneath his cavernous brows.

"What are you trying to do, Nordhoff?" he snapped. "Make trouble? Because of that story you persuaded Blaizdall to tell in Newport Beach, one sheriff has already been here to question me this morning. Wouldn't surprise me if Sheriff Dart dropped in shortly to ask more silly questions. Craziest thing I ever heard of! Why would I go out of my way to injure your business when I can take it over, lock, stock and barrel, for a dime on the dollar within a few weeks or months?"

"If you can take over my plant for a dime on the dollar," Ronnie cried warmly, "why hire Ruisant to put on that act in the Sunset Cafe?"

"Can you prove it?" Shumaker growled.

"And why hire him to buy two boxes of my steaks, set them in the sun to spoil, and slip them into Marple's pack in the hope that it will cost Marsh a customer?"

"Can you prove it?" Shumaker repeated gruffly.

"Not yet," Ronnie admitted. "But if I lay my hands on Ruisant again, he'll be glad to sign another confession—a truthful one, this time!"

Shumaker snorted, and when he spoke, his voice had unmistakable confidence. "I'm not worrying about you or Marple, or anyone else in this business! Let me tell you something,

Nordhoff. Within a few weeks I'm cutting abalone prices two and possibly even three dollars a box. Every plant on the California coast will go broke trying to meet my prices. I can buy your properties for whatever I care to pay!"

"So that's why you've been rationing customers! You've been building up your stock to fight a price war!"

"That's right," said Shumaker. "And what can you do about it?"

"But you'd lose an enormous amount selling at such prices! How could you take such losses and be able to buy anyone's plant?"

"That," said Shumaker dryly, "you'll learn about in good time."

Shumaker had not intended to reveal his plans, but his last words set Ronnie to thinking. Ronnie had suggested to Sheriff Dart that Shumaker might be stirring up trouble for him in order to give himself time to carry out some secret plans. Now the boy was sure his guess had been right.

Ronnie had done a little amateur boxing with Walter Bonnell, and now he recalled something the manager of the Inn had said, *"Keep your opponent off-balance until you can land a decisive punch."* Shumaker was doing just that! He was keeping Ronnie too busy with his own troubles to watch for the knockout punch that was coming. Shumaker needed time to deliver that blow!

Ronnie glanced at the light barge, with its topheavy mast and boom, and then at the foaming seas beyond the breakwater. The barge would be almost impossible to handle except in calm seas. It was mild weather Shumaker was waiting for! That was why he needed time!

"Thanks, Mr. Shumaker," Ronnie said abruptly. "You've cleared up a lot of things for me!"

On the drive to Seal Cove, Ronnie's mind was in a ferment as he fitted the last pieces into the puzzle. He saw that time was of even greater importance to himself than to Shumaker; to gain precious days, he would need help! Pud and Bill would assist in any way they could, but neither one could do undersea work. What diver could he trust with his secret? Mentally rejecting one after another, he concluded that there was only one in whom he could place absolute confidence. He was Marsh Marple. The clearing up of their recent misunderstanding, strangely enough, had convinced Ronnie more than ever that his old rival was to be trusted.

Ronnie was so sure that Marsh would never betray him that he did not stop at home, but drove through Seal Cove to the cottage on the outskirts where his competitor lived. Marsh's old sedan was parked outside. Ronnie walked around the house to the woodshed plant in back. Marsh was within, surrounded by open boxes of abalones. He was putting steaks through a grinding machine.

"I discovered in time," he said with a rueful smile, "what kind of a pack Ruisant was processing for me. It's either grind up my fillets and sell them cut-rate for chowders, or market tough steaks and give my pack a bad name."

"He was working for Shumaker," Ronnie declared, and described Ruisant's flight, his visit with Shumaker, and the finding of Les Blaizdall.

"This is getting thick," Marsh muttered. "You seem to think that Shumaker is making a play to control the industry, but

I can't see how he can do it. I admit he might be planning a price war, though. He's rationing his customers at a time when his freeze room is packed solid. To put the rest of us out of business by selling below cost, however, will take money. And Shumaker just doesn't have it; he's in debt to his eyebrows."

"Why would he have a barge with a grapple, Marsh?"

"I wouldn't know!"

"Well, I think I do. He's planning to raise the gold from the *Southland Star* the day it's calm enough to tow the barge. How else could he get the money, when no one trusts him any longer? With her treasure, he'd have all the cash he needs."

Marsh shrugged. "What a plant I could build with a small fraction of the fortunes that have been spent trying to find her!"

"Look, Marsh, all the treasure-hunters have searched for that schooner off Santa Barbara. And why? Because a single dying survivor was found near there after the storm that sank the *Star*."

"Where do you think she went down?"

"China Charlie found one of her lifeboats on the beach near Blacktop. It was also close to that rock that you and I and other divers heard a bell ringing underwater—*always when the swells were heavy*."

"Right," said Marsh, looking puzzled. "But what have rough seas to do with it?"

Ronnie's voice was tense with excitement: *"Couldn't the sound we heard be strong currents moving the* Southland Star's *bell against it's clapper? In open water you seldom have currents below unless you have disturbed conditions on the surface. Doesn't that explain why no diver ever heard the muffled ringing beat when it was calm?"*

Marsh's eyes widened. He whistled softly.

"Man alive, I believe you have something! But why do you figure Shumaker put Blaizdall's empty boat on automatic pilot to run in on the beach below China Charlie's?"

"For shame, Marsh!" said Ronnie with a wry grin. "An old halfback like you should understand that. It's like faking an end run when actually making a play through center."

Marsh frowned and shook his head. "I still don't get it."

"Well, look! If Shumaker found where the *Southland Star* lies, and I have a hunch he has, his play through center is the recovery of her gold. But he must be worried like crazy for fear one of us other fishermen stumble onto her before he can assemble the equipment to raise the treasure."

"But where's the faked end run, Ronnie?"

"I'm coming to that. Shumaker knew we both dived at Blacktop the day we met him there. And he had learned from experience that when it was stormy the currents would ring the undersea bell and we'd hear it. He must have worried plenty lest we make the connection between the sound and the sunken schooner. So we both fell under suspicion. The chances are he drove up into the hills above China Charlie's to see if we'd return to Blacktop the next day. You didn't, but when I reappeared and started diving, Shumaker must have been haunted by the possibility that I might continue fishing there until I discovered the *Star*."

"That's when he thought of the faked end run, I imagine. And just as in a football game, it was supposed to distract us from his real play! Shumaker set out to give us so much trouble that we wouldn't have time to solve the secret of the undersea bell. And since he was apparently more suspicious of me than of you, Marsh, I had the major share of this grief. Ruisant was hired to cause us difficulties with our customers, but we were both lucky enough to catch him at it. When Blaizdall wanted to sell his boat, Shumaker insisted that he borrow something of mine to be used to involve me in trouble. Blaizdall was even ordered to report to Shumaker if I mentioned 'Blacktop' or 'China Charlie,' which I did in the fishermen's camp on the San Simeon. Shumaker must have thought I was getting too close to his secret. So then came the pay-off —a crew of three disappears and my flashlight is found on the boat! That might have kept me in hot water for quite a while if I hadn't found Blaizdall."

"Perhaps his disappearance was supposed to serve a double purpose," Marsh observed thoughtfully. "It not only kept you hopping to clear yourself. More important, it added to the hoodoo reputation Blacktop Rock already has among abalone divers who have heard the bell."

"It's all part of the same plan," said Ronnie. "Shumaker wanted to discourage us from fishing near there. Maybe his story of the giant octopus south of the rock was invented for the same reason."

"Where there's so much smoke, there might be some fire," Marsh conceded. "But why let me in on all this?"

"I'll need help if I'm to locate the *Star* before it's calm enough for Shumaker to sail northward with his barge to recover the gold."

Marsh looked at him steadily for several moments. "You'll have it," he promised. "How will we divide?"

"You divers will be taking the greatest risks as usual," piped a thin voice from the doorway. They turned in surprise to see Hammerhead. "If we're using two boats," went on the old tender, "why not split the usual shares to avoid argument? One-fourth to each of you divers. One-twelfth in addition to each of you as the boats' owners. And one-twelfth to each of the boat-operators and tenders."

"Round up our crews at the bank, then," said Marsh. "We'll have Mr. Romano draw up the agreement."

"If we sail while it's blowing like this," Hammerhead observed bleakly as he left, "I'd sell my share right now for a dime!"

The two small boats left the cove an hour later. Within a few minutes the pounding seas opened seams that Bill had tried to caulk well enough to keep the *Sea Spray* afloat until Ronnie could afford an overhaul. Water swished across the engine-cabin with every roll. It was necessary to keep the pump running constantly to prevent the inflow from flooding and stopping the motor. The *Bubbles,* having less horse-power, also had a miserable southward passage. Both boats made such slow headway that they did not sail by China Charlie's weatherbeaten old house until early afternoon.

The seas broke white around Blacktop Rock, and as the two little boats sailed past its seaward side, pitching and rolling, only its black dome was exposed. Bill pushed on several hundred yards to the south before shifting into neutral. After a lingering glance at the foaming turmoil below the cliffs, he turned to Ronnie, shaking his head.

"I'd say conditions were impossible if I didn't know you

and Marsh!"

"We'll be making only short dives," Ronnie reassured him.

"I've heard that one," said Bill skeptically.

From the *Bubbles,* now bouncing on the swells near-by, Marsh called, "Where do we start looking?"

"The *Southland Star* couldn't have been very close to shore when she sank, or her masts would have been visible," Ronnie observed. "We sure won't find her at a depth of less than thirty feet."

"Let's start there then, and make short dives out to a hundred," Marsh suggested. "By taking turns, it won't be too hard on either of us."

"Good enough," Ronnie agreed. "Let's explore in a straight line from shore. If we fail to find anything, we can move southward a short distance and make another series of dives."

All that day Ronnie heard the muffled beating when he was below, but because he believed it was the *Southland Star's* bell being rung by the strong currents, it no longer startled him. Hour after hour he and Marsh took their turns struggling against brutal currents while floundering around on their short dives. They stopped at dusk, thoroughly exhausted, without having found any sign of the sunken vessel. It was the same the second day, and the third. Pud and Hammerhead had such difficulty maintaining their balance while tending line that both were by then ready to quit.

On the morning of the fourth day, however, the seas rolled in shallow, glittering swells, and the light breeze was almost balmy. Everyone felt more hopeful. Silt stirred up by the recent storm still made it difficult for Ronnie and Marsh to see any distance after reaching the bottom, but at least they were not buffeted by the currents. Yet the day wore toward its close with nothing encouraging to mark their efforts.

Marsh looked at the sun setting in a glow of crimson, and said wearily, "Guess I can make one more dive."

He went down in kelp, often an indication of a rocky bottom. He remained below so long that the color began to fade from the sky. When at last he came up to have his helmet removed, he gasped for breath for several minutes before he could speak.

"Hulk . . . down there. Buried in marine growth. It's a schooner, for sure . . . but I'm not certain it's the one we're looking for."

"I can't wait to find out," Ronnie cried. He strapped an abalone-bar to his wrist, knowing it might be useful in clambering over rocks.

Pud picked up the helmet, and then looked doubtfully at the darkening sky. "Don't stay down too long, Ronnie," he pleaded.

The moment his helmet and air-hose were secured, Ronnie lowered himself down the ladder. After a final adjustment of his monel valve, he waved, and began to glide down through weaving strands of kelp. When his feet touched bottom, he looked around, and made out what appeared to be a ridge of rocks. Disappointment swept through him. Marsh had mistaken that barrier for an old derelict!

As his eyes became accustomed to the semi-darkness, however, Ronnie made out the vague shape of a sailing vessel beneath the masses of sea-growth covering her. Against the lighter upper water protruded the broken stub of a mast. And beyond the prow a bowsprit was silhouetted dimly in the

230

gloom.

Pulling himself up over the rocks with his abalone-bar, fighting his way through snarls of hold-fasts, Ronnie at last reached the schooner's bow. Breathing heavily, he paused for a short rest, and then signalled Pud. Scarcely had he begun to ascend when he jerked his line again, bringing himself to a stop suspended alongside the hull. Gripping sea-plants to hold his position, he pried away abalones, starfish and algae until his abalone-bar struck a distinct projection.

This was unexpected luck! The vessel bore her name in raised letters, not paint! With gloved fingers, Ronnie traced a letter *S*. Clearing away more marine growth, he found an *O*. Now to see if the schooner had a second word in her name! Pulling himself forward along the hull, and working in almost complete darkness, he discovered a break in the line of letters. Again he cleared away marine plants and animals until he could trace the *S* and the *T* which began the second word. That was enough! He gave three tugs on his line.

"I'm certain it's the *Southland Star!*" he announced exuberantly, when Pud slipped off his helmet. He described the four letters he had uncovered.

Marsh had a worried frown as he stared across the water from the other boat. "Ronnie," he called, "the old stories say the gold was in a safe in the captain's cabin. How can we hoist it aboard without a winch?"

"Good grief!" groaned Hammerhead. "After going to all this trouble to find the old hulk, Shumaker will get her gold!"

"No!" Ronnie declared emphatically.

"Well, how can we raise the safe without any hoisting apparatus?" asked Marsh.

"I've been thinking about that," said Ronnie. "We can use the lifting power of the tide. Look, it's simple! We move the safe out on deck, and secure lines from it to one of our boats at high tide. Then we run the boat inshore until the old strong-box strikes bottom. We can take up slack on the lines at the next low tide. The following high tide will raise both the boat and the safe suspended beneath her. We can sail in closer to the beach before the box again hits bottom. By repeating that operation as many times as necessary, we'll have our treasure in shallow water."

"That will do it!" Marsh cried. "And we can heave it up the cliff with block and tackle."

At daybreak Marsh went below with a crowbar to start the work of moving the safe out on deck, providing he were successful in finding the box. He had discussed the problem with Ronnie after dinner the previous evening. They had decided the steel bar would be useful. But what they really counted on was the fact that any object was lighter in water, which made it possible for a diver in a buoyant dress to lift or shove immense weights.

Ronnie waited on the ladder of his boat, watching the white boil of Marsh's bubbles. Dressed except for his helmet, he expected to go down immediately after the first part of the work was completed.

At the wheel of the other craft, Ken Carlson was following the bubbling movement of air rising to the surface. When the milky flow became stationary, he shifted into neutral.

"Marsh must be in the captain's cabin on the poop deck," Ronnie guessed.

The life line suddenly bobbed, then began a spasmodic

jerking. Hammerhead gave a tentative pull, but could draw in no slack. Another rapid series of tugs made him try once more to heave up the line. But in vain!

"It must be fouled!" Ronnie cried. "I'll clear it, Hammerhead!"

Bill Ballard moved their boat alongside the *Bubbles* while Pud was locking on Ronnie's helmet. Ronnie left the ladder in a sidewise leap. Swiftly he was lowered through the swaying stalks of bull kelp. His cast-iron shoes soon struck the schooner's deck. He closed his air-valve slightly to make himself more buoyant. The timbers of the long-submerged vessel might give way under any undue stress!

The silt he had stirred up was settling. Rippling shadows from the swells above did little to dim the brightness of the sunlit water. As he headed aft, Ronnie saw the hold-fasts of kelp entwined about rails and pipes. Large sea-anemones and masses of smaller shelled creatures covered everything. Rising from deck was the splintered end of a mizzen mast; aft of it, a superstructure of cabins.

Marsh's line and air-hose disappeared into one of these. From somewhere beyond the partially opened door flowed a steady stream of silvery bubbles.

Ronnie pushed back the jammed door, still having not the slightest suspicion of any serious trouble. But the next instant he grew aware of the roiled water, the stirring current. Still unable to see in the darkened cabin, he was taken wholly by surprise when something lashed out of the gloom and struck his shoulder. Instantly he felt himself seized in a tight grip.

Only then did his eyes adjust to the darkness. Dimly he

made out a rippling arm studded with a double row of suction disks! A chilling sensation trembled through him. Shumaker's account of meeting an enormous octopus south of Blacktop Rock had been true!

Ronnie could see the creature now, rearing up on its snaky arms, spewing its sepia defense fluid. Through the clouded water he could vaguely distinguish two oval eyes—the most evil eyes he had ever seen! Without conscious thought, he opened his mouth to scream. But no sound passed his tight throat; he heard nothing but the roar of his air.

The arm gripping his shoulder relaxed slightly. Clammy beads of sweat broke out on Ronnie's forehead as the tentacle explored his back. Then, with a force the boy couldn't resist, the sinewy arm curled around his neck and drew him rapidly across the cabin. The creature's parrot beak could rip his dress like tissue paper unless he freed himself! For the first time, he remembered his knife. While still being dragged forward, he grasped it and placed the fine steel of the blade against the tentacle. Quickly he jerked downward.

The octopus released him before the stroke could be completed. Wildly it lashed the water with its partially severed arm. Through the swirling cloud of defense fluid, Ronnie at last saw the other diver. Two tentacles were entwined about Marsh's body. Ronnie believed he must be crushed and lifeless until he observed that Marsh was making short stabbing thrusts at the octopus' body with the crowbar. Since he could use only hands and wrists, Marsh was in reality doing more to infuriate than injure the devilfish.

Ronnie recalled a discovery of his father's. In his first fight with an octopus, Thor Nordhoff had by sheer accident learned that it could be killed by driving a knife between its eyes. It was the creature's only vulnerable spot!

But for Marsh's desperate position, Ronnie would willingly have abandoned all the gold on the *Southland Star* rather than attempt to find that weak point in his adversary. Yet he fought down the repugnance he felt, forcing himself to move cautiously toward the octopus. When a tentacle once more struck his shoulder, he slashed at it before the suction disks could grip his dress. Currents eddied about him as the creature flailed the water in fury.

Dense clouds of sepia fluid swirling before his vision plate made it impossible to see anything. Ronnie plunged his knife where he thought the eyes might be. And then, shaken by panic, fearing he had missed the vulnerable spot, he brought his knife down again and again.

Tentacles beat the water. The frenzied writhing and twisting of the beast's arms, however, seemed like the reflex movements of a death flurry. Ronnie turned to escape, hoping the knife thrusts had given Marsh his chance to break away.

Before he could reach the entrance, a tentacle dealt him a glancing blow, hurling him against the edge of the door. A second blow followed the first. Ronnie felt as if some terrible weight had fallen on his stomach. Too dazed to realize his dress had been ripped, he gulped for breath—and swallowed salt water!

Swimming waves of blackness washed over him. Yet he was not quite unconscious. His ebbing senses registered a startling fact. His forehead felt hot. Some air must still be compressed into the upper part of his helmet!

He tilted his head back, scarcely believing it could be true.

But he was not mistaken—*he could breathe!* Although he had lost much of his air, the portion he still retained was holding the water to the level of his nose. Yes; he could keep from drowning—but only while he held his head well back! And in that position, he was nearly helpless because his vision was severely limited.

Currents no longer swirled against him. However, for a moment he thought the octopus must have revived when he felt a grip on his wrist. Peering anxiously downward through his plate and grill, his eyes brought into focus a small section of Marsh's face. As his vision cleared a little more, Ronnie could see the other's puzzled glance. Looking through water himself, Marsh could not at first grasp the fact that Ronnie's helmet was partially flooded. The position of Ronnie's head eventually gave him a clue.

Quickly he seized a hand, leading Ronnie out on deck. Then, placing his helmet close so that the sound of his voice would carry, he shouted, "Relax, Ronnie! The worst is over!"

Marsh, with his longer experience as a diver, knew exactly what to do. He closed Ronnie's air-valve so that the inflowing air created enough pressure to drive the water below the redhead's lips, his chin, then almost to the collar-plate. After that, he signalled on Ronnie's life line. Ronnie saw the superstructure of the wreck dropping away, and then everything grew hazy.

He remembered nothing more until he gained consciousness many minutes later. He lay in his sleeping bag, and above his head he could hear the steady popping of the air-compressor. Turning on his side, he saw Marsh standing on the ladder of the *Bubbles*.

"How are you feeling?" Marsh called anxiously.

"Great." And he grinned faintly. "Did you want to fight?"

Marsh laughed. "Not with a guy who can kill an octopus! I'm rested, and I'll have to go down now and drag that safe outside and secure lines to it. The tide is beginning to rise."

Marsh went down, and within an hour he signalled Hammerhead to pull him up. "The lines are secured beneath my boat," he reported, when he could speak. "Any sign of the bends, Ronnie?"

"No. But I got a slight squeeze, and feel as limp as a warmed-over meal. I can get up any time, though."

"That's what you think," said Bill good naturedly.

"Better run in, Bill," Ronnie said. "We'll put Pud on the beach, and he can go for the truck and the block and tackle we'll need."

Presently the *Sea Spray* nosed into the lapping surf. Pud lowered his big body over the bow and splashed ashore. He headed northward, clambering over the big rocks blocking his way to the zigzag trail ascending the cliffs below China Charlie's.

Bill sailed alongside the *Bubbles*, and let go both anchors. The two boats lay pitching lightly in the glassy swells, and for a while nothing happened.

Then the *Bubbles* began to creak as the tide raised her, putting a strain on the lines supporting the safe. When this creaking ceased, Marsh assured the others that the old strong-box had been hoisted from the deck of the derelict where it had lain hidden through so many decades. When water laved the base of the cliffs, and they were sure the tide would rise no higher, Carlson started the *Bubbles'* engine and chugged slowly toward the beach. He advanced two-thirds of the distance to shore before the supporting ropes swung aft.

"Hold it!" Marsh shouted. "The box struck bottom."

"It works!" exulted Ronnie.

"Why shouldn't it?" asked Marsh with a grin.

At low tide slack was taken up on the lines until they were once more taut. They creaked as the tide rose, awakening Ronnie frequently. Anxiously he scanned the mirror-like sea at dawn. There was no boat, let alone Shumaker's barge, on the southern horizon. An hour short of noon, when the tide was at flood stage, the old safe was again moved inshore. It grounded in shallow water. From there it could be hauled ashore with the block and tackle that Pud had brought in the truck.

Ronnie was feeling normal once more, and when this equipment was secured to a boulder at the base of the cliff, he heaved on the lines with the others. Foot by foot, the old strong-box was dragged over gravel and sand and rocky terraces, until it rested below the precipice. The safe was not an impressive object. It was slimy with sea-growth, and provided a lodging place besides for barnacles, limpets and even a few starfish.

When the block and tackle was removed, Pud and Marsh packed it up to the truck. Motive power was used to pull the box up the cliff. Then the crews of both boats ascended China Charlie's trail to employ the tackle a third time in hoisting the treasure into the van. The old Chinese and two of his helpers came to watch this final operation, but their excited comments in their own sing-song tongue were lost on the fishermen. It was quite clear, however, that Charlie had never before suspected the waters he had looked out upon for so long concealed anything like that strong-box.

"You'd better go along with Pud," Ronnie suggested to Marsh. "And see that he doesn't dally on the way to the Seal Cove Bank! The safe had better remain there until we can all be present to open it."

The crews, each now lacking one man, returned to the boats and headed out to sea. As Bill was about to swing around Blacktop Rock, he spied two abalone boats sailing northward, with bones in their teeth. They had a barge with a topheavy mast in tow.

"There's Shumaker!" he yelled. "I'll bet he's brought along dynamite charges and is planning to kill the octopus before he starts looking for the gold. I'd like to see his face when he enters the captain's cabin and finds it gone!"

"So would I," replied Ronnie. "But we'd better hurry back to Seal Cove, in case Pud should have a breakdown and need help."

Several days passed before the corroded safe was opened by a white-haired locksmith in a back room of the bank. The crews of both boats, Joseph Romano as manager of the bank, Sheriff Dart, and a number of officials, including representatives from the Treasury Department and the Assay Office, were there. When the locksmith finally burned away the hinges with an acetylene torch, and pried off the door, Ronnie and Marsh peered in consternation at what appeared to be a sodden mass of leather. The others crowded forward for a look; there was a chorus of groans.

"All that work—!" wailed Hammerhead.

"Wait a minute!" put in nervous little Mr. Donaldson of the Treasury Department. "It's possible that—"

Gingerly he lifted out what might once have been a leather poke. It fell apart, showering gold dust and nuggets on the rotting bags beneath. It took a long time after that to examine the contents of the safe. Raw gold had to be weighed by the Assay Office man, and placed in bags. There was besides a sizeable sum in American and Canadian coins to count.

At length Donaldson struck a total on a list he had been making. "Close to nine hundred thousand dollars," he declared, even his dry voice betraying his excitement. "We'll leave this under seal with you, Mr. Romano."

"*Nine hundred thousand!*" Ronnie gasped. "But, Mr. Donaldson, I thought there was only a little over half a million—"

Joseph Romano smiled. "Gold was worth twenty dollars an ounce when the *Southland Star* sank," he reminded Ronnie. "It's priced at thirty-five dollars now. There's no telling, off hand, what amount the court will grant you as a salvage award, or how much that will be reduced by taxes. The chances are, however, that the shares you two divers will receive may approach six figures. Your tenders and boat-operators won't get as much, of course, but nevertheless each one can be sure of a comfortable sum."

"I can clear all Dad's debts, and own our own home and abalone plant absolutely clear," Ronnie exulted. "Now, just let Miss Prindle try to tell people I'm not able to care for Skip and Mardie!"

Hammerhead pushed back his battered cap and rubbed his grizzled chin. "I take back that offer of a dime for my share," he said, beaming.

Pud smacked his lips, his blue eyes glowing. "I'm going to order myself a triple-decker sandwich. Porterhouse steaks, smothered in T-bones, smothered in sirloins, and the whole thing topped off with fillet mignons and mushrooms!"

"You would!" said Bill with a laugh.

The banker chuckled. "Ronnie could even buy Shumaker's plant if he wanted it. The morning paper will carry a story that our Morro Bay branch has taken over his property. His loans are long overdue. Apparently he's been spending too much buying a barge and keeping a big pack on hand in the hope that when he recovered the treasure he could create an abalone monopoly."

The crews of the two boats left the bank, a little dazed by so much good fortune. They talked for a while, and then, as they dispersed, Ronnie squeezed Pud's arm and Bill's.

"I'll be seeing you two early. It looks like good fishing in the morning."

"Have a heart!" wailed Pud. "We've been working so hard that I'm down to my last two hundred pounds!"

"You'll survive," said Ronnie, heading toward his truck.

He was about to step in when Marsh hailed him, and hurried over to speak once more.

"It's been fun working *with* you for a change, Ronnie!"

Ronnie grinned. "Couldn't we make it permanent?"

"How do you mean?" Marsh asked.

"You could buy Shumaker's plant from the Morro Bay Bank, and we could become partners. With two good plants, we could afford to hire the right man to manage both and market our packs for us. Then we'd be free to spend all our

241

time fishing." Ronnie paused as a trim green figure in a pert little green hat stepped from a roadster and started up the steps of Plimm's Grocery. "Or maybe the *right girl* could do the job," he added thoughtfully.

Marsh turned and watched the green-clad figure disappear into the store. "Ginger would be perfect for the job," he agreed.

"If she wouldn't be a cause of disagreement," Ronnie amended.

Marsh laughed. "I'll tell you the truth, Ronnie. I don't think there's anyone like Ginger. But I'm getting a little tired of going to square dances with a girl who can't talk about anything except . . . *Ronnie Nordhoff.*"

Ronnie's eyes widened in astonishment. "Are you serious?"

"Never more so, partner." Despite its rugged lines, there was a youthful eagerness about Marsh's face that Ronnie had never seen before. "So you see there's no obstacle to our going into this together . . . Say, what's the hurry?"

"We can settle our partnership later," Ronnie called back, as he strode briskly down the street. "I have something important to see about at Plimm's!"

6584